FROM HOLT, WITH PROMISE

BRITTANY TAYLOR

Cover Design by Amanda Shepard of Shepard Originals
Editing by Vicki James
Proofing by April Pallett
Formatting by Brittany Taylor

DEDICATION

*To the ones who haven't given up on a
promise of forever*

Hello dear reader!

I hope you enjoy this *spicy billionaire best-friend's brother* romance. Holt and Selene's story is the third in the NYC Billionaire Series.

Please be aware this book is highly emotional and contains scenes and topics which may be sensitive to some.

Topics include discussion and on page descriptions of alcoholism, depression, murder and murder/suicide.

I sincerely hope you enjoy reading Holt and Selene's love story!

Xoxo,
Brittany

TEN YEARS EARLIER

SELENE

The puddle of blood inches closer toward the toe of my sandal, and I somehow hold back the roil of vomit climbing up my throat, noticing how the color I painted my toenails matches the blood creeping closer.

I wish I could swallow the red pill. Or is it the blue one? Whichever one it is that wipes your mind clean and takes you out of the nightmare you're living in. I believe it's the only thing that can save me from what I witnessed only seconds earlier.

My skin is ice cold as I press my back firmly against the wall. Silent tears stream down my face; my watery gaze refusing to break away from the two lifeless bodies in front of me. Bodies that don't belong to just anyone. Within a matter of seconds, I've witnessed the people who brought me into this world leave it.

Footsteps pound up the stairs, muffled by the decades-old carpeting. I know who they belong to. I want to stop her and shield her from the darkness of this room, but I'm frozen stiff, unable to move.

I shouldn't have followed the shouts. I shouldn't have followed their voices.

Would it have been better if I'd just found them this way? Him on top of her, their faces sprayed with each other's blood. The shiny metal of their wedding rings glinting in the afternoon sun, now coated in crimson.

Or is the pain of what I've just witnessed worse?

The only thing I know for certain is that my life will never be the same.

They taught me to believe in the fairy tale type of love, everlasting and true. But this isn't love, and I won't ever be able to think of it the same.

I'll never look at love or death the same, because when I see their lifeless expressions, his body draped over hers over a pool of damaged flesh and freshly spilled blood beside an empty pistol, I know that's all I'll see forever.

I'll be haunted by this memory for the rest of my life.

I'm frozen stiff against the wall when my sister appears in the doorway. It only takes a split second for her to register what she's seeing before her ear-piercing scream floods my ears. All I can do is stare at my mother's now-vacant eyes staring back at me, giving me all the answers I couldn't answer for myself.

Love is the master manipulator, existing only in storybooks.

Death lives on in real life, and, I think in this moment, I'd rather be dead than suffer with the memory of this for rest of my days.

ONE

SELENE

The giant, shimmering rock in the palm of my hand is heavy and meaningless. I turn it over several times, staring at it as though it isn't a real, tangible object resting against my skin. Blinking, I'm convinced I'll make it disappear, like some sort of naïve, twisted magic trick.

Love can't be trusted—a lesson I learned a decade ago.

While my life may be lacking faith in love, there's one thing it certainly isn't short of: death.

Death is real. It's an aching fact we spend our entire lives pretending it isn't coming for us, hunting us down. It's the elephant in the room we pretend doesn't exist.

From the moment we take our first breaths, death is humankind's fate. We're all doomed to die one way or another, whether by natural causes or someone else's hand. Torturous? Peaceful? No one knows how they'll leave this world. Still, it doesn't change one simple truth: no matter if it's expected or not, death still catches you by surprise, dragging you into a spiral of pain and grief, no matter the circumstances.

When I think about my life, I suppose the same could be said about love. Love, like death, only brings heartbreak.

That's where the similarities end, though.

Death is reliable, and love can't be trusted.

After dropping the pale blue, gleaming stone from my palm, I dangle the long chain from the ends of my fingertips and trudge up the last flight of stairs leading to my apartment floor. The stone swings like a pendulum, reminding me of the weight of its meaning. Do the dead miss the living like the living miss the dead? Does it even matter in the end?

I will the dark cloud hanging over me to disappear, thankful to be out of that jewelry store and heading home.

"Strange, isn't it?" my sister asks through the phone, tearing me from my thoughts.

"What is?" I hitch my purse higher on my shoulder and blow a loose strand of hair away from my face, but it flies back, shielding half my eye. I jerk my head and fish my apartment key out of my purse, keeping my grandmother's necklace tight in my grip and my phone pressed between my cheek and shoulder.

"That they can turn ashes into stone. It's strange, right?" London's voice quivers, and I imagine her shuddering at the thought.

"It's not strange to me." I frown. "I find it fascinating."

"Of course you do. You've always been a romantic like that."

"Me, a romantic?"

"Yeah, you know. You wear your heart on your sleeve. You're the writer, expressing yourself through that book you spent nearly all your adulthood writing. You have a way with words, and everything you touch has meaning to you."

I snort on that last part. "Not everything I touch has meaning to me, London." My voice is softer than I intend. Fuck, maybe my sister is right. Maybe I'm not as mysterious as I think I am.

But I don't agree with her about wearing my heart on my sleeve. If anything, I keep it well covered and protected.

Although London isn't my sister by blood, sometimes I wonder if my parents secretly had her and accidently gave her up to the orphanage before they'd found her again and decided to adopt her back into the family. Despite our closeness, though, we couldn't be more different. Where she is sleek, with rich black hair, pale grey eyes, and full lips I'm certain her fiancé West constantly reminds her how much he appreciates them daily, I have near platinum blonde hair, green eyes the color of swamp water, and lips half the fullness of my sister's.

Despite our differences, sometimes I think London knows me better than I know myself. Except for the part where she says everything I touch has meaning. With that, she couldn't be more wrong.

"You had Grandma's ashes turned into a necklace so you could keep her with you, Selene." Her tone is flat, no hint of judgment. "In my opinion, it's a little strange. Also romantic in a weird, slightly morbid way, I guess."

I know London is sad over our grandmother's death, but neither of us are naïve to how her death has hit me harder than her.

London has been through some shit in her life. Aside from bouncing from foster home to foster home until our parents adopted her the day before her fourteenth birthday, she'd gotten into an accident that caused her to lose her memory. She only recently regained it a few months back after reuniting with the love of her life, Weston Knight—the love she'd been forced to leave behind at the foster home. He also happens to be in our friend circle, as well as being her ex-husband's brother.

Oh, and there's the teeny, tiny, minor detail of him being a billionaire.

Regardless, London is absolutely head over heels in love with West, and his obsession with her is enough to make even the most hardened of hearts jealous.

Or their stomachs sick with nausea.

With my key hovering in front of the deadbolt, I stare down at the gem in my hand. Is it strange my grandmother's ashes have been turned into a gem? Maybe. It's not like I kept a lock of her hair or anything and made it into something weird. This is a necklace. A gorgeous one. I can't help looking at the gleaming stone and admiring how something so dark and depressing can be turned into something beautiful.

Maybe London was right. Maybe I am a romantic.

I square my shoulders and lift my chin as if she's standing in front of me instead of being on the other side of the city, speaking to me over the phone. "I think Grandma would have thought it was poetic."

A few moments of silence pass before her heavy sigh hits my ear, laced with a nostalgic tone. "You know, sis, I think you're right. She would have."

"Thank you." I smile softly, even though she can't see it.

After sticking my key into the deadbolt lock, I turn it, ready to shed out of these sticky clothes and into something nice for tonight's event, but my stomach flips, not feeling the lock's usual resistance.

"Oh shit." I groan under my breath.

"What?" London quickly catches on, the panic in her voice raising.

I drop my grandmother's necklace into my purse and shift the phone to my hand. "I'm sorry. I have to go."

"What?" she squeaks out. "Why?"

"I'll see you tonight."

I know *exactly* who is in my apartment without even opening the door. Still, I place my keys between my fingers to create a makeshift weapon, just in case. Even if it is who I think it is, and not an intruder, I'm likely to use them to stab him in the neck anyway.

"Selene, you can't just say things like that and hang up—"

"Everything is fine. I'll see you later tonight," I insist, ignoring her plea yet again.

"Wait! Before you go, Julianna had your dress—"

I stab my thumb against the red button on the screen, cutting my sister off before giving her the chance to finish her sentence. I just want to get this over with.

Twisting the doorknob, I push the door open and find him sitting exactly where I expect him to be: slouched on the sofa, long legs spread apart, hands lazily draped between them. One hand is cupping his admittedly small bulge under his gray sweatpants.

Such a waste considering what gray sweatpants can do to a woman's imagination.

My eyes rake over his whole body, and I somehow resist the urge to roll them dramatically when he turns his head in my direction, and his tired eyes find mine. His hair is disheveled and unkempt, and his five o'clock shadow has stayed well past its welcome.

"Hot water isn't working again." He raises his arm lazily, gesturing down the hallway.

"Great," I mutter, dropping my purse on the end table near the front door. "Thanks for letting me know." Brushing my hair off my face, I cross over to the kitchen and pour myself a fresh glass of water.

Adam watching me the entire time, burning a hole in my back and my brain.

My silence is deafening. I know it's driving him crazy that I'm not giving him the sort of reaction he wants. The only reaction I have is wishing he was anywhere else but here in my apartment.

I swallow a huge gulp of water and finally eye him over my

glass. He doesn't move from his position, his admittedly pretty eyes still staring at me.

I place my glass on the counter and inhale a deep breath. I guess we need to have a talk. Begrudgingly, I plant both my hands on the counter and straighten my arms, using them as an anchor. I know Adam won't leave willingly or easily. If he was even the slightest bit considerate and understanding, he wouldn't be here in the first place, taking up space in my apartment.

"Well?" His eyebrows rise. "You're not going to say anything about the burst water pipe? I couldn't take a shower, Selene."

I scoff, taking in the acrid scent surrounding him and his overall greasy appearance settling in the small space of my tiny New York apartment. "Obviously."

"Wow." He tucks his chin in and shakes his head. While pulling himself to a stand, he blows out a hot breath and angrily parks both his hands on his hips. Chip crumbs tumble down his chest, falling to my floor, getting lost in the fibers of my living room carpet. "I'm going to pretend you didn't insult my ego just then. It isn't my fault I couldn't shower."

I stare at him with pinched brows, gripping the edge of the counter tighter. My broken pipes have nothing to do with his lack of cleanliness and self-care. *It's just him.*

I can feel my head expanding, ready to explode. Not because I'm heartbroken over him. I'm just annoyed by the fact he's still here. I open my mouth to point out the obvious, but I wait to see if the light bulb will flick on above that greasy head of his. I scan my apartment and see empty soda cans and chip bags littering the floor. A mysterious, dried brown liquid is caked to the wooden surface of the coffee table. I already know it will take entirely too much time and muscle for me to scrub it clean. Sure, I'm aware my place isn't the best and is on the verge of falling apart, but the fact Adam thinks he can crash at my place like it's some college frat house during rush week, sets me off.

"Adam." I close my eyes and force myself to focus on my breathing before the next words find their way out of my mouth. When I crack my eyes open, I find him standing in the same position, refusing to budge. "You don't live here. This isn't your apartment and this isn't your food. We also aren't together anymore, remember?"

He jerks his head back again, brows rising. He looks like a wounded puppy. His eyes soften as he rakes his fingers through his greasy hair. It doesn't budge when his arm drops to his side. "I thought you were joking when you said things were over between us."

I curl my lip, wondering how I could be any clearer when I told him only last night, using the most straightforward language you can to break-up with someone.

We're over, Adam. I can't date you anymore.

"I honestly don't know how you're confused. I made my intentions very clear." I shrug and tear off a piece of paper towel from the holder next to the sink. I fish a bottle of spray cleaner out from under it and move to the coffee table. I spray a good amount of the pungent, citrus-scented liquid on the sticky-brown stain and wait for it to soak in.

Adam's hand lands on my back, and I freeze.

"I figured you were only saying that because you've been going through a lot lately." His voice is soft and tender. "With your grandmother passing and all."

I stand, blinking back the tears welling in my eyes. The familiar knot of grief winds itself into my chest.

Dammit, Adam

I look at him and know I made the right decision in ending things with him last night. I first met him a few months ago through a book blogging account. He sent me a message—the first to strike up a conversation. I found his forwardness endearing. I'd never been big on relationships, and I'd most definitely never been the most outgoing person. After talking for days through social media, we agreed to meet at a coffee shop. He was kind and soft, with an innocent charm about him, despite him being in his late twenties. Most men our age are all sharp lines and edges made for intimidation. Adam wasn't that.

It was then, at that first meeting, he'd told me the truth about how he'd lied to me in our messages. He wasn't a writer, per se. *According to him.* He was an editor for the New York Times. I'd brushed off his lie, excited by the idea of finally talking literature with someone other than my eighty-nine-year-old grandmother.

That day in the coffee shop, he'd quickly inserted himself into my bubble. A bubble I've been careful about protecting and monitoring who gets access to my whole life. I let him in too easily. Maybe it was the common ground I found with him in that moment. As a rising New York Times editor, we connected on a level most others in my life haven't been able to.

But I had been a fool, blind to all the other qualities he possessed, including the one where he only thought of himself. Oh, and the fact that he looks like he's just crawled out of a trash can unless he is forced to get cleaned up for the sake of work.

He pushes out his bottom lip, and his eyes soften even deeper, looking at me with pity.

My stomach turns. "Adam..."

"Sometimes, when tragic, unexpected events happen in our lives, we make rash and poor decisions for ourselves." He gently presses his thumb to my chin, smiling at me with sympathy.

I jerk my chin away. "Are you implying I'm not capable of making rational decisions?" The knot tightens, gripping around the base of my throat.

"Well, no." He blinks, sighing, and takes a step back.

"Then, what part of what I said last night left you confused?"

He lazily lifts a shoulder. He smells like stale Doritos. "You didn't ask for your key back."

Several beats of silence pass where we simply stare at one another.

I stick my hand out, palm up. "I want it back, then."

He doesn't flinch.

"I want my key back, Adam." I stare at him pointedly, then raise a brow. "Is that clear enough for you?"

His face quickly transforms from soft and hopeful to angry and bitter. I knew it was a poor decision to give him the spare key to my apartment, but it had been so long since I'd been in a true relationship with someone. Not the kind where they have a phobia of putting a label on it. Adam was quick to put a label on us. In fact, he was too fast when I think about it now.

Giant red fucking flag.

He stomps across the living room to the end of the sofa, searching through his suit draped over the arm. It's been a habit of his to change out of his suit and tie after work, lounging around in nothing but his white undershirt and cotton briefs for the rest of the night while binging on sports documentaries and junk food.

He digs into the pockets of his pants before he stalks back over to me and drops the key into my hand with an angry grunt. He reminds me of a child who has been told he can't have his ice cream before dinner.

"Thanks," I mutter, dropping the key into the side pocket of my leggings. Then I begin scrubbing at the brown stain on my coffee table.

"So, that's it then? We're through?"

Stopping, I groan and straighten my back once again. I've never been much for talking, reserving my words for those I'm able to write down versus speaking out loud, but Adam is challenging me today, forcing me to be someone I'm not. Which is part of the reason I knew we weren't going to work out. He never has understood me.

"Yes." I deadpan. "We are over. Now, kindly leave." I gesture toward the front door, then bend back down to wipe the rest of the brown stain off the table. I try not to gag when it mixes with another mysterious white substance I don't even want to attempt to identify.

"I don't understand. I thought we were going somewhere. I imagined proposing to you one day."

"Seriously?" I shoot up, shocked by the sudden turn in conversation.

"Yes. I was going to tell you that I loved you."

I press my hand to my forehead, running his confession over in my brain. We've only been dating for six weeks. How can he possibly love me? "We are seriously so far apart, it's quite astonishing the distance."

"So, you don't love me?"

Oh. My. God.

"No, Adam, I don't love you." I make my point clear before returning to my cleaning. Silence descends upon us, the only sound coming from my scrubbing.

"You wouldn't want to get married?"

I shake my head. "Someday, and with the right person." *But even then...*

"And that person isn't me?"

"No."

Tension builds in the air. I can practically feel him stewing beside me.

My rejection must irritate him further because he finally breaks the silence when he says, "Unbelievable. You are unbelievable."

My teeth dig into the side of my cheek, biting back the tears welling in my eyes. How did I end up here? I refuse to let Adam see them. I don't want him to think they're for him.

I really wish my grandmother was still here. Closing my eyes, I try to think of what she would say to me in this moment.

Straighten those shoulders of yours and hold your head high. Don't ever allow anyone to walk all over you, Selene. You're too beautiful, inside and out, to put up with shit like that.

I've never been the confrontational kind, but Adam has me testing even my own limits.

Aluminum cans crush under the weight of his feet as he stomps his way back over to his suit. I watch as he dramatically shakes out his suit pants before stepping into them with a huff. His cheeks are flaming red, and he won't stop shaking his head. He's so unkempt, even his hair still refuses to move.

"It's going to take me almost two hours to get home at this time of day so I can get ready for the auction tonight." He narrows his eyes but still refuses to look my way as he gestures toward his face, waving his fingers around. "I can't go looking like this."

I keep my thoughts to myself, that it's his own fault he looks that way, because I don't have the energy to fight him anymore. I'm hoping the fewer words that spill from my mouth, the fewer reasons there are for him to drag out this breakup more than it already has been.

He scoffs with disgust as he drapes his suit jacket over his arm and fists his tie in his large hands. He's still covered in orange chip dust, so it's hard to take him seriously, but if it wasn't for the anger blazing in his stare, I would think he was joking.

"Again, you say nothing." He curls his lip in disgust. "Is this how you've always been?"

I roll my eyes and pick up a handful of empty soda cans

before dropping them into my trash can, which is already filled to the top—another mess Adam has left that I'll have to clean up.

"Please just leave, Adam." I mutter, returning to the sticky mess on my coffee table.

The one my grandmother insisted I keep after my parents died.

I didn't plan on taking it then. I was angry for the way they left London and me behind, but my grandmother said that if I didn't keep anything from them, I would regret it. Lord knows why I chose their coffee table of all things.

"If this is how you've always been, then it finally all makes sense."

Heat blooms up my neck, and I stop wiping as I stand to face him, this time narrowing my eyes on his. "*What* suddenly makes sense?"

He lifts his chin, working his jaw. "Your sense of entitlement."

I take a step back, feeling as if this puny little, Dorito-dusted man child is giving me whiplash.

"I'm not entitled. You've seen where I live." I want to laugh.

In fact, I do. I let out a sarcastic huff of air as I look around, waving my arms at my cheap apartment. Sure, the paint is chipping and the hot water heater craps out at least once a month, but this place has become my home since the day I graduated college. It's the place where I curled into the corner of every room, pouring my heart and soul into my first romance novel. Every penny I earn working at Charleigh's flower shop goes to this place. It may be shit, but it's mine.

"You are entitled. Entitled and pretentious." Adam sticks an accusatory finger in my direction. "You walk around as if you think you're better than everyone else in your little yoga outfits." He gestures up and down the length of my body.

What the fuck is he talking about? "Yoga outfits are pretentious?"

He gives a sarcastic laugh, ignoring my question. "You think because everyone in that little group of yours are billionaires that it somehow makes you one of them too? Because you aren't, Selene. You never will be. You live in this shithole apartment that not a single one of them would ever bother to step foot in. You're just as lowly as me—the people who are the blood of this city. Those billionaires don't keep this city alive, we do. To them you're nothing but another piece of gum stuck to the bottom of their Armani shoes."

"You don't know what you're talking about, Adam." I try not to let my voice waver because, even though I hate to admit it, Adam's accusations hit me harder than they should. I've lived a lifetime of trauma, and my best friends are who have kept me afloat for the last decade of my life. While working at Charleigh's flower shop isn't my passion, at one point in time, she was the only person who managed to bring a smile out of me every day. Then entered Julianna, before London finally moved to New York City permanently. For a time, my world was isolated and lonely. But now, even though I may be shy to my core, I'm certainly not lonely. I'm simply grieving.

Adam hurling endless insults my way about my life sparks anger in my gut. Aside from the confusing grief surrounding my parents, I miss my grandmother. Fuck, I miss her.

I cross my arms and stare at him blankly. "We're over, Adam. Leave."

He nods and steps over a pile of cans trailing between the sofa and the coffee table. He stops beside me and leans forward, bringing his face closer to mine. I look into his eyes but try not to gag at the smell of stale corn chips when he breathes.

"Your so-called friend Julianna had her one of her cronies drop off a dress for tonight's auction." He glances toward the hallway. "I would say I'm surprised you're going tonight, but I'm not."

"You're going to the auction too, so don't act like I'm someone special. I'm not."

"I'm going for the *paper*. It's my job. What's your excuse?"

"I don't owe you any explanation. Especially not after you've trashed my apartment and refuse to accept that I ended whatever this was."

"You're right, you don't need to explain." He holds his hand up, backing away from me and toward the door. "There's that sense of entitlement I'm talking about. But let me guess... the Capuletis are your friends, and you owe them your support?"

He wraps his hand around the doorknob and jerks the door open, tearing it from the frame. Before leaving, he stops and glances over his shoulder. "You aren't one of them, Selene. You never will be. When you're ready to stop playing dress up, call me, and maybe we can try this again."

Adam slams my door shut with such force it causes the key hook by the door to rattle against the drywall. A piece of damaged wall flakes off and falls to the floor. I stare at the door and squeeze my eyes shut when my vision waters. Despite the strength I have and the mantra I'm repeating in my head, I can't stop the tears from forming. Finally, one breaks free, slipping down my cheek.

I'm not sad over my breakup with Adam. I'm relieved.

He's the first person I've dated in a long time, and while it sucks that it didn't last, I'm thankful we're through.

Maybe we can try this again.

His final words linger in the air, letting me know that if I were to even give him the slightest hint of another chance, he'd take it.

I shudder at the thought. My stomach flips, though it could be from the lingering scent of stale chips and soda in the air.

Once I've gathered myself, I open the two windows in my living room to air out the stink, then lock the chain on my front door, just in case Adam made a spare key without my knowledge. I doubt he would have gone to those lengths, but I wasn't expecting him to find him lounging on my couch like a vegetable when I got home, either.

Remembering the errands I ran before I came home, I grab my new necklace out of my purse and carry it to my bedroom. I set it on top of my dresser and find the dress Adam said Julianna's assistant dropped off earlier. I shoot a quick text to Marvin, the maintenance manager in my building, to let him know my hot water isn't working again, then I turn my attention back to the dress hanging on the back of my bedroom door.

I have no idea what it looks like since it's wrapped in a black bag. Orange streaks of chip dust coat the outer edges, and I grunt in frustration before I brush them off, then pull the zipper to reveal the stunning dress inside. Nothing but butter yellow silk fabric pours out. It reminds me of the gown Kate Hudson wore in *How to Lose a Guy in Ten Days*. I gasp and check my phone, opening my girls' chat. I send Julianna a thank you and preemptively promise to send her a picture of me wearing it once I've showered, done my hair, and applied my makeup, knowing she'll ask for it. Funny, considering she'll see me wearing it within a matter of hours, too.

Warmth spreads across my body, the heaviness of today waning with every passing second. I admire the gown Julianna is letting me borrow, knowing Adam couldn't have been further from the truth with his accusations. Sure, I don't have a lot of money, certainly not as much as my best friends, but I'm capable of taking care of myself. I can afford my own place, and regardless of the money they have, my best friends are incredible. They shouldn't be judged based on how many digits are in their bank accounts.

Adam's words echo in my mind, though. I'm not entitled or pretentious. Maybe he was hurt that he wasn't the one for me. I'm still rocked with disbelief that he considered *proposing to me*... even after I broke up with him.

And society calls women clingy.

A little twinge of guilt sits at the back of my mind for hurting him, though not too much. I know what I want and won't settle for just anyone. The right man is out there waiting for me. I just have to be patient and focus on what I know makes me happy now. He'll come along when I'm least expecting it. At least, that's what happens in all the great romance novels, right?

Marvin gets back to me twenty minutes later, letting me know the hot water heater should be fixed enough for me to take my shower now. So, I turn the water on, sit on the toilet, and wait for it to heat up. While scrolling through my phone, I pull up the social media post, announcing the auction Julianna's putting on tonight for Scribe Magazine—her brother Holt's magazine.

The post has nearly half a million likes. I double tap the heart icon before scrolling through the comments, nearly all of which are asking if Holt will be there and if he's single.

I mean, I can't blame them. He's handsome as hell and has a jaw that could cut glass. His eyes make the muscles on the insides of your thighs twitch with every glance your way. The man is hot as sin if not a little arrogant.

Blinking away my wandering thoughts, I smile to myself. Holt Capuleti will forever be single. He never allows a woman to stay long enough to give the media an opportunity to speculate.

Steam billows out from behind the shower curtain, letting me know I have precisely five minutes of hot water time, and to make the most of it. Leaving my phone open to Julianna's auction post, I shed myself out of my pretentious yoga pants and bra and step inside the shower, but not before glancing once more at the buttery yellow fabric spilling out of the bag on the back of my bedroom door.

Pretentious and entitled, my ass.

I just have incredible friends.

TWO

HOLT

Every single asshole is looking at me, talking about me.

I may as well be standing in the middle of the room naked, waving a neon sign that reads: *look at me!*

Furtive glances. Muted conversations. All eyes aimed my way.

Okay, maybe some aren't, but it sure as fuck feels like it.

Sweat gathers at the base of my neck and I swallow the ever-growing lump in my throat. I shouldn't be this nervous. I never am, but my current legal predicament has me on edge. I need a drink. Preferably one that's stiff and guaranteed to take the edge off.

"Sir?" A tap on my shoulder has me spinning around.

I find my publicist Treena looking up at me with soft, brown eyes. She's nearly twenty years older than me and, despite her kind heart, she's a hawk when it comes to protecting my brand with the magazine. Just the type of person I need in my corner right now.

I rake a nervous hand through my hair and eye the others in the room before turning back to Treena.

"Vanessa Burrell is here and wants to meet with you," she

whispers, sliding her gaze to the side as though someone might be listening.

"Where?" The lump swells in my throat, and I try to clear it away.

"Conference room, down the hall."

I blow out a heavy breath, hoping to catch a glimpse of my favorite blonde wallflower before leaving the ballroom. I search the black linen-topped tables with guests gathered around them, hoping to find her stunning face, but they're all covered in shadows. Mainly thanks to the dim lighting filling the enormous ballroom my sister picked out for her auction venue.

I've got to hand it to Julianna, her work is impressive. But right now, I'm cursing her for choosing the lowest lighting possible, making it difficult to find who I'm looking for.

Her. The one I search for in every room I enter.

Seeing her will settle my nerves. At least I hope it will. Every other time, my heart gets this jolt of electricity that shoots straight for my dick, begging to know what it feel like to sink between her luscious thighs.

Fuck. Focus, Holt.

Disappointment eats away at me when I can't find her, but I keep my cool.

"Let's go," I mutter, following Treena out of the ballroom and down the hall.

Stuffing my hands into my pockets, I steel myself for this conversation, knowing it won't be easy. Piano music plays quietly in the distance, melding with the sharp echoes of heels clicking against the marble tile of the Omni Plaza Hotel. We walk down to the opposite end of the hallway before Treena stops in front of an indiscriminate door and holds it open for me. I give her a curt nod and enter the tiny room.

Carpeted and covered in bland, off-white paint means

there's nothing special about this room. It's as if the auction is a million miles away in a completely different world.

Keeping my hands stuffed into my pockets, I stop just inside the door and square my shoulders.

My lawyer, Vanessa Burrell, is standing near the back corner of the room, with a black briefcase resting at her side. But it's the flash of bright blue sequins that has me shifting my attention. My sister Julianna is standing beside her.

"Mr. Capuleti. Thank you for meeting me on such short notice." Vanessa holds her hand out for me.

I accept her gesture but don't take my eyes off my sister. "No problem," I mutter quickly, then to Julianna ask, "What are you doing here?"

Julianna arches one of her eyebrows and purses her lips. Her brown hair is pulled back tightly, revealing her sharp, venomous stare. "I was greeting the auction attendees when I saw Vanessa. Anytime she's involved, I know shit is going down. If you thought I wasn't going to follow her and see why, you're crazy."

"You told Julianna what's going on?" I shift my focus to Vanessa.

"No." Vanessa clears her throat. "She hasn't stopped asking what's going on, though. She insisted on attending this meeting."

"Of course she did."

Julianna plants her hands on her hips and sticks out her chin. "When I'm on a mission, I don't give up easily."

"We know." I run my hand down the front of my face while still standing by the door, not wanting to drag out this meeting longer than it needs to be. Treena hasn't moved from her spot near the propped open door, either.

"Anyway." I wave my hand in a *let's get this going* motion.

"Right." Vanessa nods once, then gestures toward the black bag in her hand. "I went over the lawsuit you were given."

Julianna's jaw drops immediately, and her once narrowed eyes widen in horror. I ignore her.

"And?"

"It's legit."

"Fuck." I hiss, raising both my arms in the air to rake my fingers through my hair as my stomach sinks to a pit I didn't even know existed. I'm going to be fucking sick.

"I did what you asked. I tracked down the law firm representing the plaintiff, and they have a proper, valid complaint," Vanessa continues. "I tried to see if they were willing to discuss this outside of court, and they refused. The lawsuit will move forward."

"Lawsuit?" Julianna shouts. "What lawsuit?"

"Will you keep it down?" I glance over my shoulder.

Without instruction, Treena shuts the door to the hallway. The loud laughter and chatter from the hall is muted instantly.

"Um, excuse me?" Julianna crosses her arms over her chest. "My brother is being sued, hasn't mentioned a single word of this to me, and now you're asking me to keep it down?"

"Yes," I clip, angrily. Annoyance simmers under my skin. My sister always manages to twist every situation to reflect how she's feeling. "This isn't about you, Julianna." I growl, spinning and resting a hand on my hip while my other rubs at my mouth.

An ear-piercing silence swells in the room as everyone waits for me to react.

My sister breaks the silence.

"Who is suing Holt?"

"Not *just* Holt," Vanessa answers weakly. "He's suing Holt's magazine Scribe as well."

"*He?*"

"Rome Montogomery." His name spills from my mouth fast and bitterly, and I raise my head high enough to face my sister.

She laughs in disbelief. You think she'd just been told her favorite makeup brand was going bankrupt and she was ready to riot. I should know, because that's exactly what she did when she was fourteen years old.

Julianna wasn't bullshitting when she said she's relentless in her pursuits.

Her head is tipped back as her laughter pours free and tears well in the corners of her eyes. Eventually, she calms enough to stare straight at me with her glassy, humor-filled gaze. "You're kidding, right? Is this another one of your pranks?"

"No."

Her face falls. Then it turns red.

Our family has had a long, sordid battle with the Montgomerys—a classic tale of competing families—but the personal vendetta my sister holds against Rome Montgomery, the prodigal son, takes our family rivalry and jacks it up on steroids. Her hatred for him runs deep.

"Rome is suing the magazine?" She's shooting daggers at me, but I know they're really meant for Rome. "Why?" she squeaks out. "*Why* is Rome suing the magazine?"

"Defamation, apparently." I wave my hand flippantly. "Some article in my anonymous column."

"Our legal team is working on the case right now and gathering details to decide where to go from here," Vanessa interrupts. "We don't have the full story just yet, but we'll build a strong case in your defense, Mr. Capuleti."

"Defamation." Julianna's neck bobs as she swallows, and for a moment, she avoids my stare, biting down on her lip. The reality of the lawsuit must be hitting her. She knows the damage this will do to me and my company. "When did he bring this lawsuit on?"

"The night West and London held The Veiled Door reopening."

Julianna's eyes widen, her memories of that night evident. The night all of us watched our best-friend's brother get demolished by a New York City Tour bus after finding out he'd faked his own death due to giving poor investment advice to members of the Irish fucking mob.

"Don't worry about the details," I offer Julianna, not wanting to think about that clusterfuck of a night any more than the rest of us.

"Oh, um, okay." She nods once with a faraway glaze to her eyes.

"You shouldn't be surprised. This is Rome Montgomery we're talking about. I've tried to soften the hatred our families hold for quite some time now, and it doesn't seem to have worked, so this doesn't exactly come as a complete surprise. His blades are quite sharp."

"Wait," Julianna says. "Is this why you've been cozying up to him lately? Not-so-chalantly inviting him into our friend group?"

"Yes."

The corner of her mouth lifts. "So, it wasn't just to piss me off?"

"No. That was an unexpected perk, however."

"I hate you."

"Feeling is mutual."

She seems to let go of wanting to know the details, and I'm thankful.

The slight lightness in our conversation is momentary. The beige, bland walls close in on me, and I'm suddenly dying to leave this room. The weight of Rome's lawsuit is tearing me up and I'm starting to not recognize myself. My life is measured, tucked, and folded neatly into a box. I'm not a celebrity in the sense of an acting or music career, but I am a well-known face in this city. The face of a magazine willing to dig deep and write about a multitude of topics which matter to people.

A stack of metal chairs is pushed against the far wall, but my mind wanders to the one person I truly came here to see. Instead of these stupid fucking chairs, I wish I was looking at a head of blonde hair, green eyes, and a body of full hips instead.

"But... wait," Julianna blurts, tearing me from the thoughts of her best friend. "Your magazine is sponsoring this auction, Holt. If this gets out, your reputation will be ruined, along with mine."

"The auction is the perfect diversion actually," Treena cuts in. "You need to do whatever it takes to preserve your reputation, Mr. Capuleti. Once this news hits, and it will, it will be rough. You need a distraction."

"I wouldn't exactly call this auction a distraction. The magazine is just a sponsor," I argue.

"We'll figure it out." Julianna shrugs a shoulder.

"Just be present tonight," Treena encourages me. "We'll work on damage control later. Honestly, I'm surprised we've kept this lawsuit quiet for this long."

"Rome won't keep his mouth shut for long," Julianna practically growls. "The man loves to hear himself talk too much."

"Actually," Vanessa announces, holding her phone up to the three of us. "Seems we've manifested his big mouth already."

I lean forward, reading the headline to the article she has pulled up.

Venture Mogul Rome Montgomery sues Scribe Magazine and its CEO Holt Capuleti for defamation in new major lawsuit.

The article was posted ten minutes ago.

"Well, shitballs!" Julianna hisses. "Here we go. Terrible timing when this auction is set to start in twenty minutes."

"I'll read over this article and see what the public knows." Vanessa tucks her phone into the front pocket of her briefcase. "I doubt it'll effect tonight's auction since it's for various charities. You may be the number one topic for gossip, but it'll all be in secret."

"Great." I sneer. "Because it's better to have those talking behind your back instead of out in the open."

"Everything will be fine, Mr. Capuleti," Treena tries to reassure me. "Just go about your night as usual. Lay low and try not to get dragged into the spotlight. We'll get this sorted and reconvene on Monday."

"That'll be difficult." Julianna snorts.

Treena turns in her direction. "What do you mean?"

Julianna glowers at her. "You're my brother's publicist, but you don't know he's supposed to be bidding tonight?"

Treena snaps her mouth shut and inhales a long breath through her nose.

"What sort of auction is this?" Vanessa asks, stepping closer into our circle.

"Scribe and a few other organizations are sponsoring it, but it's an auction to raise money for children's research hospitals throughout the five boroughs and Jersey. The way I organized tonight's auction was meant to draw in a large crowd, and when I say large, what I mean is *massive*."

"What's so different about this auction that has it drawing such a large crowd?" Vanessa's penciled brows pull together.

Julianna's expression transforms. She's practically bursting with excitement, proud of herself. "We're auctioning off dates."

"Dates?" Vanessa's eyebrows unravel, rising across her forehead.

"Yeah." Julianna shrugs, turning her hand over and inspecting her nails as though Vanessa's questions are boring her, but I recognize it as her defense mechanism whenever she feels someone judging her. "Both women and men volunteer themselves, some models, and local celebrities for a night out with the highest bidder. There's no pressure for them to follow through on the date, and those bidding know that."

"Well, it's solved, then!" Treena blurts out. "Holt just won't place any bids."

"Oh, come on." Julianna's shoulders sag. I can practically see the air deflating out of her chest like a sad, day-old party balloon.

"I wasn't planning on following through with the date anyway, Jules," I tell her.

"Of course you weren't."

I let her sarcastic comment slide. "If Treena thinks it'll only shine a brighter spotlight on me by participating, I won't. I'll still donate money to the charities. You know I will."

Julianna stares at me without saying a word, her eyes reminding me of our mother's. Soft yet strong.

Though it doesn't come easy to her, she concedes. "Fine." She blows out a heavy breath, crossing her arms over her chest.

A soft knock on the door catches our attention. We all snap our heads in that direction as the door softly opens. A woman with an earpiece stuffed into her right ear, the kind with a spiraled cord that disappears under the back of her shirt, pokes her head between the door and doorframe. She winces, then finds my sister.

"I'm sorry to interrupt, but we have an issue we need your help with."

"I'll be out in a minute, Hannah."

The woman, apparently named Hannah, anxiously glances around the room. "It's sort of an emergency."

"Okay." Julianna runs her hands down the front of her dress before leaving the room, but not before she brushes past me. She stops and wraps her small hand around my arm, giving it a squeeze. "This will all work out. We'll get through this."

"It doesn't exactly feel like it right now."

"This is Rome Montgomery, remember? You said it yourself. If this rivalry has taught us anything, it's that our family name won't allow us to be defeated. He won't win."

I close my mouth and nod.

Julianna gives me a weak smile before leaving, and her absence is felt immediately.

I must appear to be on the brink of falling apart because Treena is now looking at me as though she's worried I'm going to snap. She could be right. My head feels like it's going to explode and paint these bland walls with crimson.

"Your sister is right, Mr. Capuleti," Treena says. "Just go out there and act normal."

"Right." I laugh sarcastically. "Like I can just go out there and pretend my entire world isn't about to blow up."

My world is about to change the second I step foot out of this room. The paranoia of secretive glances won't just be in my head, they'll be real.

I try not to let panic set in, but I know it's too late. My palms are sweaty and the floor shifts underneath my feet. I've fought for years to keep myself together and not let my past dictate my future. I've built a life for myself and my magazine, focusing on what I need to do to succeed. Now, Rome Montgomery is threatening to ruin it all over a stupid article I had no idea was even published.

Treena's phone rings from her pocket. She plucks it out, reads the screen, then looks up at me. "I need to take this. I'll meet up with you later at the end of the event."

I nod in acknowledgement, and she slips out the door, leaving Vanessa and me alone.

I adjust the cuffs of my suit and shake out my nerves. If I'm going to walk back out into the ballroom feeling like I'm knee-deep in legal metaphorical horseshit, I need to at least do it with my head held high.

Then an idea occurs to me.

I tug my phone from my pocket and type out a quick yet massive email to my entire writing staff to meet with me first thing Monday morning. I don't care if Vanessa and her team of lawyers are working the investigation. I'll work my own and figure out who the anonymous writer was. We're set to meet anyway to discuss a story idea for an editorial column I think will catapult my magazine to the forefront in a city where it's easy to slip into the background.

After hitting send, I brace myself for the fallout of tonight, knowing I'm basically marching straight into the lion's den that is my sister's auction.

"I need to get going as well," Vanessa says, walking toward me. She holds her briefcase in front of her, the top of her full breasts swelling beneath the gap of her open blouse.

I don't tell her about my email to my staff or how I'll be secretly conducting my own investigation, too.

"I'll walk you out." I don't waste any more time rejoining the auction. I'm ripping off the Band-Aid, so to speak.

I swing the door open and step out into the hallway, only to immediately crash into a delicate frame that has me knocking her off her feet. I'm quickly surrounded by blonde hair, various shades of bright yellow, and a sweet floral scent that makes my stomach clench in delight.

"Shit!" I hiss, wrapping my arms around her to catch her before she falls to the glistening marble floor. One of my arms is wrapped around her waist while I have her head cradled in the palm of my other hand.

My eyes search her beautiful face and then it hits me. It smacks me directly in the face. I've never been this close to

Selene. I quickly take inventory of the tiny golden flecks in her otherwise intense green eyes, counting every lash surrounding them. I note the way her bright red-painted lips part as she breathes in a shaky breath. She's a bright fucking ray of sunshine in my arms.

"Holt." My name falling from her mouth on a whisper sounds like fucking heaven.

"Are you okay?" I ask, not even attempting to straighten either of us up. We're caught in suspension in the middle of this hallway, bent over as if I've dipped Selene in the middle of a dance. The bubble we're in is a nice delay from what I know is coming when I step out into that ballroom.

"Yeah." Her chest heaves before she swallows. "Thank you for catching me."

I smirk before chuckling. "I didn't think I had a choice."

"What's that supposed to mean?" Her eyebrows pinch, and her mouth dips into a ghost of a frown.

"I didn't think you lying on the floor with a split skull and a pool of blood would have complimented this dress." My smile widens, and my gaze flicks to her chest.

Her mouth falls open, but her eyebrows lose their tension. "Oh, right. No... it wouldn't. My day has already been quite shitty, so that would have been the icing on the cake."

Shitty? Why has her day been shitty?

I want to ask her, but I don't. I'm at a loss for words while staring at her beauty. She's always been stunning, but being this close to her feels as if I've been launched into another galaxy. Selene has stolen the breath from my lungs—a feeling I've never felt before. Not this intensely, anyway.

Her eyes search my face. The tip of her tongue pushes out, and she sweeps it across her bottom lip. Then she looks up and over my shoulder.

After following what's caught her attention, I see Vanessa standing behind me, watching us.

"Can you let go of me now?" Selene asks, still draped in my arms.

I whip my head back to her, and my face falls. "Yeah, of course."

I lift Selene, and her grip slips away from my arms, the absence of her touch almost immediate. Smoothing her hands across the front of her silky, yellow dress, she straightens herself out before fixing her hair and sweeping it away from her face.

Her dress clings effortlessly to her body, gliding against the full curves of her hips. The front dips between her breasts, revealing the soft, supple flesh and the pale blue stone resting there.

She tilts her head to the side. "Thanks again for catching me."

"Well, I owed it to you." I run my hand through my hair, trying not to notice the eyes of passersby clinging to me longer than necessary. "It was me who bumped into you."

"Right." She smiles. "You did."

Raking my eyes over her once more, as if I haven't already gotten my fill, I gesture toward her. "You look beautiful tonight, by the way."

Her cheeks flush red. *Always so modest, Wallflower.*

"Thank you. You two look great as well." She gestures between Vanessa and me.

My eyebrows pinch, and I open my mouth to tell her Vanessa and I aren't an item, that we didn't come here together, and I sure as fuck don't think of her like that. I'm done with using other women as a distraction, hoping that this feeling I have for Selene will go away. My hardened dick beneath my Armani slacks can attest to that.

She hitches her thumb over her shoulder and half turns

away. "I was searching for the girls, so...." Her words are clipped, and her eyes widen. She does a double take when she eyes the man stepping out of the men's bathroom at the end of the hall, near the entrance to the ballroom.

The man emerges, tucking in the front of his button-down white shirt before closing the single button of his bland, generic gray suit. He stops, glances up and down the hall, then looks down at his phone.

I recognize him. He's the man Selene had her arm wrapped around the night of The Veiled Door's re-opening just weeks ago.

A lump lodges itself in my throat, but I force myself to keep my cool and not let my inner feelings show.

"How are you, by the way?" I ask Selene, not wanting her to leave just yet. If she does, I'll be forced to face my reality unfolding in real time.

Selene turns and looks up at me. Her expression softens. "I'm sorry, I really should get going." She gestures over her shoulder again toward the man she's been dating.

The fucker is still standing outside the bathroom, engrossed in whatever is on his phone screen.

Selene backs away, her lips spreading into a wide grin. "I'll see you out there later, right?"

My grin returns. "Absolutely."

Her gaze knocks me off my feet until she's spinning on her heel, marching down the hall toward the ballroom. I watch the sway of her hips as she weaves in between the countless auction attendees and guests, not looking away from her even as Vanessa says her goodbye and leaves me standing there alone.

The way Selene's blonde hair is twisted, with tendrils resting against the base of her neck, and the silky yellow fabric shaping her silhouette makes me think I've seen it somewhere before. A movie, maybe.

Whatever the fuck it was. The one with Matthew McConaughey.

"*How to Lose a Guy in Ten Days*," my sister's whispering voice hits my ear.

"What?" I turn, shocked by her sudden appearance, shoulder to shoulder beside me.

"That's where the inspiration for her dress came from. You know, the movie with Kate Hudson and Matthew McConaughey?"

"Oh, yeah, sure."

A grin stretches from ear to ear. "Isn't Massimo great?"

"Yeah." I swallow.

"I'm just thankful she isn't with that asshole Adam anymore."

I try not to show how this new revelation makes me feel inside.

"She deserves someone better," Julianna simply states, not giving me any more details.

I'm still watching Selene walk away. "She does."

I feel my sister's narrowed gaze, her suspicion piquing.

Shit. My honesty catches both of us off guard.

"Need I remind you of Rebec—"

"She was looking for you, by the way," I cut in, wanting to drop this conversation faster than a burning piece of coal.

My sister doesn't trust me when it comes to women, especially as far as her friends are concerned. Honestly, I can't blame her. Deep down, she's probably thankful her other two friends are spoken for. As if I was ever interested in them, anyway.

"I thought you had an auction to get underway," I add.

Julianna takes a step forward but abruptly stops before whipping back around to me. She's no longer in her usual playful mood. Clearly, she's irritated with me. She stares my way for several beats before her body language softens slightly and she lowers the daggers she has pointed at me. "I just wanted to tell you the rumor mill has already started around here. I've overheard several conversations, all with yours and Rome's names being uttered. I think you should heed Treena's advice and stay under the radar tonight. Don't do anything you would normally do."

"Seriously?"

"Yes, and you know exactly what I mean." The corner of her mouth curls. "Just try not to be Holt Capuleti tonight."

I try not to take her comment to heart but, fuck, it's hard not to when she's not only said this, but she's also bringing up my past. Clearly, my history hasn't been forgotten around here, and now I'm afraid it's only going to be thrust further into the limelight with this lawsuit hanging over my head.

I'm fucked.

THREE

SELENE

Holt Capuleti has never been one to show emotion, but under his flippant attitude about almost everything in his life, there's a heart that's guarded behind a shield of iron. He's kind when he needs to be and never takes life too seriously. Unless it's his business ventures, including Scribe Magazine.

I've heard the mutterings and hushed whispers of his name and magazine ever since leaving him standing in the hallway, but I haven't been able to pay too much attention to them because everything about him still surrounds me. The familiar scent of his aftershave has been following me like a shadow since leaving him standing there in the hallway. I can still feel his body hovering over mine as his deep blue eyes peered straight in to my soul. I don't think I've ever felt more exposed than in that moment. It was as if Holt had cut my chest open without even trying.

I'm touching my grandmother's necklace, hoping it will bring me resolve to the heat stirring in my body, but it's of no use. Nonetheless, I welcome the distraction because Adam is here... somewhere. I saw him earlier near the men's restroom, after Holt saved me from becoming an unwelcomed decoration to the marble-lined floors of the Omni Plaza Hotel.

Tonight's auction sponsorship banners hang from either side of the ballroom, displaying those who are bidding in tonight's largest fundraising charity in years. Or so Julianna claims. For someone whose claim to notoriety has been her interior design business alone, Julianna seems to have a knack for pulling out all the stops with her event organizing, too. The Omni Plaza hotel is already one of New York City's luxury hotels and event centers, but she's managed to amp it up to another level. With it decked out in glitz and glam, the mystery of tonight has caught the attention of celebrities and high-level politicians throughout the city.

"I ran this idea by Julianna earlier but wanted to see what you both think," Charleigh says, glancing between London and me. Asher, her fiancé, is standing beside her with his hand wrapped around her waist, pulling her as close as possible to him. Charleigh is wearing a form-fitting pink ball gown decorated in tiny, black sequined flowers scattered like polka dots. Her hair is twisted into a side braid, revealing her gorgeous face.

"What's that?" London asks, lifting her glass of champagne to her plum-painted lips. Her equally dark purple gown blends into the shadows. London's fiancé, and my future brother-in-law, West, is staring at her with hearts bubbling in his eyes. He's so enamored with her, even when she isn't paying him any attention. He's the perfect complement to her in his black suit, complete with dark navy-blue lapels.

"Now that Asher and I have set an official date for the wedding in the spring, we've started planning all the other events leading up to it, including the bachelorette party." Charleigh beams, practically bouncing on her heels.

"You want a bachelorette party?" I furrow my brow. "I didn't think you were into that."

"I'm not, and I wasn't really thinking of this as a bachelorette party as more of a girls' pre-wedding retreat."

"Oh." London perks up. "A retreat? I like the sound of that. Where to?"

Charleigh swallows a mouthful of her cocktail. "At first, I was thinking somewhere close to home, but I only plan on getting married once, so I'm thinking we go a bit bigger, which brought me to think of a place known for their flowers. Paris."

"Paris?" London's jaw drops. "I've never been before. I love that idea."

"Yeah?" Charleigh's eyebrows rise, then she's looking at me. "What about you, Selene? What do you think?"

I grin at my best friend-slash-boss and chuckle at her seeking of our approval, when the truth is I'd go wherever she wanted me to go if it made her happy. "I would love to go to Paris."

"Yes!" She squeals. "Oh, this is going to be so much fun."

"Hopefully, Charleigh will fall in love with Paris so much she'll agree to get married there." Asher wags his eyebrows playfully.

"Is that what you're wanting to do?" West asks. "Get married in Paris?"

Charleigh shifts her attention between West and Asher, uncertainty marring her expression. "I'm considering it."

"Honestly, I'd get married to Charleigh anywhere." Asher laughs. "Hell, we would have been married *years* ago if things had gone our way. But since this will be the only time we both plan on getting married, I'll give Charleigh whatever wedding she wants."

Charleigh's mouth splits into a grin that stretches from ear to ear as she looks up at Asher. She has the same hearts in her eyes that West has for London. My stomach somersaults, wanting only the best for them. Hoping for it, in fact.

Originally high school sweethearts back in Connecticut,

Charleigh and Asher haven't always had it easy. They were forced apart after a family tragedy for years, and only recently did they happen to find each other again by chance, when Julianna and Holt connected Charleigh with a realtor that would help her find a bigger flower shop. Seeing her before Asher came back into her life compared to the way she is now has been beautiful to watch. She's genuinely happy.

Asher kisses her deeply, and then Charleigh begins rattling off the rest of her ideas and other pre-wedding plans. My mind wanders to Holt and the situation that unfolded in the hallway. I'm still thinking about his blue eyes when I spot him across the ballroom, standing close to the door, immersed in conversation with the woman I saw him with earlier. I've never seen her before, but knowing Holt, it isn't completely out of the realm of possibility that she's here with him tonight.

Holt knows *many* women.

My gut clenches at the sight of him, the low lighting of the ballroom highlighting his features thanks to the shadows cutting across his face.

Everything about Holt screams money.

He's tall and fit, clean cut, sharp jawed, with defined muscles straining under his black Armani suit.

My gaze drops to his black Armani shoes, and I bite back a chuckle, thinking back to what Adam said to me earlier.

Holt's heavily cedar-scented skin still lingers in the air, fogging my mind. Ridiculous, considering he hasn't even come over here yet. He's standing nearly fifty feet away from me, but his presence is dominating. The room is quickly filling with more attendees, and the air grows increasingly stifling. I press my hand to the back of my neck and inhale a steadying breath.

While animatedly talking with the woman in front of him, Holt's gaze flashes in my direction.

I suck in a sharp burst of air, his attention striking me like a bolt of lightning. Heat blooms inside me, radiating down to my lower stomach, then between my thighs. How is it that I'm physically reacting this way to my best friend's brother? I *shouldn't* be feeling like this.

His mouth curls, and he barely lifts his hand in the air, his long fingers relaxed as he gives me a small wave in acknowledgement.

"I'm fucked." Julianna's face is suddenly in front of mine, blocking the view of said brother. Her long, silky, maroon dress hugs her curves, and it has a long slit driven up the length of her leg.

"Julianna always knows how to make an entrance," Charleigh mutters jokingly from the corner of her mouth, but Julianna doesn't find it amusing.

Asher and West are no longer standing in our circle. They must have left while I was distracted by Holt.

"What do you mean, you're fucked?" London asks.

Julianna presses her hand to her forehead and quickly looks at each of us. "One of the women that was supposed to be up for the auction got sick in the bathroom. Literally vomit everywhere."

The three of us scrunch our noses in disgust.

"I hope she's okay," I tell Julianna. I can't fight the urge to see if Holt is still behind her by tilting my head.

He's gone.

"I do, too," Julianna sympathizes. "We have EMTs here, so they're tending to her now, but this means I'm short an auction participant."

"Can't you just continue the auction without her?" I ask. "I'm sure you'll still get a considerable amount of donations."

Julianna looks around, as though scanning the room before snapping her mouth shut. She wrings her hands in front of her.

I've never seen her like this before: unsure, anxious, fearful, even.

"Jules..." Charleigh senses her uncertainty, pressing a reassuring hand to her arm. "What's going on?"

She sighs. "I can't really go into the details right now, but major news broke out about Holt and the magazine being sued for an article that was published anonymously."

Charleigh lifts her hand to her mouth, and London's jaw drops. The blood drains from my face, and without another thought, I'm searching for Holt again. The attendees have filled the room, and at this point it'll be impossible to find him from where we're standing. But now that I'm taking a moment to look around, I notice a few more hushed conversations happening around us, everyone cautiously looking at our group circle, their mouths barely moving to hide their whispers.

"His publicist told him to remain out of the spotlight tonight, which is fine, but I know if anyone gets even the slightest hint that the auction is falling apart, the media will be all over it and it'll make this shit worse." She chews on her bottom lip.

"What do you need us to do?" Charleigh asks.

Julianna's face turns hopeful. "Can one of you fill in for her?"

The three of us stay silent. Too long. Excruciatingly long.

"Come on." Julianna clasps her hands together. "*Please.*"

"Can't *you* just fill in for her?" Charleigh asks.

Julianna worries her lip again. "I'm the organizer. Plus, I think if I were to go up there, it would only add more fuel to the fire that's blazing about Scribe and this lawsuit. I'm too close to the gossip. I need someone else." She swallows nervously. "Charleigh?"

Charleigh scoffs. "You know I can't, Jules. Could you

imagine someone bidding on me for a date? Asher would kill the poor innocent soul."

Julianna turns to London and me.

London holds her hands up, laughing in disbelief. "West wouldn't even let the man draw another breath if he tried. Remember how Club Verona turned out?"

My stomach flips. I do remember that night, even though it led to West and London confessing their true feelings for one another.

My mouth spreads into a ghost of a smile. I may not trust love, but I love that my sister does. I'm glad both she and Charleigh found love.

Julianna hasn't found that kind of love, and for months I remember her paddling deep into the dating pool. It seemed every few weeks she was introducing us to someone new. But she's apparently swam back to shore for now, too preoccupied with work and dampening family scandals.

"Selene?" Julianna's voice strains as it passes her lips.

All three women are staring at me with bated breath. The air is tense, and suddenly, I'm wishing I could fade into the background like I usually do.

"What?"

"Could you?" Julianna asks, her eyes lining with tears on the verge of spilling. "Could you do it?"

I laugh, shaking my head. "I can't."

"Why not?" She steps forward, wrapping her hand around mine and holding onto it. "You're single, so you won't have anyone wanting to kill whoever bids on you. Also, not like it needs mentioning, but you're fucking gorgeous. The men will be fighting over you."

"Sounds barbaric." I scrunch my nose in disgust.

"It isn't." Julianna jerks back, offended by my comment. Then her gaze softens. "It really isn't as bad as you're making it out to be. You don't have to do anything but stand up on stage and smile."

"But what happens when someone bids on me? Aren't the winning donors supposed to take us out on a date afterward? Isn't that the incentive for them to bid?"

"It is, but you don't have to." Julianna squeezes my hand. "The winning bidder will join you on stage, kiss you on the cheek, then there's the option for a date afterward. No one is forced to go through with the date, though. The bidders understand the rules going into the auction. They know whoever they bid on has the choice to follow through on a date or not. They're doing it for the publicity and to bring attention to their name, along with their donation."

I swallow the enormous lump in my throat. Wow, I didn't realize Julianna had put so much detail into this auction.

My gaze drifts over her shoulder. Some of the auctioneers have already started filing onto the stage, a mix of men and women of various ages. I imagine myself standing up there beside them.

My skin is sticky, and my hands grow clammy.

"I don't know." I shake my head and shift my attention back to Julianna. She's standing close, her hand still wrapped around mine. "I don't think I can do it. It's already been such a weird day. This will multiply that by a million."

"I know it's ill timing considering your breakup with Adam earlier."

"I'm not torn up about Adam. I'm glad that's over, but it's just been strange, you know? I don't date or open myself up to anyone really. Love is complicated, and if this relationship with Adam has taught me anything, it's that love is not for me. I decided that a long time ago, and somehow allowed myself to get distracted."

I can feel London's eyes on mine, sensing her thoughts just

by her body language, her softened gaze, her bottom lip sticking out in a sympathetic pout.

I spilled all the details to my best friends earlier, describing my breakup with Adam. About him crashing my apartment and not taking the hint that we were truly over. His comments still linger in the back of my mind, and I've tried to ignore the prick to my chest when he said I don't belong with my friends. It's hard to believe him, though, when I'm surrounded by these three incredible women.

I avert my attention momentarily, looking around the crowd surrounding us. Adam is here. I knew he would be here, but I'm hoping we can make it through the night without seeing or speaking to one another. The last thing I need is Adam begging me to take him back, convincing himself we aren't over.

"I don't necessarily agree love isn't for you, but this doesn't have to be serious." Julianna hitches her thumb over her shoulder, pulling me back to the crisis at hand.

"Don't pressure her, Jules, if this isn't something she feels comfortable doing," London defends.

Julianna reluctantly shifts her attention to London but nods softly. "I'm sorry, Selene. I don't want to pressure you or make you feel like you have to do something you don't want to do. I truly understand. But just know that if you did, it'll go by quickly, and you won't have to say or do anything other than stand up there during the bidding. This really is just for charity."

"I don't feel like you're pressuring me, but..." I trap my bottom lip under my teeth. "I don't really like being put in the spotlight. I wasn't kidding when I told you I'm an introvert. I'm all for supporting you, Jules, but I don't think my nerves can handle it. I'm sure whoever places their bid and wins expects a date. I'd feel terrible if they donated all this money only to get a few seconds on stage with me."

"Like I said, they know the rules, Selene. Once the bidder has won, they come up on stage and take a photo with you, then you're free to leave." Her voice is still tight with anxiety. "Promise."

I stare into my best friend's eyes, and my love for her aches. I've never seen her like this. My gaze bounces between my two best friends and my sister, searching for affirmation, even a semblance of input or opinion, but I don't get it from any of them. They're silent. Most likely because they know this is a huge deal for me. I keep my circle small, and I keep my life relatively quiet, causing the least amount of waves possible. Life is safe and more predictable that way. A lifetime of death and heartbreak will do that to you.

But I love Julianna, and I want her to be successful. She has an enormous heart and passion for helping others. I may not agree with the morality of this auction, but I have to hand it to her, she's damn good at what she does. The last thing I want is for this night to fall apart.

Her and Holt's reputation is on the line. I know it isn't practical for Charleigh or London to fill this role. I'm the best and most logical option.

I quickly glance around at the packed ballroom, then the lighted stage before looking into Julianna's vulnerable eyes.

Then, with as much conviction as I can muster, I square my shoulder, and finally say, "Fine, but a kiss on the cheek is all they're getting. Then I'm out."

I've barely drawn another breath in before Julianna's arms are wrapped around me and she's whispering a million *thank yous* into my ear.

FOUR

SELENE

I immediately regret my decision to help Julianna the second I step on stage.

The spotlight beaming down on the dates up for auction, including me, is bright as the fucking sun. Not only do I regret my decision to offer myself up like a piece of meat to a pack of wolves, but I also regret my decision to wear a bright yellow gown. With the light beaming down on the stage, I feel like a beacon of light in the middle of the ocean.

Nerves slither down the length of my spine. With my pulse racing, my eyes adjust to the light, scanning the shadow sea of people gathered below.

Breathe in. Breathe deep. Breathe out.

"All right, everyone!" The announcer emerges from side stage.

He's tall with a smile brighter than the gold rings around each of his fingers. His black bow tie is slightly crooked, but he adjusts it as he saunters over to center stage as effortlessly as a duck paddling through water. "My name is Scott and I'll be your announcer for this evening. Welcome to New York City's largest charity organization, City Angels' first annual Auction of

Love. Where several lucky bidders will win a date with these stunning singles, all while donating to some incredible charitable causes!" Scott half turns, holding out his arm to showcase the ten of us standing in a row.

The ballroom erupts into applause.

Clinking champagne glasses and cheers echo from below. Now that my eyes have finally adjusted to the lighting, I search the crowd for London and Charleigh, desperate to cling onto to the sight of them for survival. Instead, my gaze lands on two blue eyes piercing through the darkness—ones I was staring into thirty minutes ago, when they were only inches from mine, melting me into a puddle.

Holt's gaze is unwavering and hard as stone, but his mouth is clamped shut, and his sculpted, sharp jaw ticks, his muscles twitching beneath his smooth skin, indicating he's as surprised as I am to see me standing up here.

"Before we begin," Scott booms into the microphone wrapped tightly in his grip. The blood drains to my feet, stealing my attention. "We would like to send a thank you to all our event coordinators and sponsors. Without them, this night wouldn't be possible. Let's give them a hand."

The crowd explodes into another round of applause before the auction gets underway. I stand at the end, debating whether it would be in my interest to go first or last. I'm standing at the end of the line, near the edge of the curtain. Behind the ten of us, a small quartet is set up. The drummer starts a slow and hushed beat before the rest of the band joins in. First, the guitarist, then the bassist. The beat vibrates across the stage, matching the speed of my heartbeat, ramping up my anxiety.

I sigh with relief when Scott starts at the opposite end of the line.

He calls the first woman forward: a tall, queenly woman in a gorgeous, black velvet, floor-length gown. She moves to

join him at the front of center stage, and he asks her to intro-
duce herself. She gives her name, age, and occupation—all the
basic details you would learn from an online dating profile.
Then he opens the bidding up. I try not to show my stunned
expression when the bidding starts out with a four-digit
figure.

By the end of the bidding, I have to force my mouth shut
when it closes at just under six figures, and the winner is asked
to come on stage. A young man appearing the same as the
woman he's just won a date with weaves his way through the
crowd to join her. He passes by the line of us waiting, on a
mission to meet his date. He shakes the woman's hand with a
large grin, then leans forward and presses his lips to her cheek.
She giggles when he whispers something in her ear. After one
more round of applause from the crowd, the couple return to
the line, standing hand in hand.

Then Scott moves effortlessly onto the next single. An older
man dressed in a perfectly tailored black tux. Julianna managed
to cast a wide range of candidates. Each one of us is of different
ages and genders.

The auctions go faster than I expect, and, for a moment, I'm
drawn into the excitement of it all. I listen intently to everyone's
bios and stare blankly into the crowd once the bidding begins.
Every time I turn back to the crowd, I can't help looking at Holt.
He remains where he is near the back, with his handsome,
unwavering expression.

I'm almost caught up in him, but my neck prickles with
nerves the faster the bids start to go. Before I've even had a
chance to ready myself, Scott is standing beside me.

"And last, but certainly by no means least, is this stunning
woman in yellow. She's a golden ray of sunshine, am I right?"
Scott grins, revealing his blinding white, straight teeth. The
crowd hums and hollers in agreement. Scott nods, riled up from

the crowd's reaction, then he turns to me. "Tell us, young lady, what's your name?"

He shoves the microphone toward me, holding it close to my mouth. I want to jump out of my skin. A lump swells in my throat and my heart races. There's only ever been one other moment in my life when I found myself wishing to be anywhere other than where I was in that moment.

Vastly different circumstances, yet similar sensations humming in my body.

I clasp my hands in front of me and blankly scan the crowd, swallowing my nerves before answering. "My name..." I clear my throat and sweep my tongue across my suddenly dry lips. "My name is Selene Walker."

"Selene Walker, everyone!" Scott shouts. The crowd erupts into applause. "That's a beautiful name, Selene."

"Thank you," I mutter, unable to look at Scott.

"Tell us, what's your age? What do you do for a living, and where are you from?"

"I'm twenty-eight years old," I start, my voice shaky and uneven. "Originally from Long Island, though I currently live in Manhattan. I'm a florist."

"Florist, huh?" Scott clicks his tongue, eyeing me suspiciously.

My skin crawls.

I stare at Scott, wondering why he's looking at me with a cocked brow when he adds in a surly voice, "Something tells me there's more to you, Selene Walker. Come on. Tell us something interesting and unexpected."

"Um," I mutter, frantically searching my brain for anything remotely interesting about myself until the first idea pops into my head. "I've written a novel." Once I realize what I've just said, I curl inward, shrinking under the spotlight.

"An author?" Scott's mouth falls open before he turns

toward the crowd, encouraging them to react. He swings back to me, waiting for my answer.

Fuck, why did I mention my novel? Stupid nerves.

I shrink even further. "Yes."

"It's not often you meet someone who's written a full-length novel."

I give Scott a trepid smile.

"I love it," he quips. "Means you're smart and have a way with words. Your date will no doubt find that an endearing quality."

I don't know what to make of his comments. I feel lost in this sea of madness, a nightmare of Julianna's making. I've now made my way through half the battle of doing her this favor, but I'm desperate for an off-ramp escape before I get snatched up by some stranger with a bottomless wallet.

"All right, time to open up the bidding on Selene Walker, the twenty-eight-year-old florist and author from Long Island!" Scott announces to the crowd. He reminds me of a game show host. "She's gorgeous and successful, and whoever wins tonight will be incredibly lucky. We'll open the bidding at five thousand. Do I hear five thousand?"

He waves his arm in front of him.

I immediately start to scan the crowd again. I still haven't found London or Charleigh's faces yet. Hell, I can't even see Asher or Julianna close by.

The one person I do find again... is Holt. Easily. Towering over nearly everyone in the crowd, he isn't hard to find, but his expression catches me off guard, making Scott's voice fade into the background.

Holt's eyes are hardened like two shining pieces of glass in the shadows. At first, I think he's standing frozen in the same position against the wall, near the back corner of the ballroom, but he's closer to one of the small cocktail tables now. At least I think he is. My brain is foggy, and my memory can't be trusted. My anxiety is firing off a torrent of nerves in my brain, making everything I'm witnessing unreliable. I'm questioning my own memory at this point, begging for this to end and be over.

Holt's hands are stuffed into the pockets of his Armani suit, and his lips finally part slightly. I'm clinging onto the vision of Holt when someone shouts out the first bid from the other side of the ballroom. All heads turn in that direction, including Holt's. My fog-filled brain takes a second to register the voice of the bidder. It's familiar, and one that makes my stomach somersault. I hold my breath when I follow the stares from the crowd to the lone man sticking his arm straight up in the air.

Adam.

His hair is considerably tamer than it was just hours earlier. He's clean shaven, and as far as everyone else here is concerned, he's put together. But I know the truth of what he's like outside of work hours. Both in appearance and personality.

He's wearing the same suit he'd slipped into before leaving my apartment, and compared to the other men in this same room wearing their expensive suits and tuxes, Adam sticks out like a sore thumb.

Reality slams into me like a gut punch. Adam just bid five thousand dollars on me.

What the fuck?

Rapidly blinking, my worry sets in, causing the lump in my throat to drop in my stomach.

"We have our first bidder, folks!" Scott announces, his voice echoing throughout the ballroom. "Five thousand. Do I hear six thousand?"

"Six thousand!" someone else shouts.

"We have six thousand!" Scott says, pointing to the next bidder. "Do we have ten?"

"Ten thousand!" Adam bids, his arm flying into the air.

My jaw drops. I force myself to snap it shut, frantically bouncing my attention between Scott and Adam. I don't know where to look. All I know is that I don't want Adam to win this bid. Mostly because I know he doesn't even have that kind of money.

What happens if the person who bids doesn't have the money? I think of Julianna and the reputation she's trying to uphold tonight. If the public find out Adam has placed a bid he has no intention of paying, Julianna's name will be in jeopardy.

Anger simmers and builds beneath my panic. How could Adam declare a bid he can't afford when that money is intended for charity?

My eyes widen when another round of challenging bids go back and forth through two others, then Adam's hand flies into the air again, and bidding *fifty* thousand dollars.

I suck in my bottom lip and nervously chew on it. I want to crawl out of my skin and leave the stage. I don't understand Adam's motive. Worry builds, and I'm ready to walk off the stage, when someone else's hand shoots into the air. Everyone's heads turn on a swivel to the man standing near the back of the room.

The man with piercing glass blue eyes, wearing a lush black suit.

"One hundred thousand!" Holt declares, his gaze glued to mine.

Audible gasps ripple across the sea of others. Holt was supposed to remain in the shadows. Julianna didn't go into detail about his lawsuit, but I do know he wasn't supposed to make a show of himself. Yet here he is, doing exactly that.

The spotlight moves, landing directly on him. The people gathered around him back away, as if they're suddenly remembering the gossip surrounding Holt Capuleti. Whispers over shoulders break out.

"One *hundred* thousand!" Scott repeats. "Do we have a challenger?"

"One fifty!" Adam announces.

Heads snap in his direction.

"Wow." Scott snorts in surprise. "Selene Walker seems to be the catch of the night here, folks, with the highest bids on record for our event."

I worry my lip, tears building behind my eyes. I don't want to cry. I can't. Not when I'm on stage at the center of a bidding battle. But memories of pooled blood at my feet and the idea of love literally shattering in front of me has me in a chokehold. Memories of Adam's accusations earlier, telling me I'm only playing a part digs at the shield I've held up for years. The thought of talking to Adam again has my stomach roiling.

The panic coursing through my veins is overwhelming, and then I lock my eyes with Holt. The options laid out before me are clear. I understand Julianna's rules set to the auction bidders, but I know if Adam were to win, aside from his lack of ability to pay, he would expect more.

I stare at Holt and shake my head slightly, just enough for him to notice, then I mouth the word, "Please."

"Two hundred thousand!" Holt shouts.

More gasps and whispers.

He's moved closer to the stage now. The crowd parts, opening a path for him to make his way over. Adam still hasn't moved from where he is, and his face falls with disappointment and defeat. Anger too.

He knows Holt is in our friend circle, and while I wouldn't exactly consider us close friends, Holt is the poster boy for the type of people Adam was disparaging earlier.

Adam's defeated expression shifts when he looks back up to me on the stage. Fire-fueled eyes coupled with the echo of his accusations become pin pricks to my heart. He doesn't need to use his words to tell me what he's thinking. He's proven a point with this bidding war with Holt.

Shaking his head, he firms his jaw and rakes his fingers through his freshly-washed hair, stamping his foot. He presses his lips tightly together. I swear, I see steam shooting out from his ears and flared nostrils.

"Two hundred thousand!" Scott cuts through the silence that's descended across the packed ballroom. "Do we have another bid? Going once..."

Silence.

"Going twice..."

Hushed whispers.

"Sold!" Scott booms into the microphone. "Two *hundred* thousand for the gorgeous and talented Selene Walker of Long Island. Come up on stage, sir, and claim your date with a kiss."

I look down at Holt, my pulse racing.

He pauses, trading glances between Scott and me, wearing an expression that suggests he's only just realizing what he's done in the past three minutes. Three minutes of bidding, placing the spotlight on himself.

He removes one of his hands from his pockets and adjusts his tie. Then he's smiling.

Smiling.

A dimple presses into his cheek, and a sparkling glint flashes in his eyes as he moves to the side stage before bounding up the stairs. Smooth and assured, he stands beside me, meeting me center stage.

"Well," Scott says, addressing the crowd, then us. "I'd ask your name, but I'm almost certain all of us here know who you are. Congratulations, Holt Capuleti, CEO and owner of Scribe Magazine."

Holt's grin doesn't slip even a fraction. He's treating this moment as if his life isn't under intense scrutiny. I can't say I'm disappointed. He did just save me from interacting with Adam and prevented the humiliation he would have endured if he'd won and never been able to actually pledge the money to charity.

"Now that you're here with Selene, you may kiss your date," Scott says, grabbing my hand and placing it in Holt's, the same way he did the other couples.

All eyes are on us as Holt holds my hand. It's large yet tender as his thumb rests over the tops of my fingers.

I turn to face the crowd, leaning a bit to my side to offer my cheek to Holt, but my breath is yanked from my lungs when Holt tugs on my hand and pulls me toward him. My body slams against his, and then I'm staring at his chest. His fingers hook under my chin, lifting my gaze effortlessly with his touch. The same scent of cedarwood surrounds me, bringing me back to our moment in the hallway.

He's so handsome.

It's the only thought wandering around in my brain. I must be disoriented from the whiplash of tonight. The past twenty-four hours have been more dramatic than anything I've experienced in the past ten years. Well, except for the night I witnessed my sister's ex-husband get squashed like a bug by a barreling New York City tourist bus.

Holt's searing gaze sends a shiver down my spine and heat radiating to the space between my thighs. It's as if every nerve ending has been awakened by his sudden appearance and closeness.

"Nice to see you again, Wallflower." He smirks, the corner of his mouth curling. A chuckle rumbles from his chest before his grip tightens on the small of my back. "Are you ready?"

Then his mouth melts into mine.

FIVE

HOLT

You know that feeling you get when you're told not to touch something, but you do it anyway, tossing all fucks out the window? Like staring at a flashing red button with a million signs hanging above it reading: *Danger: Do not press.*

You press it anyway, and the whole fucking building explodes.

That's what I've done.

I was supposed to keep my mouth shut. I was supposed to stay hidden in the shadows, pretending Rome's lawsuit isn't hovering over me like an ominous dark cloud, fueling the gossip of tonight's event.

But without a single thought or consideration, I pressed the button.

I've never been very good at following orders.

The crowd is eerily quiet for a ballroom filled with hundreds of auction attendees and media outlets. I can hear the constant clinking of flashing cameras, capturing the moment I decided to kiss Selene Walker.

Holy shit. I'm kissing Selene Walker.

Her chest is pressed against me, her back bowing under the

palm of my hand. It rests just above the top curve of her ass, her silk dress sliding against my touch. My other hand is gripping the back of her head. My fingers get lost in the threads of her shiny blonde hair.

I hold her against my mouth, not wanting this moment to end. I've caught her off guard, stolen her breath away. I wasn't supposed to kiss her on the mouth. It was supposed to remain innocent—a show of cuteness for the public, a gentle peck to the cheek. But I couldn't help myself. She's insatiable with absolutely no effort. One look, and I'm caving, tossing all fucks out the window, reputation be damned.

See? I'm not very good when it comes to following orders.

The hushed whispers and gasps from the crowd grow increasingly louder with every passing second, but I still hear the moan that rumbles from Selene's mouth. She melts under my touch, bending into me and pressing her mouth harder to mine. Then her hand wraps around my arm, clutching onto me for support. I dig my fingers into the small of her back, supporting her. My skin crackles at the thought of making her literally weak in the knees.

Kissing Selene Walker is something I've imagined for entirely too long, and now I'm actually fucking doing it. She tastes and feels like heaven. Utter perfection against me.

But even in this moment, when I will it to last forever, it doesn't. Our kiss is fleeting.

I tilt my head, wanting to deepen our kiss, but Selene's grip on me tightens. Then she's pushing me back. Our mouths tear apart, and she distances herself. Her green eyes stare at me, wide-eyed, the golden flecks in them reflecting off the spotlight still shining down on us.

She shivers, her breath quivering between her now swollen lips. "What the hell?" She inhales, her chest caving in with a dramatic breath. Her wide-eyed gaze shifts to her right, out to the gossip hungry crowd. With her cheeks enflamed, she presses her hand to her stomach.

Guilt crashes into me. Not for kissing her. But for kissing her this way in front of hundreds of people, knowing I'm the one who's caused the panic that's now clearly pouring out of her.

I squeeze her hand, hoping it will ease her reaction, but my confidence fractures when her wide eyes narrow and she winces.

She tears her hand from my grip and leaves me where I'm standing on the stage. She's shaking her head as she walks but stops when she reaches the outer edge of the curtain backstage. I'm staring at her back when she lifts her hand to her forehead.

"Selene, wait."

Her hand falls away, ignoring me, and she takes several more steps farther backstage.

I finally catch up to her. "Selene."

"What the hell was that, Holt?" She spins on her heel, eyebrows slanted in anger.

"Not quite sure why you're so upset." I narrow my gaze. "You were clearly asking for my help out there. Pleading for it, in fact."

I can't forget the way she mouthed her plea to me with her gaze locked onto mine.

"I was not pleading."

"Right, because you mouthing the word 'please' from across the ballroom isn't pleading." I smirk. "Tell me, Wallflower, why would you rather have me bid on you than Adam when you came here together?"

She pauses, her neck bobbing as she swallows. "We aren't together."

Her confirmation of what my sister told me earlier makes me feel better. Not that I didn't believe Julianna, but sometimes my sister can run with a rumor and twist it.

She crosses her arms defiantly over her chest. She's shutting me out, but I can't help noticing how I've never seen her like this. I've lit a fire in her, and I want more of it. My stomach and dick delight at the thought of bringing this side of her out.

Her cheeks are flushed red, and her chest rapidly and dramatically rises and falls as she attempts to fill her lungs with air.

"You kissed me."

"The winning bidder gets to kiss their date."

"On the cheek." She scoffs. "You missed by a few inches."

"Oh, come on." I lean forward, stuffing my hands in my pockets to keep myself from touching her. I won't do that again unless she asked me to. "Admit it, Wallflower."

"Admit... what?" she stammers, straightening her back. Her arms unravel.

"Admit that you just experienced the best kiss of your life."

Her mouth falls open, but then her head snaps to the left.

"I don't know whether I should be pissed or happy right now, Mr. Capuleti." Treena bursts through the event coordinators gathered backstage.

"Apparently, you aren't alone in that sentiment." I give Selene the side eye.

"Well, the crowd apparently loved it." Treena gestures toward the ballroom. "At first, I was pissed you didn't listen to my advice, but it seems to have distracted everyone from talking about the lawsuit."

"Great." Selene huffs, crossing her arms over her chest again. She turns to me, the wall between us growing thicker. She's angry but still beautiful. She's all soft curves and piercing green eyes. "You shift the narrative regarding your reputation at my expense. You're welcome for the PR boost, Mr. Capuleti."

She storms off, disappearing down the stairs leading back to the ballroom. Passing Julianna along the way, she doesn't even bother stopping.

Julianna looks over her shoulder before snapping her head in my direction.

"I don't blame Selene for being irritated," Julianna says. "You weren't supposed to kiss her on the lips, Holt."

I open my mouth to explain why I did it. That the feelings I've harbored for my sister's best friend bubbled over like a pot of boiling water, and the opportunity was staring me dead in the face, but I stop myself. Mostly because I know anything I say won't help matters. Julianna will continue to see me as the villain, crushing hearts of those she cares about since we were kids.

But despite my true motives, Selene has a point. I push away the roiling sensation in my gut at having hurt her and focus on what happened out there moments ago.

Kissing Selene on stage was a PR stunt. A good one.

"You know, for someone who never keeps his opinions to himself, you sure picked a hell of a time to be silent."

I stare at my sister, her words driving into me like a knife to the chest.

"Don't worry, Jules. I'm certain you have enough opinions for the rest of us, so does it truly make a bit of difference?"

Her jaw drops as I curl my hands into fists tightly in my pockets. Apparently, that's about the only good thing I've been able to do tonight—make everyone's jaws drop. Somehow this night has turned from barely tolerable to incredible, to a raging fucking dumpster fire within a matter of an hour.

I leave backstage as fast as my feet can carry me. My sister shouts behind me, demanding to know what the hell I mean, but I don't stop to fucking answer. Julianna's words may cut deep to my core, but it's the hurt in Selene's gorgeous green eyes that haunt me most as I slip through the ballroom, dodging questions from left and right from gossip hungry reporters.

I've seen a similar hurt in someone's eyes before. A hurt only caused by me.

I slip into the backseat of car and tell my driver Howard to take me home as fast as humanly possible, realizing one single fact.

I'm a fucking masochist.

SIX

SELENE

Aside from spilling words out into an open blank document on my half-broken laptop, only two other things have the power to bring clarity to my mind: yoga and flowers.

Surrounding myself with flowers on a near daily basis for the past several years has forced me to grow an appreciation for the beauty in them and the way they're nurtured, blossoming from the love and attention they're given. It's the way I used to think about love in real life.

Now, I only reserve that sentiment for love stories typed out on blank word documents.

"These bouquets turned out beautiful, Selene," my best friend and boss, Charleigh, coos beside me.

I've been fussing over a bouquet of orchids for the past twenty minutes—a specialty in Charleigh's flower shop during the colder months.

Charleigh leans forward and brings her nose toward the vase next to mine before she closes her eyes and breathes in.

I feel the corner of my mouth lifting in awe of my best friend and how she never questions the love she has for her work. Opening her eyes, she fingers the petal of the orchid. I look back at the mess I've been attempting to turn in to something beautiful.

"I think you made me fall in love with orchids even more, and I didn't think that was possible."

"Thanks, but I didn't put that one together. Astrid did." I nod toward the back, where Charleigh's newest employee disappeared nearly thirty minutes ago.

Charleigh half turns, glancing over her shoulder.

I stare blankly at the white flower in front of me, running my thumb over its velvety petal.

"Everything okay?" Charleigh's soft voice filters into my thoughts.

I snap my head in her direction, tucking strands of blonde hair behind my ear as I inhale a deep breath, the weight that's been sitting in my chest since I slithered into bed last night rising with it. "I'm fine." I lick my lips, knowing she won't buy my lie.

It's an unwritten rule. No one who says they are fine is *actually* fine.

Charleigh scrunches her nose. "Is this about what happened last night with Holt?"

I open my mouth to object but know she's right. "Holt," I say, rolling my eyes. "Adam. Me caving to my best friend because she gave me puppy dog eyes and going up on stage for that ridiculous auction. All of it." I shake my head and give up on the orchid arrangement. After wrapping my hands around the blown-glass vase, I carry it over to the table set along the far wall. Dropping it on the table, I move between the tables and stop behind the checkout counter, to boot up my computer.

"Selene," Charleigh says, urging me to stop.

My teeth cut into the side of my cheek, and I swear I can still taste Holt on my mouth. Should be impossible considering he didn't even stick his tongue past my lips.

"You know you can talk to me, right?"

I reluctantly shift my gaze toward hers.

She frowns. "I know you have your sister, and Jules, too, but we've been close for so many years. How many is it now?" Tilting her head to the flower wallpapered ceiling, she narrows her eyes in concentration.

"Six years," I answer for her, remembering the day we met.

I'd passed by her store after having the worst last shift of serving at a small pizza place a few blocks over. I was covered in pizza sauce after a co-worker spilled an entire can of sauce on the floor. The tin had bounced off the tiles, sending a splatter of red liquid across my white T-shirt. Once the manager stepped out from his office to see what had happened, my co-worker pointed an accusatory finger in my direction. I didn't even argue when he'd fired me on the spot, no questions asked. I was tired of working with co-workers who constantly teased me for being too quiet and reserved, anyway.

I'd reeked of garlic and dried pizza sauce when I'd passed Charleigh's flower shop on my way to the subway station back home. I'd stopped outside and found myself smiling at the flowers displayed in the front windows. Then I'd glanced down at my food-stained T-shirt. I'd never been more certain walking into Charleigh's shop and asking her for a job was what I was meant to do. At least in the meantime while I'd gained my bearings in the city and figured out how to gain a foothold within the publishing industry.

Temporary. That's what this job was supposed to be.

Now, six years later, I'm fussing over a bouquet of orchids, with a fully finished manuscript that I'm uncertain I ever want to see the light of day. Self-doubt is a bitch.

"What's going on in that head of yours?" Charleigh tilts hers and reaches out, tucking my hair behind my ear.

"I don't know." I shake my head. "Life has just been weird lately, and the events of last night only made it worse."

"Yeah." Charleigh nods. "I love Julianna, but sometimes she doesn't read the room. She means well but—"

"No," I interrupt. "I don't blame her at all. You and London obviously weren't an option. I'm the single one, and if it wasn't for me being debilitatingly shy, she probably wouldn't have had to do so much begging."

"Have you talked to her since last night?"

I stare back at my computer screen. "Not yet."

"I talked to her this morning. She feels terrible and thinks you're upset with her."

I turn back to Charleigh. "I'm not."

"I told her that, and I told her she should just call or message you, but she's been oddly silent."

"That is strange. Julianna Capuleti is *never* silent. I should have messaged her or called. I've just been distracted and in this weird space, you know? I haven't even talked to London."

When I'm caught up in my own head, unable to sort my thoughts, silence is normally my MO, not Julianna's.

"I think she understands that. I think we all do." Charleigh shrugs a shoulder. "Maybe Holt kissing you is bothering her. Remember how much she used to warn us to stay away from him?"

I tug my bottom lip under my teeth, thinking back to Julianna's comments about Holt with women. She's always been critical of him and the women he's dated over the years, warning us, her best friends, to stay clear of him because he's trouble. I never truly understood what she meant by trouble. Considering I never date, though, I never put much stock into it.

My stomach somersaults, tasting him on my mouth again. I've had two cups of coffee, brushed my teeth, eaten a mini spinach and feta quiche from the bakery down the street, and I can *still* taste him.

Maybe it's all in my head.

His large hand wrapped around my waist, pulling me toward him, slamming his mouth to mine. The taste of mint and aftershave permeating my lips.

Yep, it's definitely all in my head.

I inhale a deep breath and blink the memory of last night away. It's no use thinking on it much longer.

My phone vibrates on the counter beside my keyboard. I pick it up and flip it over, reading the message bubble at the top of the screen.

Holt: Can we talk?

"Is that her?" Charleigh perks up, eyes dropping to my phone.

"No." I groan. "Holt." I place it back on the counter, face down.

She jerks her head back in surprise. "Holt? Really?"

"Yeah, he messaged me earlier, but I haven't responded. He wants to talk. I'm assuming about last night."

"I asked if you were upset with Jules, but I didn't think to ask..." Her eyebrows rise, widening her gorgeous sparkling eyes. "Are you upset with Holt?" The curl to the corner of her mouth is hard to ignore.

Her question slams into me like a ton of bricks. Am I upset with Holt for kissing me? I haven't been able to stop thinking about him or the kiss, but I'm uncertain why I haven't stopped thinking about it.

Part of me is thankful the store hasn't opened yet. A fury of conflicted feelings is raging inside me. I feel for my grandmother's necklace for clarity, but my mind wanders to Holt before, like a pendulum motioning at full speed, it swings to my parents. I've been thinking about them more than usual lately.

Tears sting the backs of my eyes. I swallow them away and basically give my best friend an unhealthy dose of word vomit—an unusual occurrence for me. "I'm only upset he made the situation worse than it already was by kissing me. He knew the reaction he would gain from the crowd, and that only made my anxiety about being up on stage amplify. I've never been great at handling situations where everyone's eyes are on me. Holt's used to it."

"True... but something tells me Holt is struggling with this lawsuit more than he's letting on," Charleigh argues. "Rome may be public enemy number one, but now I think back on the past year, it seems like Holt was at least attempting to diffuse the tension. Now, all hell has broken loose."

A nagging little itch in the back of my mind tells me Charleigh might be right. Holt may seem like a prick on the outside, but he does have a heart. I've seen it in the way he hated seeing how his attempt to bring Rome into our friend circle hurt his sister. He would never admit it out loud, but anyone who was truly paying attention could see his heart isn't entirely made of stone.

Charleigh gives me a gentle, soft smile, then reaches out to grip my bicep. "I'm here for you if you need me. If you want to take the rest of the day off, you can."

I shake my head, brushing off her comment about Holt and shifting my attention back to the damn orchids sitting on the far table, mocking me. "No, my yoga class isn't until this evening, and if I go home now, I'll either be thinking about my manuscript or last night. Being here is a welcome distraction. It's better than being left alone with my thoughts."

Charleigh nods her agreement, which I'm thankful for. "I'll message Julianna and see if she's okay after last night. I've been avoiding social media, but Asher told me the news of Rome's lawsuit is spreading like wildfire. I'm just not sure how much of this is affecting Julianna. Her and Holt have had a hot and cold relationship over the years, but I can imagine it's affecting her at least a bit."

"Okay." I inhale a cleansing breath and click back into my computer, opening up my latest invoice to send to Charleigh for approval.

I'm typing in a few numbers and calculating the cost of our latest shipment, but I can't help the uneasiness growing in my stomach. It's a nauseating feeling I can't shake—one that has me thinking of my grandmother, my parents... their blood touching my toes.

Then all I see are blue eyes. Intense blue eyes peering into my soul right before feeling their owner's lips against mine, stealing my breath. Heat radiates across my chest and down my arms, pooling between my thighs. My skin hums, the pressure points of his fingertips on my bare back searing me, marking me.

My phone vibrates on the counter again, twice in quick succession. I gasp for air and startle at the sound. My eyes snap open. I hadn't realized I'd closed them.

Picking up my phone, I turn it over.

A text from Julianna in the girls' chat is at the top.

Julianna: Girl's night, ASAP. We need to talk.

After reading the message, I lift my gaze to find Charleigh staring at me, her phone resting in her hand.

Then I look down again, reading the message that came in right behind it, seconds apart.

Holt: We need to talk. Don't make me beg, Wallflower.

It seems the Capuletis are just as unsettled about last night as I am.

Charleigh quickly taps out a response to Julianna's text.

I don't look at my phone long enough to see her reply. I don't need to.

As for the other text—*his* text—I swallow the heat brewing inside me and turn my phone over in my hand before slamming it back down on the counter.

SEVEN

JULIANNA

My mother used to tell me love made you crazy.

She was wrong.

Hate makes you crazy.

I'm staring at her picture resting on my brother's polished, mahogany desk. Mahogany wood that's been derived and crafted from a legendary designer located in Sweden, no less. I would know because I helped him decorate this office years ago when interior design was my main focus.

I run my finger over the curved edge, barely lifting my eyes to her picture. It's hard looking at her. An invisible string tugs at my core, reminding me of the giant hole her absence has left on our family. The one currently being torn apart by scandal after scandal. Then the string pulls again, this time harder than before.

I adjust in Holt's office chair, the back of my bare legs peeling off the leather, burning my skin. I delight in the feeling. It's a distraction from the impending conversation I'm about to have with Holt—one I don't want to have but that's needed.

"Who? Who the fuck wrote it?" my brother's booming voice echoes from the other side of the double mahogany doors.

Again, I know this because I helped with the remodel. There are two entrances to my brother's office. The main one, which is connected to his secretary's entrance leading to the main entrance of Scribe Magazine's level, and the other through a conference room. A conference room he only uses in the direst of circumstances.

There are several muffled voices at a lower octave than Holts', surely telling my brother they have no idea who submitted the anonymous article, because that's the whole point. It's anonymous.

Years ago, after Holt acquired Scribe Magazine, he wanted to push the boundaries with his work. Holt is *always* pushing the boundaries. But the first course of action he'd taken had been to create an anonymous column—one where anyone could submit a story or opinion completely anonymously. The source could never be traced, and the writer could never be held accountable for their submissions if they were published. Most submissions have been confessions about themselves or others. Some have been to ruin reputations.

I place my hand on my stomach and massage the sickening feeling that's growing.

With a side glance, I stare at the rich, dark wooden door, wondering when the fuck my brother will end this clusterfuck of a meeting. One minute he's rattling off about the anonymous article Rome is suing him over, and the next he's talking about something to do with Rhys O'Connell—a name I swear I've heard before.

My patience is wearing thin when the sound of muted footsteps comes from the other side of the door. Then the doors are flying open. Holt pushes his way through them, coming to a screeching halt when he sees me sitting at his desk.

His hair is perfectly styled, as it always is, and his Armani suit is polished, with not a single speck of dust to be seen.

Unlike usual, though, his cheeks are flamed red, and the muscles in his jaw are strained under his freshly-shaved chin.

"You know what I told you about hanging out in my office."

I swallow thickly, averting my gaze to the front door of his office. "I need to talk to you."

"If you don't mind, I'm a little busy."

"Too busy for me?"

He sighs and pinches the bridge of his nose. His nostrils flare before he lifts his gaze back to mine with narrowed eyes. "In case you've forgotten, Rome decided to sue me, and the magazine is on the verge of collapsing. So, yes, I'm a little too busy to hear what gossip or lecture my sister is deciding to lay into me today."

I grind my teeth. Fine, I deserve it, but only a little.

I do lecture my brother more than I probably should, but he usually deserves it. History tends to linger, lending to a certain air of distrust, even when it comes to him.

I cross my arms and fight back the bile crawling up my throat. "Of course, I haven't forgotten Rome has sued you."

"Great." He sighs, smoothing a hand over his thick, dark hair. "Then, if you'll excuse me, I have one of my writers following an important lead."

"Important lead?" I know I'm supposed to be here to talk to him about the lawsuit with Rome, but color me intrigued. "Does this have to do with Rhys O'Connell?"

Holt's head snaps in my direction, his eyebrows slanting. "What do you know about Rhys?"

"Nothing." I widen my gaze, then nod toward the confer-ence room. "The doors I installed may have cost six figures, but they aren't exactly the best when it comes to being soundproof."

"Oh." Holt clears his throat. "Don't worry about Rhys."

"Right." I snort. "Because that's reassuring. Why does his name sound familiar?" Holt's silence gives me time to recall before it finally hits me, and my jaw drops. "Wait. Isn't he the one Heath, West's brother, got wrapped up in to cause him to fake his own death? The leader of the Irish mafia or some crazy shit like that?"

Holt looks away from me, his expression refusing to confirm or deny.

Worry settles in my bones. "Whatever mess you're getting you and your magazine into, don't. You aren't an investigative journalist, Holt. This is serious shit."

He squeezes his eyes shut and shakes his head. When he opens them again, he's clearly annoyed with my presence. "What exactly did you come down here for? To lecture me on how to do my job, or is this about last night? Let me take a wild guess. You're here about Selene."

I open my mouth to tell him exactly why I came here, that I need to make a confession, but he doesn't give me the opportunity.

"Not that I'm ever in the mood for your opinion on my personal life, but I'm especially not in the mood for it today, Julianna." The cloud of tension surrounding him swells.

I stand from his chair; his words cutting me deeper than usual. Now my annoyance is bubbling over. I step forward, bringing myself closer to him as I look up and stare into his eyes. Eyes like mine. Like our mother's.

I chuckle, the sickness is my stomach still apparent, but the memory of the shit my brother pulls time and time again shoves it aside. "Why did you kiss her?"

Holt scoffs and shakes his head. He moves around me, takes his place in his seat, leans back, and rests his elbow on the desktop.

"Why did you kiss Selene, Holt? You were only supposed to kiss her on the cheek. Those were the rules."

"What rules? I'm an adult, Jules. Fucking thirty years old.

You don't have the right to gatekeep who I'm allowed to kiss, talk to, or, hell, even fuck. As much as I know you love to control the narrative. You don't see me butting in when it comes to the petty bullshit games you play with Rome, do I?" He pauses, curling his lip. "This little tit for tat game you both play is a little childish, don't you think?"

His mention of Rome lights a series of fireworks beneath my skin.

"First of all, you don't date, you only fuck. Fuck with women and their hearts." I set aside my frustration with Rome, recalling how my brother hasn't always been the best when it comes to relationships. I remember how it felt to have my arms wrapped around my best friend in the bathroom during prom, sobbing uncontrollably. "And I don't love to control the narrative. We agreed."

"Agreed to what?"

"To you not getting involved with my best friends. After Rebecca—"

"Fuck." He curls his hand into a fist and slams it against the mahogany wood. "*We* didn't agree to anything. That was all you. You made those terms yourself, and it's been eleven years. Are you seriously trying to crucify me for the rest of my life over one fucking mistake?"

"Rebecca was more than a mistake. She was destroyed because of you Holt. *Destroyed.* So, excuse me if I'm trying to prevent you from doing the same to all my friends. I would like to keep this group intact without any of them being touched by you."

He presses his lips tightly together and massages his fingers over his mouth before huffing out an exhausted breath. "You're unbelievable."

"I just care, that's all."

"Care about who?" he shouts, shooting daggers in my direction.

I open my mouth to answer but again, he shuts me out. His pain and stress is evident. Clearly, this wasn't a good time to talk, and I bury my confession beneath all the hurt he's piling on.

"Because it sure as fuck doesn't seem like it's me you care about," he continues. "If you did, you'd be more worried about this lawsuit than interrogating me for kissing Selene last night. You know as well as I do that I wouldn't hurt Selene."

I swallow back the tears threatening to spill over. Straightening my spine, I take a few steps forward and feather my fingertips across the glossed wood. I stop close enough for Holt to see how serious I am just by looking at me. "Selene just lost her grandmother—the only real family member she felt truly understood her—and she's been through a lot of shit in her life. Horrifying things no one should ever experience. You took advantage of her last night."

"Like you didn't?" He tilts his head. "Like you didn't ask her, practically beg her to go up on that stage to help you?"

I pause, allowing his words sink in for a moment. "Break her heart or hurt her in any way, and I'm not sure the outcome will be the same as last time. My forgiveness only goes so far."

"You truly think that low of me?"

I arch a brow. "Track record speaks for itself."

"Jesus Christ, Jules." There's a vulnerability in his usually contained appearance. His expression relaxes, and his lips part to take in a breath. His eyes shift toward the full-length glass windows overlooking the city. He's attempting to conceal his hurt. "Get out," he grinds, clenching his jaw.

But he's also hurting me.

I came over to his office, first thing, to tell him the truth. That it was me. That it's all my fault.

At one point in time, I thought Holt and I were as close as a brother and sister could be thanks to the endless nights as kids spent sneaking into our secret hideout in the garden of our manor on the outskirts of the city. But we're no longer those kids trading secrets. Instead, we're keeping them guarded, locked inside a vault having tossed out the key.

"Leave," he says, turning his angry eyes back on me. "Leave before I lose my patience all together and say something I might regret, forgetting you're my little sister."

The lump in my throat is unbearable. Everything is fucked.

I keep my confession to myself as Holt holds on tightly to his secrets. Rhys, the development of Rome's lawsuit, and his feelings for Selene.

Because as much as I don't want him anywhere near Selene, deep down I know he's different when it comes to her. I see it in his eyes. I hear it in his voice when he talks about her.

But through the glimpse of softness and vulnerability, reality hits me: I can't confide in Holt. I never have been able to truly count on him.

I leave his office without another word, allowing the guilt to wrap itself around me. I won't be able to contain the truth much longer—I can't.

I'll tell him soon, it just won't be today. Not when we've traded cuts and wounds, exposing each of our vulnerabilities, knocking each other down until we're at our lowest.

Selene for him.

Rome for me.

His mention of my and Rome's tit for tat being childish is the biggest cut of all. He doesn't know it, but he's widened the wound that's festered for years, opening the sore and allowing it all the spill out of me like the breaking of a dam. I try to keep it contained, never showing that the rivalry between Rome and me isn't simple. It never has been.

EIGHT

HOLT

"Tell me you have a handle on this, Holt."

I stop dead in my tracks and hang my head, pinching the bridge of my nose so tightly, I think I might fracture it right down to the bone.

A sea of people continue to surround me. They check me with their shoulders and elbows, but I don't give a shit. I'm just trying to make it through this phone call without blacking out or taking my frustration out on an innocent bystander.

"It depends on what your definition of handle is, Dad," I grit, moving my fingers from my nose to my forehead.

"Please," he scoffs. "Don't be a fucking smartass."

"I'm not, but I've been working all day to contain this, and you're talking to me as if I have no clue what I'm doing or like I'm just letting this shit happen to me."

"That's not what I'm saying, but I'm not certain this *can* be contained, Holt. It's all the city is talking about. You and the magazine are plastered across every headline," my father seethes. His anger is evident through the speaker pressed to my ear, and it's a rare sound for someone who has spent his entire forty-year political career containing scandals. The majority of those being while he was the mayor of New York City. Every statement and act was a strategic chess move, doing whatever it took to keep the media's attention off the shiny object while flashing another object to distract them.

"Any situation in which our name is tied with those fucking Montgomerys needs to be shut down immediately," he continues. "It's been twenty-four hours since this news broke, and that's entirely too long. The media has posted the article written by someone accusing Rome of holding sex parties at his multiple estates, among other details I'd rather not repeat. This accusation will no doubt leave a bad taste in the mouths of those who'd ever want to do business with Rome. What I don't understand is how you could publish that piece in your magazine. You know the Montgomerys won't let gossip such as this just slide."

"It's an anonymous column," I explain gruffly. "I personally don't vet every single article. The anonymous column has its own editor and staff."

"You should have told them."

"Seriously?" My anger ramps up, and I feel like I'm back in my office with Julianna standing in front of me again, questioning my life choices as if it's her fucking place. I narrow my eyes at absolutely no one. "Told them what, exactly?"

"Told them not to ever mention a single Montgomery. Ever."

The Capuleti and Montgomery rivalry goes back generations. The exact start date is unknown, but every generation as far back as I know has been raised to never question the last. From birth, we're told the Montgomerys are our sworn enemy— something to do with a Capuleti son being caught having an affair with a spoken for Montgomery. As retribution, the Montgomerys gifted the Capuleti family the son's head on a spike. From there, the domino effect began, with a river of bloodshed following for centuries. Or so the story has been told over the years. We've been told to never question it.

We don't dare get involved with them or even attempt to cross their paths, or we'll be exiled from our respective families or perceived as a traitor, no questions asked. Over the years, the lines drawn between our families have weakened, and I guess you could say Julianna and I have worsened it between my attempts to cozy up to Rome and Julianna's constant string of pranks. I can't blame her, though, when Rome continues the cycle, pushing Julianna to take it a step further.

A Capuleti never could let a Montgomery have the last word.

Julianna played with fire the moment she decided to entertain Rome's interventions and teasing. I danced in it the second I convinced myself we could fix a centuries-old rivalry just by simply playing nice.

What a fucking joke. My ancestors would be rolling over in their grave if they saw us now.

I tilt my head back and squeeze my eyes shut. Dusk has set in across the city. The sunlight is nearly gone.

"I'm not going to tell my staff to avoid publishing the Montgomery name over a stupid family rivalry."

"Tell that to the countless lives lost and blood spilled at the hands of that family over the years," my father hisses. "Our family rivalry isn't a joke, Holt."

I open my mouth to point out that the Capuletis are just as guilty as the Montgomerys but stop myself. There's no point. There never is a fucking point. Instead, I settle on muttering, "I understand."

"Good."

"I have one more question." I blow out a heavy breath. I've debated having this talk with him, but curiosity gets the better of me. I should drop it, but I've never been very good at listening to the rational part of my brain.

"Always," he says confidently. "You can always talk to me."

"Okay." I inhale a deep breath. "About Mom's death—"

"That's not a question, Holt," he interjects quickly. A little too quickly. "But what is it?"

"I know it was a long time ago, but something never sat right with me about it." I swallow around the lump in my throat. Suddenly, I'm nervous. "I remember the police saying it was a common type of death. A random shooting on the subway, but—"

"But nothing, Holt," he clips, his voice hardening. "We've been over this a million times. There's no reason to go down this rabbit hole. I was almost certain it had to do with the Montgomerys, but the police did their investigation. Some random drug addict or criminal decided to cut your mother's life short for absolutely no reason. While I have the urge to question it myself sometimes, I don't. That's all there is to it. Understand?"

I rake a hand through my hair and hang my head, looking down at the pavement beneath my feet. Honestly, I'm not even sure I have the bandwidth to argue with my father at the moment. We've been through this conversation before, and we always end up circling back to the beginning.

Unlike him, I don't think the Montgomerys had a hand in her death. They hate us, but I don't think they would stoop that low.

I'm exhausted, and I only have myself to blame. This is all my doing. In truth, there's only one thing I know will make this feeling go away, and it sure as fuck isn't talking to my dad.

Especially when he convinces me to believe that my mother's murder was random.

I can only tackle so many battles at once. I don't have enough fucking weapons to fight this one.

"Understood, Holt?" my father presses.

I hesitate but ultimately decide to give in. For now. "Understood."

Honestly, my mind isn't completely in this conversation with him anyway. It's on someone else. While I've been tackling the lawsuit and Julianna's surprise visit to my office all day, plus this random thought about my mother's murder, I've been doing it all with only half a mind. My thoughts are too tangled up in a green-eyed wallflower.

It's as if kissing her has opened the floodgates. I surrender to the current, allowing the torrent of waves to whisk me away. The feelings I've kept bottled inside have exploded, Selene's luscious lips the key to the lock.

"Listen, Dad," I blurt out. "I'll talk to you later."

"Wait!" he calls out before I pull my phone away. "I can tell you're pissed at your circumstances, but I didn't call you to criticize you for what you've done in the hours after this media leak about the lawsuit."

"No?" I bite back a bitter laugh. "I couldn't tell."

"No," my father huffs. "While the lawsuit seems to be the main story, there's an emerging story coming out about what happened at the charity auction last night with Selene."

"Seriously?" I ignore the way my pulse skips a beat at the mention of Selene.

"Yeah." I can practically hear the hope in my father's voice. "It seems the public has more interest in this mystery woman that caused you to break the rules than the lawsuit."

Wow. Sounds like Treena was right.

Rome's lawsuit has been overshadowed by me kissing Selene on stage at the auction.

"Not sure how you're going to work this out, considering she's your sister's close friend."

"I'll figure it out," I tell him, wanting to end this conversation right fucking now.

She's more than Julianna's close friend. She's her best friend—one Julianna hasn't stopped telling me, practically begging me, to stay away from.

"Talk to her. Maybe take her out just the—"

"Dad, I said I'll handle it. I'll talk to you later and update you about the lawsuit." I hang up before he has the chance to steer the conversation back to our family rivalry or drudge up any more mistakes I've made in my past.

Fuck, what is it with Julianna and my father today?

I don't need either their help or advice, especially when it comes to Selene. Because the truth is, I don't need a fucking new storyline to use as an excuse to get close to her.

Truth is, this is what I've always wanted. I've just been too deep in my own shit to make a move. But I made mine last night, and now there's no going back, no matter how much Julianna likes to keep me drowning in the past.

I've never let Julianna's nagging get to me, but for some reason, I let her today.

I'm impulsive, I know. It's been both a strength and a weakness throughout my lifetime—an attribute I've learned to live with—but I'm probably allowing her nagging to get to me because she's sticking her nose into my love life as if I have one.

Truly, I can't blame her. After what happened with Rebecca, I understand her fear, but that shit bothers me. It's been eleven years. I was still a kid back then, and there's so much she doesn't know. I've protected her from hearing the truth about that day she claims I destroyed Rebecca Henry's life. But she wasn't the only one hurt that night. I tried to mend things with Rebecca, but it's difficult when the person you're trying to help wants nothing more to do with you. So, I let it go, just as she had. That still didn't stop me from making sure Rebecca was living the life she deserved.

Several years ago, I searched for her on Instagram and raked through a profile filled with images of her wedding day, the birth of her first child, then her second. The most recent pictures at the time were family pictures she'd had taken at the beach, drenched in sunlight and love.

I hardly destroyed Rebecca's life.

Frustration over the past three days is still blistering beneath my skin when my phone vibrates in my hand, and I read the message bubble.

> Cory Editorial Writer: At the docks now. I'm scoping out who to talk to first, keeping an ear out for anything that might give me a lead or hint at where to start.

> Holt: Thank you for doing this for me. If it wasn't for this fucking lawsuit with my name and face plastered all over the news, I would have gone myself.

> Cory Editorial Writer: I know you would, Boss. But don't worry, I've got it covered.

> Holt: Thanks. Be sure not to use your real name, and don't let anyone see where you're headed when you leave.

> Cory Editorial Writer: Roger, Capuleti. I'll report back when I have any new information.

I shake my head as I drop my phone back into my pocket and shove down the sinking feeling in my stomach.

Cory, my youngest editorial staff writer, is tracking down a lead on Rhys O'Connell's ties to Boston. I considered talking to

West about what Heath said the night he'd risen back from the dead and confessed why he'd faked his own death but thought better of it. West is one of my best friends, and I think the second death of his brother is still too fresh for me to start asking personal questions such as those.

Julianna's warning earlier still rings in my ears. My sister may be dramatic about my track record of destroying women, but she isn't being dramatic when she's warning me about following this story on the O'Connells. But I can't tell her about this gut feeling I've been having. About how hearing the O'Connells name hasn't just spurred on this sudden need for a story on the Irish mafia. There's an itch in the back of my brain telling me there's a connection to my mother's death. I know I heard it that night.

City air fills my lungs as I take a deep breath and run my hands across the front of my suit before smoothing my palm over my hair and brushing off any thoughts of work or Rhys O'Connell.

My foot meets the crosswalk, but the breath is knocked from my lungs before I've taken another step when, through the glass window facing the street, I see her.

Her blonde hair is pulled back into a tight ponytail—one I immediately want wrapped around my fist. Her sage green yoga pants leave nothing to the imagination when it comes to her full, tight ass. Six inches of bare skin is exposed between the top of her leggings and her matching sports bra. She adjusts the top of her leggings before bending over to stretch, touching her toes.

Fuck. Me.

It's the first time I've seen her since kissing her.

I've kissed plenty of women, but seeing Selene now, knowing her lips have been pressed against mine stirs a new sensation in my gut. There's a raging firestorm burning through my veins that shoots straight to my dick but also to the left side of my chest. I massage the delightful pain away, having never felt anything like it.

Well, shit. This is new.

She turns her head, glancing out at the busy street. It's crazy how she can take a yoga class with thousands of people walking past. The thought of others seeing her in multiple contorting positions, ones that have her ass on full display, sets me on edge. I'm in no position to be jealous of strangers.

Her eyes sparkle through the clear glass. The last bit of orange sun peeking from between the buildings shines across her soft, gorgeous face. I want to reach out and touch it. I want to feel the way I felt last night with my skin on hers, lighting a match inside my dark chest that's felt empty, hollow and, at times, robotic.

I feel like I've woken up after discovering I've been in a deep sleep my entire fucking life.

Ignoring the searing sensation spreading across my chest, burning me from the inside out, I take another step and, for the first time today, I'm looking forward to what I'm about to walk into.

NINE

SELENE

Yoga is the favorite part of my day.

Thirty minutes I dedicate to clearing my mind and stretching parts of my body I didn't even know existed. When I'm finished, I leave feeling more complete than I did when I walked through the front doors.

After the death of my parents, my grandmother insisted I go to therapy. I resisted at first, telling her there was no amount of therapy that could erase what I'd witnessed. The agony of my parents' death wasn't just tragic; it was a fucking nightmare. A nightmare that changed not only my life but who I am at my core. My world used to feel surrounded by a protective glass case until it shattered that day. Shards of what remained scattered at my feet, removing the veil of security that had been in front of me that my parents had created.

It wasn't long before I faded into the background of my own life, allowing myself to descend into the darkness. Every situation life threw at me I proceeded with caution. I was no longer outspoken. I was no longer impulsive. Life became a series of calculated moves taken with careful measure. My grandmother caught on to my sudden shift in personality and became concerned for my wellbeing. It didn't matter how many times I told her I was okay and that I was still me, just a different version, she wouldn't let up. She'd nagged until I'd given in, hence the therapy.

I barely spoke during the first few sessions, opting to sit in tortured silence instead. Until my therapist suggested calming ways for me to clear my mind of the intrusive thoughts. Yoga was her first recommendation and, ever since my first class, I've been hooked.

I've been coming to this same yoga studio for the past year. At first, the floor to ceiling windows facing the busy street intimidated me. But once I'd set my knees on my yoga mat, bent forward, and pressed my head to the floor, I no longer cared. I slipped away into my own world. A world of my own making.

The sun beats against my skin, and I close my eyes, soaking in its last bit of warmth. Evening sessions are the best. Inhaling a deep breath, I sink to the floor and press my knees to my favorite purple mat. I adjust the top of my sage green leggings, then lift my arms over my head. Keeping my eyes closed, I bob my neck from side to side, immediately feeling relieved.

Yes, this is exactly why I'm here.

The intrusive thoughts that have clouded my mind all day begin to dissolve with the fading sun.

My finished novel collecting metaphorical dust that's sitting in a word document on my half-broken laptop.

The gaping hole left behind from my grandmother's death.

The embarrassment of standing on stage last night, with everyone's eyes on me while I could only focus on one pair.

Holt's blue eyes staring at me from the center of the crowd, then him making his way toward me after being declared the winning bidder.

The feel of his mouth pressed against mine.

His hand clutching my hip.

A rush of air passes between my lips. My thighs clench, and I run my palms against the tops of my legs.

Why is my heart beating so fast? It should be slowing down, not racing. Yoga is supposed to be calming, like the sound of small tides rolling onto shore. Instead, I feel like I'm gripping the railing of a ship headed toward a hurricane. Why is my stomach in knots at the memory? Not in a way that makes me feel sick but in a way that has me *feeling*.

I cock my head to the side and swallow, telling myself to get a grip. I forced myself to stop thinking about Holt at work. It worked for a while, but now he's back, distracting me.

Raising my shoulders, I tilt my head to the side and force the feelings away. I open my eyes and glance around at my fellow classmates. I've become friends with a handful of them over the past year, but not so much that we take our friendships past the front doors of the yoga studio.

"Welcome, everyone," the instructor, Alison, begins, clasping her hands in front of her. "We're going to start with a bit of gentle yoga today, intended to calm your body and mind. I'm going to start with a half lotus position and lift my arms out and over my head, making sure to take in deep breaths along the way."

I mimic Alison's movements while closing my eyes. Calming meditative music plays overhead, but it's quickly drowned out by the thunderous sound of applause. A small groan crawls up my throat as a flickering memory of blue eyes invades my mind. His deep, velvety voice hits my ear as his hand wraps around my hip, pulling me toward him.

Nice to see you again, Wallflower? Are you ready?

"Okay, now that we've loosened up, we're going to transition into a tabletop position."

My heart jumps into my throat at Alison's sudden

announcement. Peeling my eyes open, I shake the memory away and blow out a heavy breath.

What the fuck is wrong with me? One kiss from Holt, and now I'm suddenly unable to think of anything or anyone else?

I shift from my seated position, placing both hands near the front of the mat. With straightened arms, I press my knees into the mat, ensuring my back is straight and my arms are even in front of me.

Looking up, I wait for Alison's next instructions, but they never come.

Her focus is directed squarely over my shoulder.

"Um, excuse me," she says, sitting back on her heels, her eyebrows pulled together. "Can I help you?"

Blinking, I slowly glance over my shoulder. My neck prickles and nerves dance down my spine. Uneasiness with a dash of excitement settles in the pit of my stomach. Gasping, I stare , wide-eyed, at the tall, handsome, blue-eyed menace in a suit. He stands behind me, toward the back end of my yoga mat. Sensing he's caught my attention, he looks down and sends me a wink.

My face immediately falls.

Am I dreaming? Is he truly here, crashing my yoga class?

"Sir." Alison breaks our trance, stealing Holt's attention. And mine! *"Can I help you?"*

"Oh." Holt runs his hand through his hair and smirks before planting his hands on his hips. "I'm here for the class."

Alison surveys him, clearly not understanding, considering he looks like he's ready to do anything but take a yoga class.

"I don't think so." She presses her mouth together in disapproval. "You can't just come in here without—"

"Don't worry." Holt waves her off, hitching his thumb over his shoulder. His too-wide grin widens. "I paid for the session."

He shrugs out of his suit jacket and carefully folds it in half before dropping it at the foot of my mat.

Alison stares at him deadpan before her eyes flick around the classroom, apparently waiting for someone to speak up and demand that Holt leave, but no one does. Aside from the quiet tunes filtering in the warm air, there's not a single word of objection. Even I'm left speechless.

My mouth is still agape as Holt kneels between me and the woman beside me. He has no mat, and he looks ridiculous in his suit. I stifle a laugh at how out of place he looks. Something about a man as clean cut and expensive looking as him surrounded by meditative music and burning incense is comical. It's like trying to fit a square peg into a round hole.

He leans forward, pressing his hands to the strip of hardwood between my mat and the woman's next to mine. Looking up, he waits for the next instruction from Alison.

She blinks and shakes off the interruption, then continues on with the class.

But I'm not so easily moved.

Seeing Holt here has my mind swarming with heavy, clouded thoughts. The thoughts of last night come rolling back in, thick and heavy, stronger than they were moments only earlier. My stomach is still doing that stupid fluttering thing, and the memory of how he humiliated me last night echoes in my mind.

"Come on, Wallflower," he whispers from the corner of his mouth. "I thought yoga was all about finding different ways to twist yourself into a pretzel, not people watch. Don't tell me that's why you come to these classes."

I scoff, watching him in disbelief. Curling my hands into fists on top of my thighs, I inhale a deep breath and settle back into my tabletop pose, then roll my neck and squeeze my eyes shut. "So, what, are you, like, stalking me now?"

I have no idea if Holt is still following Alison's instructions, but I don't care.

He chuckles, and the sound shoots straight to those damn butterflies raging in my stomach. The sensation is so strong, I open my eyes and turn my head to look at him.

He's sent me endless messages today, asking to talk, but I haven't responded to any of them. Mostly because I haven't been able to get a handle on the way I'm feeling about it just yet —another perk to therapy. Suddenly, you're aware of every feeling and spend extra time analyzing and figuring out how to cope with them.

"What makes you think I'm stalking you?"

"Oh, I don't know. Let's start with you gatecrashing my yoga class in a ten-thousand-dollar suit for one."

"Five thousand."

"What?" I slip into the next pose, trying not break my concentration. I'm failing miserably. The scent of his aftershave drowns out the incense burning throughout the room.

"The suit was five thousand, not ten."

"Whatever." I rest my forearm on the floor while turning to the side. I engage my core, tightening as I reach my arm up into the air while breathing out.

Holt's eyes never leave me. He isn't even bothering to follow the moves the class is making. He's simply lying on his side, propped up onto his elbow, watching me.

"Don't tell me you came here just to eye me like a creep," I whisper, tossing his words back at him as my arm starts to shake. I really need to get my arm strength up. This is pathetic.

The humor in Holt's expression has faded. He doesn't even care that Alison is launching daggers in his direction every few seconds.

"You haven't been answering my texts." He loosens his tie a little more. His sculpted collarbones peek out from the top of his shirt with the first few buttons undone, and I have the sudden desire to drag my finger along them. Heat pools in my lower belly, and I hate it. At least I do in this moment.

"There's a reason I was ignoring you," I say in a low voice, going back to a tabletop position.

Holt still hasn't moved.

I begin rolling my hips from one side to the other. I arch my back, then pull it back in, stretching my spine and legs, the muscles in my lower stomach and inner thighs contracting. My entire body warms under Holt's searing gaze.

"You're torturing me." He clears his throat, his gaze moving up and down the length of my body, taking in my position.

"My silence is torturing you?" I ask, chuckling.

His blue eyes dart straight from my lower body to my face. He lifts his hand and drags his thumb slowly over his bottom lip. "Yes."

I roll my eyes. "I doubt that."

"Why is it so hard to believe?"

"We never talk much, Holt. We aren't exactly friends."

"I never said we were."

I roll my eyes again. "You're my best friend's brother."

"So, what, that means I'm not allowed to care whether you shut me out or not?"

"Oh, so this is about your ego?"

"Ego?" He jerks back, clearly offended.

"Yep." I nod. "You used our kiss last night to divert attention away from the news of your lawsuit. Your publicist didn't waste any time letting you know how effective it was. Bravo. You hated that I didn't play along with that stunt you pulled last night, and now my silence is bothering you. So much so that you tracked me down and crashed my yoga class." I pause. "Wait, how did you know I'd be here?"

This very question didn't dawn on me until now.

Ten seconds of silence, then... "Julianna. I've heard her mention coming with you to this studio a few times. I took my chances."

"Right." I nod once, accepting his answer. It's true, I've taken both of my best friends and my sister to at least one yoga class each, and it's safe to say they've never wanted to come back since.

"Selene..." He blows out a hot breath.

There's a growing tightness in my chest that's ready to snap. I can't put my finger on one single moment that's brought me to this point, but the more I look at Holt lying in front of me, the tighter the knot gets. It's suffocating. Overwhelming.

Holt's relentless searing gaze is unnerving. Enough to cause the dam I've built to break. "Look, I'm sorry my silence has suddenly bothered you enough to come down here. If I knew you'd be this inconvenienced, I would have saved us both the embarrassment and responded to you earlier."

"Selene, listen—"

"Why are you here, Holt?" I ask too loudly, my thoughts overruling all common sense. Once the words leave my mouth, I know I've broken one of the most sacred yoga rules.

"Shh!" Alison hisses. "No talking."

Both Holt and I snap our heads toward the front of the class, half of which is staring at us, the other half hanging their heads low, pretending not to be listening to our conversation.

My cheeks bloom with heat when Alison's eyes narrow sharply.

I mouth, *"I'm sorry,"* to her before slipping into the next position she wants us to in: child's pose. I bend forward, bringing my chest to my legs and reaching my arms forward, pressing my palms flat on the floor. I'm thankful for this position. It allows me to block out my view of Holt. Maybe if I ignore him, he'll go away.

He doesn't speak again. I try, again, to clear my mind, but all I can think about is him beside me. His gaze sears every inch of my body, and it's agonizing. Seconds tick by, and I wonder how long we'll stay like this. Is this normal or has time slowed?

Finally, Alison urges us to come up and take a second to breathe and stretch. When I sit back, I avoid looking over at Holt, but I can feel his gaze glued to me. I close my eyes and roll my head to each side.

"Stop watching me," I whisper.

"What else should I be doing?" he whispers back.

"I don't know… Yoga might be a good start?"

"I don't know how to do yoga."

"Oh, my God," I groan. "You coming here is the real torture."

"Spicy today, aren't we, Wallflower?"

I open my eyes and stop moving, curling the tips of my fingers into the tops of my thighs. The class continues with their next pose, but I'm no longer in the mood. Holt has stolen all the concentration and energy I had for this class today. I'd say it happened the moment he barged into this session, but the truth is, he was a distraction before he was ever even here.

I came here to get my mind off him and that stupid kiss last night, but now he's right in front of me, and not just in my head.

An ache twists inside me—something overwhelming that causes my breath to hitch.

Without a word, I pull myself to a stand and begin to roll up my yoga mat. It's completely uneven and it takes me a few tries to finally get it on the right track before I snatch my water bottle and phone up from the floor and tuck my mat under my arm. Once I leave the studio, I rush over to my tiny cubby and slip my socks and sneakers back on.

Holt is quick to follow. He watches me in silence as I slip

into each sock then shoe. Once I'm finished, I stiffen and stare at him, shooting him as many invisible daggers as possible.

The front desk clerk shifts her attention toward us before swinging it back to her screen, pretending to click on her computer.

I open my mouth to lay into Holt for ruining my class but stop short. His blue eyes have softened, and his black suit jacket dangles loosely from his hooked fingers at his side. I don't know why but one look at him and I've turned to utter mush. I was angry with him inside the studio, but now I feel my anger shifting. My body and mind are completely betraying me.

"Why did you come here?" I ask him, trying not to sound like I'm on the verge of letting him see how he's affecting me. "And don't say it was because you suddenly had an interest in yoga. You weren't even trying back there."

The corner of his mouth curls again. Dammit. "You owe me a date."

Well, that's a statement I wasn't expecting.

I jerk back as my eyebrows pull together. "I don't *owe* you anything."

"The winning bidder of the auction gets a kiss *and* a date."

"For someone as intelligent as you're supposed to be, you aren't very good at reading the fine print," I snap. "First, the kiss was supposed to be on the cheek, not the mouth. You clearly bulldozed over that rule."

Chuckling, he lifts his hand and massages his chin. His eyes spark with humor. "And second?"

"Second," I force out, annoyed. "The date is optional. I have a right to say no if I don't want to go on a date."

"Are you telling me you don't want to go on a date with me?"

I'm at a loss for words.

He steps forward, bringing his face dangerously close to mine. "Go on a date with me, Wallflower."

I haven't even asked him where he came up with that nickname for me yet. He's said it a few times, but I don't have the energy to dig into it right now.

"Holt, I can't."

"Why not?"

"Because..." I turn my face away from him so he can't read my thoughts. He's already managed to break through some of the walls I've put up. I don't want him getting any closer to how I'm feeling when I can't even make sense of it myself.

Slowly, he hooks two fingers under my chin, pulling me back to him. "You have to admit something about that kiss lit something inside you." His voice is deep and velvety, slithering across my skin with determination, like it knows exactly the kind of reaction it's drawing out of me.

He doesn't care that we aren't alone. The clerk working the front desk is clearly watching us now. She isn't even shy about it. Her mouth pops open, and her eyes spread wide.

I focus on Holt. His close proximity causes the blood to rush to my face, deepening the heat in my cheeks.

"Holt, I—"

"You need someone to challenge you."

"I don't need anyone."

"No," he chuckles, lifting his hand and tucking my hair behind my ear. "You don't need anyone. But, see? You're proving my point already."

"What point?"

"I make you feel something." His fingers graze the shell of my ear, then along the curve of my neck.

"You do not."

I've sworn off dating. Adam was a momentary lapse in judgment. Like taking a test drive that I soon decided was a massive mistake. And while going on a date with Holt would be counterproductive to my own argument, he has a point. He does light something inside me. I'm just not sure it's something I want to confront at the moment.

"What would Julianna think if we went on a date?"

He pauses and swallows. His neck bobs with the motion, and I want to press my lips to his delicate flesh just to feel his pulse beating against me.

"I hardly care what my sister thinks."

"I do," I tell him honestly, dropping my gaze to his lips.

His mouth curls into a knowing smirk and a chuckle erupts from his throat. "I think she'd understand."

"Because of the auction?"

"Yeah, because of the auction." He licks his lips. His hand is still resting behind my ear, and I realize I haven't pulled away. I haven't even tried. Not like I did last night. I'm still angry with him for humiliating me in front of hundreds of New York socialites. I'm angry with him for using me as a distraction from his own bad publicity.

But the vulnerability in his expression has me softening. My heart is betraying me, telling me to run from this feeling as fast as possible.

I don't, though.

I close my eyes and blow out a heavy sigh. "Fine, I'll go on a date with you."

His fingers drop from behind my ear, and I pop my eyes open.

His expression is blank, and suddenly, I'm aching with need. Need for what, exactly, I'm unsure. All I know is that if I roll onto my toes and lean just a fraction forward, we'll be kissing again. Would it feel like it did last night?

What the hell am I agreeing to?

I force my feet to remain where they are. "But only for the auction. You paid for it, after all. For me."

His eyebrows pinch and his chin rears back.

Shit.

I blink, waving my hand in the air. "I didn't mean you *paid* for me, but you know…"

He takes a step back as if he's realized he's stuck his hand into a raging fire. He can't pull away from me fast enough.

"Holt." I sigh, lifting my hand to the back of my neck where Holt's was just seconds ago. "I want to go on this date with you. As friends."

"I thought we weren't friends, remember?"

"We aren't."

Wait, what did I just say?

He gives me a long pause before he clears his throat and runs his hand down the side of his face. "I'll pick you up tomorrow night at seven."

I raise my brows. "At my place?"

"Yeah." He nods once. "Where else would I pick you up?"

"You've never been to my apartment." Suddenly, I'm panicking.

"So." He shrugs.

"I won't be there. I'll be working," I blurt out, coming up with a lie on the spot. I don't know why, but the thought of Holt showing up to my place sounds like the one thing I don't want. I'd rather spend the rest of my life organizing orchid arrangements than see him standing in my apartment.

"Charleigh has you working at the shop that late?"

"Inventory," I clip out, hoping he doesn't catch onto my lie.

"I'm sure Charleigh would understand. She's never been a difficult boss."

I laugh. "How would you know?"

"Seriously?" He pops a brow. "Charleigh's one of those

people that would rehabilitate a dying rat if she found one barely clinging to life in the middle of some back alley. I doubt she's some domineering, tyrannical boss."

I smile, knowing he's right. Charleigh would do something like that. "She isn't. But, yes, I guess you can pick me up from the shop. I'll be ready at seven."

"Perfect." His too-wide grin returns. He's back to being his usual smug, confident self. The type all the women in the comments of his social media posts pine after.

He slips back into his suit jacket before running his finger down the length of my face. Then he's pushing through the front doors and disappearing into the crowded streets of New York without another word.

"The rumors are true, then?" The clerk behind the front desk squeals, stealing my attention. Her hand is pressed firmly to her chest, and her eyes are glazed over like some giddy teenager. "You *are* dating Holt Capuleti."

I don't even bother asking her what rumors she's talking about. I already know.

I simply tuck my yoga mat farther under my arm and hope I can slip back into obscurity, but something tells me I won't be able to contain the beast that's been unleashed. The one that has my world quickly blending with Holt's now.

TEN

SELENE

My body hasn't stopped humming ever since I slipped into my two-piece outfit and locked the front door of Charleigh's flower shop. I smooth my hands over the front of my linen top, the cool late fall air nipping at the exposed skin of my bare arms and legs.

There's a lump in my throat, and I try to swallow around it.

Usually, when I'm in a pinch for an outfit suitable for a night out, I call for reinforcements. My best friends. Julianna's connections in the high fashion world always paid off in a crisis. But tonight, I settled on a two-piece ensemble I ordered online and have had hanging in the back of my tiny closet ever since the day it was delivered. I couldn't ask the girls for help. Not tonight, at least. This isn't one of our usual circumstances. Not only because I'm going out with Holt Capuleti, *alone*, with no one else in our friendship group, but because I haven't told Julianna yet.

Sure, I messaged her separately outside of our group chat, but she only gave me a short message in return, telling me she'd get back to me later tonight after several meetings she had prescheduled with potential clients for an upcoming interior redesign project.

I understood, considering she told me her fundraising and event planning has been overtaking her interior design firm business and she's hoping to rebuild that side of her life. For the past several years, Julianna has tried to balance her once crazy dating life with her business life. It's nice to see her pouring herself into her work. After her reply, I swapped over to the girls' chat, glad when we all agreed to meet this weekend.

I sigh and turn my phone nervously over my hand while glancing down the street for Holt. I'm not entirely sure what to be looking for. I have no idea how he's going to show up. I don't even know where or what we're going to be doing on this date for that matter.

What I said yesterday in yoga class was true: Holt and I aren't friends, despite being in the same tightknit social circle. We've never spent time alone in the eight years of knowing each other. Not any true alone time, anyway. We've never talked on the phone or texted separately. Everything I know about Holt is through the lens of his sister or the moments we spend in the group.

By the time a blacked-out car pulls up to the curb, and Holt steps out from the back seat, I realize I don't know Holt Capuleti at all. Not truly. Not deeply.

And that realization makes me want to bail.

If I wasn't wearing four-inch, pointed, black strappy heels, I'd sprint down the sidewalk and head toward the nearest subway station.

But then my remaining bit of resistance dissolves when he lifts his head and grins, and I melt all over again. His familiar aftershave wafts off his sharp jaw. Three lines crease in the corners of his mouth, revealing his blinding white, stain-free teeth.

Everything about Holt screams money. I'm suddenly feeling very inadequate and underdressed. I hate the feeling because it gives credence to what Adam said the day we broke up.

Holt takes a step forward to meet me on the sidewalk but stops suddenly. The bright lights of the city hang above, resting below the pitch-black night sky. Since we're smack in the middle of fall season, the sun has completely disappeared by six o'clock.

Surrounded by the city lights, in his blacked-out suit, Holt lifts his arms straight out in front of him, spreading each thumb and forefinger to make a frame. He joins his two hands in front of me and closes one eye as he smirks.

Flushed, my heart races. I wrap my hand around the back of my neck and avert my gaze from his. "What are you doing?"

"Look at me," he orders quietly.

With shallow breathing and flushed cheeks, I turn my face up.

I've been on dates before, and considering I just ended the first relationship I've had in years, I'm no stranger to going out with a man. But I've never had a man look at me the way Holt's looking at me right now.

I have the same mixture of excitement and dread filling my gut as I did when I was on stage at the auction. But instead of an audience of strangers, the only audience is Holt.

He still has his head tilted to the side with one eye closed, peering between the frame he's made with his hands.

"What?" I ask, stamping my heel. Instinctively, I reach up and finger my grandmother's necklace.

Holt chuckles, then lowers his hands to stuff them into his pockets. His smile hasn't faded, but he's now studying me with two widespread, blue eyes. Blue eyes that make me dizzy.

"I don't think I've ever seen anyone as beautiful as you are tonight, Wallflower. I can't look away. I don't want to."

My shoulders drop, and I snort, rolling my eyes. "Oh, come on. You've been with a million women. That's impossible."

This outfit is six years old, and I bought it for forty-five dollars. There's no way.

His eyes darken, and he closes the space between us. The air has shifted. I freeze. My breath hits the back of my throat, nearly choking me.

Holt slowly reaches up to brush my curled hair aside, tucking it behind my ear. The motion sends a shiver down my neck, heading straight for my lower stomach.

Leaning forward, he brings his mouth to the shell of my ear, but not before he drags his nose along my hair, breathing me in. "Let's set some ground rules here, Wallflower." His voice causes my pussy to clench. I know I'm already dripping. "I never say anything I don't mean. Next time you question me, there'll be consequences."

My pulse races.

"What consequences?" I breathe. Fuck, he smells so good. My mind is hazy, every thought filtering into the background, making me lightheaded.

He pulls his mouth away, and my eyes flutter for a moment with his absence. He slips his hand away from the back of my neck. My jaw fits in the palm of his hand as he runs the pad of his thumb across my bottom lip. I flick my gaze to his, even though he's staring at my mouth.

"Don't worry, Wallflower. Nothing we won't both enjoy."

I gasp, then take a step back. I look around, remembering the situation I'm in. I'm going on a date with Holt because I owe him. He paid six figures for this moment with me tonight. How much of what he is saying and doing is for the cameras that are potentially watching us? How much is he doing this for the publicity?

I glance up and down the street, but nothing stands out. It's hard to tell in the dark, anyway.

"Are you ready?" I ask him.

He stares at me but doesn't speak another word. Stepping aside, he holds his arm out before guiding me into the back seat of his car.

I slip inside and my ass glides across the smooth, supple leather. I've ridden in Holt's car before, but never without someone between us. Now, it's just the two of us.

Holt's driver eyes us through the rearview mirror and gives me a small smile in acknowledgement.

Considering the walls Holt seems to be tearing down between us over the past two days, I'm surprised when he sits as far over as possible. His arm is resting on the door, and only half his face is visible as he stares out his window.

He isn't sitting any different than when his sister has sat between us before. He must have been close to me on the street earlier on the off chance someone might be watching us, keeping up the appearance for the press.

Folding my hands in my lap, I try to focus on the view from my window, but I'm aware of everything. I'm aware of every breath passing through my lips. I'm aware of the way my chest moves up and down, the way my heart is rattling against its cage. I'm afraid the buttons of my small vest are going to pop off with how wound up I am. Everything down to the wetness remaining between my thighs from Holt's voice hitting my ear registers in my brain. I want his tongue trailing and tasting my skin. I crave his touch, even though I've never felt it. I bury the sensation and heat, telling myself it isn't worth it.

Keeping myself facing forward, I shift my eyes to Holt. His elbow is still resting on top of the door, but his fist is pressed against his mouth while he's clearly deep in thought. The muscles in his jaw tick while his other hand grips his knee.

I clear my throat and decide to sever the tension between us. "Where are we going?"

He doesn't move a muscle other than to pull his fist away from his mouth enough to speak. "You'll see."

I chuckle, wondering why everything feels different in the car than it did outside the flower shop. "I don't even get a hint?"

His nostrils flare as he breathes out. The car pulls to a stop along the curb, and he's quick to open the door. "No hints." Then he steps onto the curb, and all I'm staring at is the soft bulge under his expensive suit and his outstretched hand.

With my pulse racing, I don't immediately take it.

Holt dips his head in the open doorway, his eyes softening just a little. "You need to learn to trust, Wallflower."

My sweaty palm sticks to the leather seat beside me, and a twist in my chest aches fiercely. Despite the pain, I shove it aside and place my hand into Holt's, allowing him to pull me over the edge, dragging me in with him.

ELEVEN

SELENE

Turns out Holt has brought me to his penthouse apartment in Midtown Manhattan.

It's one of his many places throughout the city. I've only ever been to the one he owns in Brooklyn. The sight of the glamourous, modern architectural building is drastically different from the one I stepped into over the years for countless get togethers and parties.

I try to suppress my ironic laugh, realizing he lives in what those of us who live in other, less expensive parts of the city call Billionaires' Row.

Why has this place not been his go-to when it comes to holding parties and events with the social elites of New York City?

I pick up my jaw as he ushers us inside the incredibly tall building that's shaped like a pencil reaching for the sky. The inside of Holt's building is decked out in sharp lines of marble and chrome accents. He pulls me behind him, never allowing my hand to slip from his as he waves to the door attendant, then heads straight for the glaringly shiny elevator. We ride it to the top floor. Once the doors open, we're on the roof.

The view from here takes my breath away, and I barely have time to take it in before Holt is pulling me toward the open, waiting helicopter.

"Holt." I grind his name out slow and low, my stomach fluttering with nerves. "What are we doing?"

"We need to take my helicopter to get to where we're going," he says over his shoulder. "Beats sitting in traffic. Plus, the view is better."

The gravel under my heels crunches before I'm met with solid, smooth black tarmac. I tug on his hand to try and slow down his oddly quick pace.

"Wait, Holt." I squeeze his hand harder just outside the open helicopter door. There are two open seats in the back, with a headset hanging above each one. The pilot sits in front, adjusting knobs and switches.

Holt stops and spins around. His blue eyes immediately find mine, his hand still wrapped around mine. "What is it?"

I dart my attention between him and the helicopter. My stomach is queasy. "I don't know."

Nerves overtake me, and I finger my necklace, rolling the gem between my fingertips. Finally, Holt pulls his hand from mine, but he places it over mine holding my necklace.

"Tell me what you're thinking, Selene."

An odd sensation comes over me. I can't explain it other than Holt seems to have the ability to peer into my soul in this exact moment. He knows what my mind is thinking before I've even said it out loud. Strange, considering we've spent more time together in the past hour than over the years we've known each other. This Holt is completely different from the one I've always known. This one is intuitive and patient. Kinder, even.

"I've never flown in a helicopter," I admit.

The corner of his mouth lifts, and he chuckles, slipping his hand easily into mine.

I want to kiss him again. It's crazy and maniacal. Completely irrational.

His eyebrows rise. "There's a first time for everything, right?"

"Yeah, but..." I blink.

"You're safe with me, Selene."

I press my mouth together and surprise myself when I nod once in agreement.

My grandmother would be so proud.

Holt helps me inside, then follows behind. Once I slide into my seat, I look around, taking in the number of knobs, buttons, and switches. It's all too much and confusing as fuck. How is it possible to need this many controls?

"Are you sure this is safe?" I shiver. "I know you said it was outside, but now we're here..."

Holt reaches across my lap for my belt. He buckles me in as if he's done this a million times. The buckle clicks, and he's tugging on the straps, pulling them tightly across my body. Then he reaches up to the headset and places it carefully on my head.

Everything about him surrounds me again. His scent, his presence, his shining blue eyes. Nerves shoot down my spine as he smiles. He won't stop smiling at me.

"I meant what I said. You're safe as long as you're with me."

I scoff. "Not if something goes wrong. Then we're both fucked."

"What do you think is going to happen?"

"I don't know." I wave my hand in the air. "Have you ever watched the news? A bird could fly into the propeller. The engine could malfunction, then we're suddenly crashing into a bridge or the Hudson in a raging ball of fire."

Holt stiffens, staring at me with amusement in his eyes.

"What?" I scowl.

"Nothing." He laughs, shaking his head.

"That laugh wasn't nothing. Are you making fun of me?"

"I'm not making fun of you." He pauses then sighs, staring into my eyes. "Okay, fine. First of all, we aren't flying over the Hudson, so you don't have to worry about crashing into water."

I glare at him.

"Second, my helicopter goes through multiple maintenance checks." He frowns and tosses his head to the side. "Birds on the other hand, no guarantees."

I harden my glare.

"You're cute when you get fired up, you know that?" He chuckles. "No wonder you're a writer. Your mind has a wild imagination."

"I'd rather not die at twenty-eight, thank you very much." I huff, then snap my mouth shut. This is why I don't open myself up to others often.

"Is this the sort of stuff that goes through your mind all day?"

I close my eyes and rest my head back. "What if it was?"

I feel him shift beside me followed by the sound of his seat belt buckling. Then his voice is in my ear, coming through the headset.

"Sounds exhausting," he mutters.

I roll my head against the headrest and open my eyes. He's staring at me. He's sexy yet beautiful sitting beside me, with dark brown strands hanging above his brow, framing his blue eyes. "It isn't exhausting."

"Worrying about what could happen instead of living in the moment sounds incredibly exhausting."

I inhale a deep breath and force myself to think calmly. I try to use the tactics my therapist has taught me over the years when I start to feel overwhelmed and consumed by thoughts. Or as Holt calls it, *exhausted thoughts*. But none of it works. Not until Holt's hand rests on my thigh. Electricity crackles across my skin. His fingers press into the muscle of my leg, only separated by the thin linen fabric of my skirt.

"Can I ask you a question?"

"You just did." He laughs.

I playfully slap his arm. "What are you, five?"

He rolls his eyes while mine drop to the crease on the corner of his mouth. I want to drag my tongue across it.

Fire grows in my belly.

I roll my head back to face forward. The noise of the helicopter grows louder, causing a vibration through my seat and body. I close my eyes and breathe. I don't know what has me more of a nervous wreck: this damn helicopter ride, or the fact I'm going to spend the whole night with Holt, just the two of us.

"What was your question?" Holt's voice comes through the headset, breaking my concentration. It's oddly comforting.

I don't move, instead focusing on the feeling of us lifting off the ground. I don't open my eyes even to peek at the earth growing smaller beneath us.

Swallowing, I stiffen as the helicopter dips slightly, then I slap my hand on top of Holt's, hoping it'll steady me.

"I'm sorry, Selene." His voice is soft in my ear. "Please, ask your question. It'll distract you."

"Do you think our lives flash before our eyes before we die, or is that just a myth?"

I've often asked myself this question ever since my parents' death. Did my mother's life flash through her mind as she stared down the barrel of the gun? Did my father's when he turned his gaze on me before pulling the trigger?

"I'm not sure, Wallflower." Holt clears his throat, sliding his hand closer to the inside of my thigh. My skin is white hot, the electricity from his touch jumpstarting my heart. "But I guess if we're going to go down in a raging ball of fire, we're about to find out."

I finally open my eyes and turn to see Holt staring at me. We're thousands of feet in the air at this point, heading to God knows where, but I have this sudden urge to both slap him and kiss him at the same time.

Maybe by the end of the night, I'll end up doing both.

That's if we make it out alive.

TWELVE

HOLT

I'm almost certain Selene hasn't taken a breath until we've landed back on solid ground. She hasn't pulled her hand from on top of mine. I wish I could say I kept my focus on the view the entire ride over to our destination, but I didn't. I couldn't look away from her.

She's too beautiful. Like staring directly at the rays of sunshine peeking between the tree branches and skyscrapers surrounding us. Hidden in plain sight, full of sass and fire, she's show, glimpses to another side of her I've rarely seen, if only during the past two days. It's a side I want to see more often.

She kept her maroon-painted bottom lip permanently tucked under her teeth and her hand clutched over mine. My fingers ached to graze her skin, to pop every single one of those buttons on her tiny vest open and reveal what was hidden underneath. Her leg was pressed to mine, and my dick twitched at the thought of having her sitting on my lap. It also leapt, along with my heart, at the idea of me being the one to keep her steady and calm when she was obviously spiraling into an anxiety attack.

Once we land, I take Selene's shaking hand and escort her

toward the waiting, open elevator doors at the opposite end of the landing pad.

She doesn't ask where we are or where I'm taking her. I'm glad she's finally taken the advice I gave her back at the car to trust me.

She clutches onto me and glances around at the surrounding buildings in silence. But once we've stepped into the elevator to take us straight to ground level, I can't take her silence a second longer.

"Are you not going to ask where we're going?"

Her hand falls away from mine as she leans against the wall of the elevator and closes her eyes. "I'm still trying to catch my breath." She lifts her hand and presses it to her bare chest. I watch as the swell of her breasts rise and fall with her hand, like watching the tide rolling in gently across the sand.

"Besides..." She licks her lips and pushes off the wall. "You told me to trust you. Are you taking that back?" She tucks her long, blonde hair behind her ear and clasps her hands in front of her. Her breasts push together, and I want to sink between them so fucking badly.

There's the glimpse of her fiery side again. I fucking love it.

"No." I rub at my chin. "But for all you know, I could be taking you to some nondescript basement to kidnap you and chain you to a bed."

"Oh." She grins, all her anxiety gone. "I don't think you'd do that. Too risky."

"I don't know." I shrug. "I like to live on the edge. Clearly, you think so. Don't tell me that wasn't a scenario that played out in that wild mind of yours."

"Kidnapping me or chaining me to a bed?"

Her question practically knocks me off my feet. Fuck, this woman is incredible when she's out of her shell.

"I'm not down with the kidnapping, but I can't say I would say the same about chaining you to a bed."

It appears I've knocked her off her feet, too. Her mouth snaps shut, and her eyes drop. Heat blooms in her cheeks, spreading down to her chest.

"Fine, I'll ask then. Where are we?"

"The West Village," I tell her, just as the elevator stops. "Casa di Luce."

"Really?" She pops an eyebrow before she tips her head back in laughter. "While the helicopter ride felt like forever, when I think back on it, it was pretty short." Her laughter fades and her smile goes with it as her green eyes shoot white hot heat into my veins. "Why did you choose this place? Other than it probably has a million eyes that will keep this rumor mill well oiled."

Her words remind me how much she doesn't know about me, only what she thinks she knows. "This place has special meaning."

The doors open directly to the restaurant. Decorated in gold and black tones, it's wrapped up in a million memories. And now, watching Selene walk in front of me, with her head tipped up in awe, I have a new one to store away.

Her mouth twitches, and I see the thoughts clearly working in her mind. She's retreating again but not completely. Not like usual. She simply allows me to take her hand and escort her to the front desk.

I tell the host I have a reservation, and she escorts us to the back of the restaurant. I hold Selene's chair out for her. She glances over her shoulder at me before scooting forward. Something tells me she isn't used to this.

I know this date is meant to be for show, to continue the rumors I started the other night at the auction. The media is an ugly, starved beast, constantly searching for its next story. If I don't keep the story of Selene and me alive, the lawsuit with Rome will come back to rear its head.

But I won't lie, I have other motives with this date. Once I barged in to Selene's yoga class yesterday, I haven't wanted to stay away.

No. Scratch that.

I haven't wanted to stay away ever since I kissed her up on that fucking stage.

I've thought of her every fucking minute and second since. I've showered thinking of her. I've sprinted on my treadmill thinking of her. I've sat in my office, staring out at the city thinking of her. Hell, I've even tried to jerk myself off to the thought of her so many fucking times. But all I'm ever left with is this hollow sensation and an absence on my cock, wishing it were Selene instead.

Apparently, I'm weak when it comes to her.

She's consumed me without even trying.

So, at this point, I will do whatever I can to keep her closer than I've managed in the past several years. Instead of distance, I only want her near.

Standing over her as she pulls herself closer to the table, I look down. Her blonde hair cascades down her back and shoulders. As if it has a mind of its own, my hand reaches out and brushes her hair. She stiffens and inhales a breath as I tuck my fingers under her golden strands. I pull her hair back, revealing her bare shoulder. Tiny goosebumps spread across her skin as my fingers graze her delicate flesh.

I glance around as eyes wander in our direction. Even if they weren't watching, I'd keep going.

Bending forward, I bring my mouth close to Selene's ear. She smells like vanilla and sunshine.

I don't miss how she leans her head slightly into me.

"Hungry, Wallflower?" I whisper, my breath causing her goosebumps to rise again.

I can practically feel her body humming.

"St..." she starts, pausing to swallow. "Starving."

I smirk, then stand, moving around the table to sit across from her.

The table is set with two appetizer plates and cloth napkins folded perfectly in the shape of a heart. Between our plates sits a small votive candle, burning delicately inside a smoked glass jar.

I stare at her from where I'm sitting, taking note of how different she looks. Her outfit is drastically unlike than the ones I've seen her wear to other events and functions. This one isn't obvious or loud. It compliments her, and somehow it feels like I'm looking at her for the very first time when really, I've been watching her for years.

She's a vision of creamy golden tones and sunshine, like watching the sun waking up over the Hudson, just when it's barely peeking over the horizon.

Catching me staring, she levels her gaze on me and arches a brow.

"Have you ever been here before?" I ask, unable to hold back my smile.

Our server walks over, pouring iced water into each of our glasses. I point to the most expensive wine on the list and wait for Selene to answer my question.

She gifts our server a soft, warm smile, then nervously glances around. Straightening her back, she clears her throat and fusses with the silverware laid out beside her plate.

"No, I haven't."

"What?" I chuckle, relaxing back into my chair. "You're telling me Adam never brought you here? Or places like this?" I rest my elbow on the arm of my chair, mostly to keep my hands busy and distracted. All they want to do is touch the woman across the table.

I must have struck a nerve because Selene's expression has changed. Instead of an air of lightness surrounding her, she almost looks uncomfortable now.

"I'm sorry." I never apologize. Not to anyone other than Selene, apparently. "I didn't mean to bring him up." Guilt sits in my bones. A feeling I'm not accustomed to.

"But you did."

"I did."

She shifts her gaze, turning her face so I'm staring at her profile. Her lips are pressed tightly together. Then she surprises me when she says, "Adam was a liar."

I adjust in my seat as she turns her face back to mine.

Her eyes have softened, and I recognize the look almost immediately. She isn't heartbroken. It's regret in her expression. I barely knew Adam, and from what I do know their relationship didn't last long. I tried to stay out of their relationship, but if I'm honest, I probably know more about Adam than Selene thinks I do.

"He was one of those men that would bring cookies to a dinner party, telling you he spent all day baking them from scratch when all he really did was tear open the package and pour them out onto the plate."

I hum and lean forward, intrigued, because Adam sounds like a fucking prick. I cross my arms over the edge of the table, hoping I'll be able to smell her scent again. There's too much distance between us for my liking.

Selene mimics me, leaning closer and resting her arms on the table. The tiny candle illuminates her face, and her cheeks and eyes sparkle with tiny flecks of gold from her makeup.

"I recognize that look, Holt Capuleti."

"What look?" I shift to rest my chin on my fingertips.

"The look of judgment."

"I'm not judging. I'm just wondering why you were with him at all when it was clear from the start you hated the idea of spending even another minute with him. I mean, that feeling is what led us here, isn't it?"

She sits back, placing her hands in her lap under the table. "I have a question." Her eyes dance around the room. "Why this restaurant?"

"What do you mean?"

"Why did you choose this restaurant to bring me to? You could have taken me anywhere."

"Julianna redecorated it a few years ago." I point to the painting hanging on the far wall. "Our mother painted that."

Selene twists in her seat before turning back around. "It's stunning. I didn't know your mother was a painter."

"She was for many years." I nod, the memory of my mother barreling into my thoughts. I think about her every single day, but talking about her gives me a different feeling than usual. "She donated that painting to the restaurant weeks before she died."

"Random shooting at the subway station, right?" Selene tips her head, full of sympathy. "Jules told me."

"Yeah," I whisper, my voice cracking. I open my mouth to tell her more about my mother and all the memories I have of her, but our server abruptly returns, setting two empty wine glasses on the table.

Selene and I watch him open the bottle in silence. He pours a little into my glass before waiting for me to take a sip. I eye Selene over the rim as I give it a taste, then hum in approval, welcoming the warmth it brings to my throat. I didn't realize how thirsty I'd become in the past several minutes.

The server continues by filling Selene's glass, then mine before setting the bottle back down on the table.

From the corner of my eye, I see other guests leaning over their tables and whispering. I swear, a few of them even pull out their phones to snap pictures. Perhaps it's paranoia, maybe it isn't. It's true, the story of Rome's lawsuit is floating around, but being here with Selene is definitely bringing up a fresh story for the media to cover.

I've tried to push aside the stress I've been feeling over this lawsuit, but all my efforts have been unsuccessful. I've prided myself on making a name for myself outside of my father's political achievements. When you're the son of the mayor in the largest city in the country, it's almost impossible to separate yourself from that legacy. And I've done that.

Until now.

Now all the media sees is the Capuleti name tied to corruption and manipulation, all to get ahead.

I've felt like shit ever since Rome's slimy little attorney slapped me with the lawsuit outside of West's bar. The stress of my castle crumbling has taken over every aspect of my life since then. My only relief, the only medicine to this bleeding wound, has been Selene.

I watch her with intensity as she lifts her glass and drinks nearly half her wine in one gulp. Her perfect lips press to the delicate glass, and her head tips back, exposing her soft, smooth flesh. The gold chain wrapped around her neck glints under the gold lighting of the restaurant, the pale blue stone shimmering as she lowers her glass and sets it down on the table.

For as long as I've known her, Selene has been comfortable living in the shadows. She's quiet and reserved. She keeps her heart well-guarded. But I can't stop this nagging feeling inside of me from growing as I watch her. Ever since our kiss on that stage, she's opened up to me... whether she realizes it or not.

She's fiery and opinionated, unafraid to speak her mind. I

want to know her more. I want to see this side of her again and again and again.

Fuck, seeing her like this feels like taking a hit of heroine.

At this point, I'll do whatever it takes to cling to this feeling.

My phone vibrates in my pocket, but I ignore it. It's been nonstop ever since we sat down.

Selene picks up her menu and studies it. She lifts her hand and tucks her hair behind her ear, but all I want is to feel her. I want to keep her close.

I guess my plan truly will kill two birds with one stone.

Falling for my sister's best friend isn't something new for me, either. I thought I had fallen for Rebecca, but it wasn't like this. This is fucking new.

Here goes nothing.

THIRTEEN

For a moment, I forgot Holt only took me out tonight because he won this date at a charity auction.

Now, though, I remember.

He's staring at me across the table while I'm cursing my pussy for getting wet at the sight of him and the stupid way he sticks his tongue out slowly before swiping it across his bottom lip. Or the way he works his fingers across his chin, scratching at the small shadow of stubble lining his sharp jaw. Or the way his voice is like weighted velvet, floating through the air before shooting straight for my heart, making it feel like I've been struck by Cupid's arrow.

"So, what do you think?" he asks, shoving the last bite of chocolate cake into his mouth.

I watch him chew, working the food in his mouth before he swallows it. His thick neck bobs with the motion, and I cross my legs under the table, squeezing my thighs together until they ache.

Blinking away my thoughts, I force myself to take another drink of wine. We've nearly killed two bottles between us. "Think of what?"

His eyes darken as he points his fork at the plate. "Of the cake?"

"Oh." I shiver, shaking my head. I need to snap out of this. "It's good." I quickly shove another bite of cake into my mouth and force myself to eat it.

Holt's eyes fall to my mouth, watching me chew.

When I'm finished, I lick my lips and lift my napkin to wipe my mouth. "What do you think of it?"

He averts his gaze and smirks.

"What?" I ask.

He frowns as he drops his fork, sits back in his seat, and takes a deep breath, running his hands over his thighs under the table. Then he's looking back up at me. "I'm not a fan of chocolate flavored things. Chocolate on its own is good, but brownies or cake? Not so much."

"So, you don't like chocolate cake?"

"Not really." He scrunches his nose.

I laugh under my breath, realizing he only agreed after I'd suggested ordering it. I tip my head to the side. "What type of cake is your favorite, then?"

"Coconut."

I grin. Then I start laughing out loud. It feels good.

"Is that funny?" he asks, staring at me with those shining blue eyes of his.

My world spins the longer I stare at them and my laughter fades. The longer we've been sitting here, the more comfortable I've become. I'm enjoying Holt's company.

"It isn't funny. There's nothing wrong with coconut cake." I shake my head and shrug. "Just surprising."

"Well, I just shared something personal about me. Your turn."

A familiar ache builds between us, and I reach up, touching

my necklace again. "I'm really not that interesting. There's nothing to tell."

"That's a lie but, here, I'll make it easier for you." Holt pauses. "What's the story with Adam?"

"Easy, huh?" I relax with a sigh. "There is no story."

He tips his head forward as if he doesn't believe me. He must know its bullshit after I practically begged him to get himself into a bidding war with Adam.

Holt's brown strands of hair hang just above his eyebrows, and I want to run my fingers through them. I imagine tugging on them with his face between my legs, relieving the constant ache I've felt since he stepped out of his car to pick me up outside the flower shop.

I relax in my seat and tuck my hair behind my ear, working out the best way to navigate this conversation.

"Adam was the first guy I'd dated in years."

I wait for Holt to react, but he doesn't say or do anything.

Sighing, I continue. "Being with him was like trying to date that boyfriend from high school, only to realize he never grew up. Nothing changed. He reminded me why I swore off dating all together."

"Why have you sworn off dating?"

The four walls of the restaurant close in on me. Panic sets in, forcing my breathing to hitch. Then there's an echo of not only one gun shot, but two. I close my eyes and bite back the tears threatening to form.

Memories are weapons. Weapons used against you in the future to keep you from moving on with life. That's what this one has done time and time again.

"Doesn't matter, really," I murmur, shaking the chill from my body.

Thankfully, Holt seems to accept my answer with no further interrogation.

"My turn." I clear my throat.

"I'm all ears." I feel his foot inching towards mine under the table.

The tip of his shoe meets the tip of my heel, and my pulse ticks up. No, it practically leaps so hard I think it might tear straight through my flesh and fall onto my chocolate cake, crumb-coated plate.

"How are you..." I swallow thickly. "How are you, um, feeling after the news of Rome's lawsuit broke?"

"Oh." He visibly deflates but considers my question. "It's been a shitshow at the magazine, but I have my team tasked with figuring out who wrote the article."

"I thought it was anonymous?"

"It is, but there's always a paper trail," he says, coolly. "I'll find out who wrote it."

"What will you do?"

Holt shrugs. "I plan on showing it to Rome in the hopes it will get him to drop the lawsuit. Hopefully, I can convince the author to own up to it."

"Are you sure that will work?" I ask, the reality of this lawsuit hitting me. I can see the turmoil it's causing Holt just by having this conversation.

"It's my only hope." A small smile appears. "The Capuletis and Montgomerys may be sworn enemies, but I still know how to handle a crisis situation."

"Confident, huh?" I smirk and raise my wine glass, only to realize it's empty. Holt catches on and pours what's left of our second bottle into my glass.

"Always," Holt says, lifting his gaze up to mine as he sets the empty bottle down, then relaxes back in his chair. "My turn. Tell me I was right."

His words are like a bolt of lightning. "Right about what?"

"I was right about our kiss. You enjoyed it." There his voice goes again, slipping over me like weighted velvet.

"Holt..." I avert my gaze. I can't look at him. The longer I do, the more I feel like he can see too much.

"If you did - and I know you did – it's okay to admit it."

I dart my attention back to him. He's leaning closer, shoving his empty plate forward. It clinks against the tiny votive candle at the end of its life. His foot has now found its way next to mine, the toe of his shiny black shoe slipping along the inside of my arch.

"But knowing you did makes this all the easier to ask."

"Ask me what?" I gulp.

"I know you've sworn off dating but... why not date me?"

I gasp. "What?"

My heart is racing a million miles a minute. I'm almost certain it's about to be stripped from my chest at this point. I nervously look down at my plate, expecting to see my heart sitting in front of me, taking its last few beats before flatlining and becoming nothing more than a dead organ.

"Date you?"

"Well..." Holt tosses his head side to side, his eyes shifting to the side. "Help me keep up the *appearance* of dating me."

My world collapses around me.

I've been so busy paying attention to Holt and this bubble we've made for ourselves, I haven't taken the time to notice the rest of the world around me.

More eyes have turned toward us. The restaurant is packed, and I get the feeling it isn't unusual for a place as famous as this. But what isn't usual is the amount of phones pointed in our direction, followed by quick clicking sounds.

Heat radiates across my body, and I feel like I'm standing on stage again with all the hushed murmurs and peering eyes directed at Holt and me.

"You want me to fake date you?" I whisper, bitterness quickly filling me mouth.

Why am I crushed by this idea?

I've spent the past ten years holding onto one rule: I will never date. I will never allow myself to fall in love or to even feel a tinge of it. Adam was a test. But now, here I am, sitting in front of Holt, crushed because he's asking me to fake date him.

"The lawsuit has tarnished my reputation in the worst way. It's a PR disaster, and I'm working on getting that ironed out," he explains, matter-of-factly. "But ever since the other night at the auction, being with you..."

I glance around us again. "Everyone is looking at us."

"Yeah."

I pull my foot away from his, slinking back into my chair. Disappointment consumes me, and I don't have the energy to hide it. "You want to use me for a PR boost?"

"Wallflower..." He presses his lips together. The mood has shifted. We've gone from hot to cold in a matter of seconds.

"Why do you call me that?" I can't think straight. Fire simmers under my skin, and I can't tell if it's from the sudden shift between us or if I'm angry with myself for feeling like this. I shouldn't care what Holt thinks of me. I shouldn't care that he's only using me to restore his reputation.

I don't fall for anyone. I won't allow myself.

"Why do you keep calling me Wallflower?" I repeat through gritted teeth.

Ten seconds of silence pass between us before he's rolling his eyes dramatically and groaning as he scoots down in his seat a little farther to dig his phone from the pocket of his pants. He flicks his thumb across the screen, then freezes. His eyes widen, and he lifts his hand to massage his mouth. I have no idea what message he's reading, but I can tell it isn't something he was expecting.

"What is it? Is everything okay?"

"Yeah. I need to go."

He won't even look in my direction. Even as he waves to our server for the check, who barely has a chance to drop the bill before Holt's whipping out a slate-black credit card.

Then he's swiftly escorting us out of the restaurant and back to the roof.

This time when we step into the elevator, we aren't alone. There are already four others in the lift. Holt escorts me in first as he orders the attendant to press the button for the roof level. The three others eye us before turning their attention back to the phones in their hands.

Once we're inside, I stop and turn as Holt moves to stay behind me. His back is pressed against the mirrored wall, and I stay at least a foot in front of him. There is distance between us, but I can still feel his heated stare burning my back.

My mind is swimming with wine and the conversation we left at the table.

I can't piece together what I'm feeling. No matter how hard I try, my mind is too scattered. It feels like the first time I looked at my blank document, unable to put the words that were in my mind to fruition.

I inhale a shaky breath when the elevator suddenly stops on the second floor, then I dart my attention to the panel of buttons and see more than half of them are lit.

This is going to be a long elevator ride.

On the second level, two of the four get off, but another group of five joins us. The elevator fills, and a hand grips my hip from behind, tugging me backward. My back hits Holt's chest, and I'm gasping for air from the jolt of electricity. I'm frozen as his finger dips between the space of my vest and the top of my skirt. His mouth hits the shell of my ear.

"I call you Wallflower," he whispers, "because that's what you are, Selene. A wallflower."

A shiver slivers down the back of my neck, wrapping around my stomach, then dipping to the point where his fingers touch the curve of my hip.

My eyes flutter before they pop back open, remembering where we are. A man stands in front of me, too close. It's as if I'm in on a secret no one else knows other than Holt and me, but he's touching me as if we're alone.

I inhale an unsteady breath.

"But I see you. I've always seen you. You pretend to live in the shadows, quiet as a mouse, never making a show of yourself. But I see the fire inside you begging to be break free," he whispers, his breath hitting my ear again. "Don't make a sound, Wallflower."

I breathe in as his hand slips farther into the front of my skirt. His entire palm is pressed against me, the tips of his fingers teasing my delicate flesh.

"If you want me to stop, I will," he whispers, his fingers grazing over the front of my lacy thong.

I tilt my head, leaning into his mouth. It feels as if I'm caught under a spell. His voice and touch have done something to me. His explanation of my nickname, too. It feels as if I'm no longer in control of my thoughts or my heart. All I know is I don't want him to stop.

This feels too fucking good.

I place my hand over his under my skirt and push it farther down.

I feel his mouth curving into a smirk against my ear.

"Good girl." Then his fingers are shoving my thong aside and plunging inside me.

My jaw drops, and I slam back into Holt. He grunts as I

press my ass against him, feeling his reaction to me. His cock swells, straining under his designer pants. He seems to relish in me being forward, countering him when he tries to push me, like two opposite ends of a magnet trying to come together.

His palm presses against me, adding pressure to my aching clit. I gasp again.

"Shh," he breathes into my ear, stopping his hand. "We have thirty more levels before we make it to the top. If you so much as make a single peep, alerting anyone in this lift to what a naughty girl you are, there'll be consequences. And because I know you're thinking it, yes, it'll be the same consequence I promised earlier. The second I have you alone, I'll spank your ass until you're begging me to relieve you of that tension you've kept to yourself for years."

"Holt..." His name falls from my mouth, barely at a whisper.

"If you think dating me for appearances won't come with its perks, I'll tell you right now, you're wrong." He sinks his teeth into my ear before moving his hand. He uses his other to turn me slightly away from the people beside and in front of us. I'm terrified their eyes will drop and see that I'm being finger fucked inside this tight elevator.

As if Holt is reading my mind, he whispers, "Shit, Wall-flower. Your pussy is as tight as this elevator."

I squeeze my eyes shut, silently begging myself to calm down as I tuck my bottom lip under my teeth, biting down on it until it stings. His touch is lighting me from the inside out. It feels as if there's been this ball of energy I've been carrying around, and every day that's passed has made it heavier than the day before. But with one kiss and one touch, Holt has burst it wide open. I'm unraveling, and it's terrifying.

The elevator continues to rise higher, and so do I. Holt's fingers hook inside me, reaching a spot that even I haven't been able to touch in God knows how long. I was with Adam only once in the weeks we were together, and I didn't feel anything remotely close to what I'm feeling with Holt. He's standing behind me, but I feel him all around me. His scent. His breath. His touch.

My lower stomach tightens, the strands weaving into a tense ball. I want to come. I'm fully aware of where we are, but I don't want this to stop. I don't want him to stop.

Rolling my hips, I grind against Holt's hand, wanting more pressure. He catches on, riding my orgasm out until we've reached the top.

I'm wet as his fingers move in and out of me in slow, torturous strokes. I want him to move faster, wilder. I want him to work my clit expertly in time with his fingers, bringing me sweet relief. I *need* it. But I also know that if he does, the sound will be too loud. I'm dripping. My wetness coats his fingers and the entire space between my legs, covering my inner thighs.

Throughout the course of the ride up to the roof, the elevator has stopped and started too many times for me to count. As if I would be able to keep track anyway. But even through the transfer of people getting in and out, we always manage to stay concealed. We're moved farther into the back corner, and when Holt pulls his fingers out of me long enough to pinch my clit, I slap my palm against the wall.

The group of people in the elevator turn their heads in our direction, but I've already turned my hips to the side where they can't see Holt's hand plunged down the front of my skirt. My chest stills, and I freeze, but Holt's chest still moves against me, forcing me to stay upright. I'm practically boneless, melting under his touch.

Slowly, one by one, everyone turns back to their phones or to face forward, a few clearing their voices. Someone even sneezes. I chew on the inside of my cheek, forcing myself to act normal. As if having a man's fingers plunged so deep inside you in a packed elevator *is* completely normal.

Once everyone has diverted their attention away from the two of us, Holt slips his fingers over my clit and back inside me. He slowly starts working me in and out again. I close my eyes and focus on my breathing. And his hand. His back. Even his mouth still resting against the shell of my ear.

He clicks his tongue in disapproval. "Close call, Wallflower. You almost risked getting us caught."

God, his voice.

His voice has the heat quickly returning to my stomach. I curl my toes against the toe of my heels, pressing my hand to the wall to steady me.

I'm close to coming. I'm going to come all over Holt's hand. I start to panic, wondering if I'll be able to stifle my cries once it comes. I feel it cresting. I'm at the top of the peak. I'm toe to toe with the edge of a cliff. All I need to do is step out and I'll be falling. I'm practically there when Holt abruptly tears his hand away from me. My eyes snap open, and the elevator doors open with them, the group surrounding us leaving quickly. We're one level from the roof now, and the only ones left aside from the elevator attendant.

I feel the absence of Holt immediately, silently cursing the universe for denying me an orgasm. Or was it Holt?

I'm left gasping for air when he brings his mouth to my ear again and whispers, "There'll be punishment for your indiscretion later, Wallflower. Don't worry."

I want to tell him he's already punished me. He pulled me toward the edge of the cliff but jerked me back at the last second. My body is screaming at me, weeping for not getting the gratification of release.

Once we reach the roof, Holt reaches for my hand and gives a courtesy nod to the elevator attendant before leading us to his helicopter waiting. He helps me get buckled in as he did on the way here, but this time is different. He doesn't offer up jokes on my fear of flying. He doesn't offer me reassurances, either. We don't speak about what happened in the elevator. In fact, we don't speak another word the entire flight. It's as if his mind is somewhere else, not completely tethered to me in the here and now.

Sensing his shift, I don't press him. He simply stares out the window in silence until we land back at his place.

After stepping out, Holt asks his driver to take me home.

I crumble when he wraps his arm around my waist, his hand resting on the base of my spine. He pulls me toward him and places a gentle kiss to my forehead. He lingers for a few seconds, his lips causing electricity to crackle along my skin before he's bringing his mouth to the shell of my ear and whispering, "I'll text you later, Wallflower."

Then he breaks our connection.

He doesn't come with me. He doesn't give me a proper kiss goodbye. He doesn't even give me the punishment he promised when we were alone.

Once I'm finally home, lying in my bed, staring at the ever-growing crack in the ceiling, I toss and turn. I turn so much, I end up tangled in the sheets.

Disappointment over how the night ended eats me up inside. It shouldn't. I don't do love. I don't fall for anyone. Ever.

But if that's true, then why can I not stop thinking about Holt's touch and how him calling me Wallflower made me feel like this? Why did I allow myself to cross this invisible line? What would Julianna think if she knew how far her brother and I went tonight? Is Holt feeling the same disappointment?

Probably not, because even if he did, I could never trust it to be true.

Everything has changed. Or maybe nothing has at all.

Maybe it was all a dream, and when I wake up in the morning, the echo of his touch across my skin will have finally disappeared.

HOLT

It takes me precisely sixty seconds after watching Howard escort Selene into the elevator before I'm finally moving.

I didn't want to leave her the way I did, but it's for the best. I don't know what the fuck I'm walking into, and I need to keep her safe at all costs.

Checking Cory's message once more to make sure I read his emergency text correctly, I spin on my heel and head back toward the waiting helicopter. Normally, I wouldn't take this method of transportation to the office, but with Howard taking Selene home, it's the fastest way there.

I hop in and instruct the pilot to take me to Scribe.

Within fifteen minutes, I'm walking into my office to find a panicked Cory sitting on the leather sofa situated on the opposite side of the room. He bounces out of his seat. I don't think I've ever seen him so pale.

"Thanks for coming, Boss," he pants, almost as if he's out of breath. "I'm sorry to message you so late, but I swear, I didn't know what else to do."

At twenty-seven, he's usually calm, cool, and collected. As

one of my best editorial writers, he's been with the company for three years now, but I've never seen him like this.

Beside him is one of our other staff writers, Macy, who I just hired on permanently after a yearlong internship. I'm not entirely sure why she's here. I'm assuming it has to do with his emergency text Cory sent me at dinner.

Code Red.

The codeword Cory and I agreed we would use if shit hit the fan regarding the investigation into Rhys O'Connell's connection to the Irish mafia.

Cory and I were scheduled to meet in the morning to discuss what he learned from his questioning of Rhys's known associates down by the docks yesterday. I assumed all was well but apparently not. Cory wouldn't have used the codeword unless it was absolutely critical.

My suspicion is confirmed when I see the large manila envelope sitting on the coffee table between us.

"Is this it?" I point to the envelope.

"Yeah." Cory nods, running a nervous hand through his hair. "I'm sorry, but this shit freaked me the fuck out. I mean, I... I..." Shaking, he picks up the envelope and hands it to me, the ends of his fingers white from how tightly he's holding it.

I take it from him, eyeing him with concern. He looks like he's going to vomit. I shift my gaze to Macy, who looks just as nervous.

Opening the envelope, I slide out the stack of photographs. Dropping the envelope to the table, I flip through each one. "What are these?"

There's a photo of Cory leaving the office. Cory hailing a cab. Then Macy leaving the office. Them meeting at a subway station a few blocks from the office. Him and Macy walking down Fifty-first Street. They're in the distance, surrounded by pedestrians, but it's clear they were the intended targets of the photo. The next is the two of them holding hands. I flip to another one, only this one is different. It's a view from outside, looking into what appears to be the bedroom of an apartment. Cory is lying back on the bed, with Macy straddling him. Naked.

"What the fuck are these?" I snap my head up, darting my fiery gaze between them.

Macy's eyes are swollen with tears. She's nervously wringing her hands together, shifting on her feet.

"Holt, I... I can explain." Cory stumbles over his words.

"Wait." I drop my eyes to his hand. "Didn't you just get married, like two years ago?"

"I did," he says quietly.

Macy's tears are now streaming down her face.

"Fuck." I hold onto the photos as I spin and start to pace the room, pinching the bridge of my nose. Eventually I stop, looking up at the both of them standing on the opposite side of the table, cowering like wounded puppies.

"I should fire you for this type of shit," I seethe, anger burning in my veins. "It's against company policy."

"I'm sorry." Macy's bottom lip wobbles, and her chin quivers.

"How long has this affair been going on?" I ask them both. I can't help raising my voice. This is the last fucking thing I need. Another goddamn rumor about two of Scribe's staff members having an affair.

"This was only the second time we've met up," Cory explains, gulping. "Please don't fire Macy. If you're going to fire anyone, let it be me. I pursued her first."

His pathetic explanation causes a cynical scoff to climb up and out of my throat.

"What the fuck?" I shout, raking my fingers through my hair. I lift the photos to look up at them again, hoping they aren't true. But there is no denying the way her head is tilted back, Cory's arms reaching up to palm each of her breasts.

"Listen, I know you're angry about the affair, especially since Macy is an employee as well, but, Holt, this shit is scaring the fuck out of me. They left this envelope on my fucking front porch, *at my house.* And these pictures were taken just last night," Cory spills, clearly still in a panic. "I mean, they even have photos of me from yesterday down at the docks."

"Who did you talk to?" I lift the photos up. "How would they have known?"

"I don't know." He shrugs. "I kept a low profile. I didn't even give them my real name, like you said. I just asked a few of the dock workers if they had heard of Rhys O'Connell. Nothing seemed out of the ordinary, and I didn't make myself obvious. But they're clearly watching me and using this affair with Macy as blackmail, right? Or some sort of warning. Isn't that what the mafia does?"

"This is definitely a warning." I sigh, pressing my lips together.

My mind wanders to West's brother Heath and the trouble he caught himself in with Rhys's crew. This isn't a joke, and I'm now understanding the seriousness behind it. But the part of me I've never been able to resist wants to know more. I need this story. My magazine does, especially after this lawsuit with Rome. Maybe it's wrong, but I never back down from a challenge. All I know is that if I'm going to stick to cracking this story, I need to be extra careful. It has to be a delicate dance that will require a little more precision than usual.

"What are we going to do?" Cory asks. I can tell he's itching to reach for Macy's hand, but he doesn't.

I chew on the inside of my cheek. I wish I could rewind back to at least the past hour before Cory sent me the Code

Red. When I was in a euphoric state, my hands wandering all over Selene. She's the calm to the shitstorm that is my life.

She always has been, even if she doesn't know it.

Thinking of her has the fire inside me raging. I'm itching to message Howard to make sure she made it home safely.

"Listen, I took this assignment on, no questions asked. I don't know why you're wanting me to look into Rhys O'Connell, but fuck...." Cory's worried eyes grow distant.

I, too, stare off into the distance, sifting through options of how to deal with this mess I've made.

"Boss?" Cory asks, bringing my attention back to him as he raises his brows, cutting through my thoughts. His worried expression hasn't wavered, and Macy's tears haven't stopped. She's just crying silently. "What do you want us to do?"

"First, this shit ends now." I wave my hand between them. "For the sake of company policy. Also, not that it's my business, but I don't get down with cheating. You should tell your wife, and I wouldn't blame her if she left you for this shit. If I catch you, or if Rhys does, *again*"—I hold up the stack of photos— "you're both fired. But for now?" I drop the pictures on the table. "You're off the story."

The pictures scatter across the glass, Cory's affair on full display under the dim lights of my office. The entire floor outside of this room is covered in darkness, the hollowness of a dead newsroom echoing through the thin walls.

"Holt, I don't know if I can." Cory's voice tightens.

"Don't know if you can what?" I jerk back. "Which part don't you think you can do?"

Cory swallows thickly, then shifts his eyes toward Macy. "I don't know if I can... if I want to..."

"Seriously?" I trade confused glances between the two of them. I don't understand their affair, and if I'm honest, I don't give a fuck.

"I know, it's all confusing."

"Honestly." I hold my hands up. "I don't want to know. Just figure your shit out, but if you're going to be together, one of you needs to leave. I can't have you both working here if you're doing whatever the fuck this is. It causes too much drama."

I would know. Years ago, before I was appointed head of Scribe Magazine, I had a run with a fellow reporter at *The New Yorker*. Our affair didn't end well when our editor-in-chief caught us fucking in one of the storage closets.

Part of me can sympathize with Cory and Macy for their affair, but there are differences between us. For one, I wasn't fucking married.

The memory of fucking the reporter and all the other women I have in my past has my stomach roiling. It's difficult to think of other women when the only one on my mind now is Selene. I thought kissing her had made my head spin, but now I've had the privilege of touching her, I'm ruined for all other women.

"We understand." Cory nods, his shoulders relaxing slightly. "But, hey, if you decide to continue this story, Holt, I urge you to be careful. These fuckers aren't messing around."

I stare at Cory. His stark warning pulls me back to when Julianna made the same comment in this room only days ago.

His warning and the echo of my sister's sends an eerie chill down my spine.

I don't know how far Rhys is willing to go. He hasn't physically hurt us or even spoken to any of us at Scribe, but him sending these photos to Cory is a clear message—one I can't and won't ignore.

Panic sets in, and once Cory and Macy leave the office, I'm pulling out my phone.

Holt: Are you still with Selene?

> Howard: Just watched her walk into her building. She's safe. About to head back to your place to drop the car off.

> Holt: Can you stay a little longer? Watch to make sure she doesn't leave on her own, and if she does, follow her? I'll send Knox to relieve you soon.

> Howard: Knox? Didn't you just cut back on his surveillance?

> Holt: Yes, but circumstances have changed.

It takes several seconds before Howard is responding. Three bubbles appear then disappear before his message eventually comes through. He knows what this means.

> Howard: Of course, Boss. I'll keep an eye on her. You have my word.

I send Howard a quick thanks before sending Knox a message, asking if he doesn't mind also tasking another one of his security detail to my sister as well—a request I didn't think I'd need to make. The thing is, I've always watched over those that I love. Despite what some might believe, it's in my nature. There's never been any other option.

FIFTEEN

SELENE

My body hasn't stopped burning since my date with Holt. It's a monstrous fire. I've told myself over and over again that this isn't me. I'm not the one to feel this way after one date.

Holt is just like the other few I've dated in the past. He's just like Adam, too.

I'm numb to their touch. Numb to the words they speak. Numb to their lips against my skin.

Holt: I want to see you again.

"Are you sure you can make these taste like the ones at the bar?" Charleigh asks twisting in her seat, looking over her shoulder to my sister working away in the kitchen.

I look back down at Holt's unanswered text still resting in the palm of my hand.

"Trust me, Charleigh. West walked me through the recipe multiple times. I think I've got this." London raises her voice over the sound of her mixing. My back is turned to her, but I picture her lifting a large, metal glass in the air and shaking it as hard as she can.

"Okay," Charleigh sings, twisting back. "I'll trust you."

I'm still staring at the text when she clears her throat beside me.

I snap my head up and shut my screen off.

"You okay?" she asks, grinning.

"Fine."

"Right." She tilts her head to the side and studies me.

Leaning back against the couch, I cross my legs and take in a breath. "How have you been these past few days? How's Asher?"

Charleigh's grin widens, and I see it in her eyes: her happiness, the light, the love she has for Asher.

"He's good. Closing out a few properties, but nothing that isn't too consuming." She tucks her hair behind her ear. "I talked to my mom about dress shopping soon. She basically cried when I told her I wanted her to go with us. Well, we both did."

I lean forward and give her hand a squeeze. I know how much this means to her. Charleigh's worked to rebuild her relationship with her mother after she moved to New York. They grew distant when she'd moved from Connecticut, but when her mom showed up to apologize and tell her she'd left Charleigh's dad, they began to heal.

"Shit," I giggle, sniffing. "I might be crying, too."

"Oh, stop." Charleigh waves me off. "Tonight is girls' night. No room for crying."

The two of us turn our attention to the front of Julianna's apartment when the door swings open and she emerges from the hallway. Julianna recently moved. Her apartment is larger than her old one. I haven't told her, but I definitely think it's too much space for one person. I've resisted asking her if she ever feels that it might be, too.

I haven't seen her since the night of the auction, but even though it's only been a week, she looks different.

"Sorry I'm late." She sighs, a mountain of shopping bags dangling from her arms. "Got stuck in traffic on the way home."

"Woah." London stops pouring whatever drink concoction she's made up, hovering the metal cup above the martini glass. Her eyes widen as Julianna unloads the bags onto the sofa across from Charleigh and me. "You said in your text you were going out for a little light shopping."

"Not going to lie, I had to laugh at that, Jules." Charleigh giggles. "We all know you never do a little *light* shopping. I figured something was up, though, when you told me to use your spare key and for all of us to wait until you got back."

"Yeah." Julianna sighs with wide eyes, trading glances between the three of us. "Stress shopping was necessary to clear my head."

Eyeing Julianna wearily, London shrugs her shoulders and pours the remaining bit of drink into the last glass. She begins passing them out to us, starting with Julianna.

Julianna immediately shakes her head and says, "No, thank you."

"Everything okay?" London asks, handing Julianna's unwanted drink to me.

I gladly take it. Something tells me I'm going to need it. I tip it back and swallow a larger gulp than intended. The sweet and sour mixture stings the back of my throat. It burns on the way down before settling in my stomach, like the way it felt to have Holt's hand pressed over the same spot.

My cheeks heat, and I barely chance a glance up at Julianna. I brace myself for truly looking at my best friend for the first time since her brother's fingers were plunged deep inside me, building what I knew was going to be the best orgasm of my life, even if I was denied the satisfaction of falling over the edge completely.

I plan on telling her about Holt tonight. Not all the gritty details, but about our date and how he proposed a fake dating arrangement to keep up the rumors.

I haven't fully committed to dating Holt for show. I'm a conflicted mess at the moment, and maybe part of it has to do with telling Julianna first. Knowing how she's been against any of her friends so much as glancing in his direction for years, I can't imagine her being okay with it. Even if it is all just for show.

Once Julianna has her bags unloaded, she sinks into the space between Charleigh and me.

"So... what's up?" Charleigh asks, concern etched in her expression. She lifts one leg up onto the cushion and twists to get closer to Julianna. "You said you wanted to do this girls' night ASAP, but that was a week ago."

"I know." She shocks us when she jumps out of her seat between us. She paces the space between the couch and the large, wooden coffee table as the three of us exchange glances.

"I've never seen you like this, Jules," I say quietly. "What's going on?"

It's true. I've never seen her like this. It's worse than the night of the auction. She seemed off then, but it doesn't seem as if she's gotten better since. If anything, she looks more stressed and unlike herself.

She comes to an abrupt stop, anxiously wringing her hands in front of her. The tips of her fingers turn white, contrasting against her black nail polish. Her chest freezes as she inhales. "I need to tell you guys something."

Her eyes well with tears, and I'm officially freaked the fuck out. Apparently, so are Charleigh and London. We all sit forward, inching closer to the edge of the couch. I set my drink down on the end table beside me, afraid I'm going to spill it along with Julianna's confession.

With tear-lined eyes, she closes them and inhales another

deep breath through her nostrils. When she opens her eyes again, she starts hyperventilating as she blurts out, "I fucked up. I submitted the anonymous article." She slams her hands to her chest. "It was me."

"What?" Charleigh's jaw drops.

Then London's.

Then mine.

The blood drains from my face before I'm snapping it shut, swallowing the weight of her confession. Silence fills the room, suffocating and all consuming.

"Why didn't you tell us sooner?" London eventually asks.

"I wanted to..." Julianna's pacing a few feet between the table and the couch, her glazed eyes frantic as she explains, "But I didn't know how."

"I don't understand," Charleigh cuts in. "What do you mean you were the one who wrote the article?"

"Remember how I told you Rome and I have been playing these pranks on one another?"

"Yeah..."

"Well..." Julianna tips her head to the side, then presses her hand to her forehead. "We'd been falling into this pattern of tit for tat. He was pissed about the erectile dysfunction newsletter I'd signed him up for, so he got back at me by breaking into my office at work and littering it with a million pieces of notebook paper. Like, tiny, little, cut up pieces of paper everywhere. They covered every single surface. And I don't know... it got to me. I just saw red and..."

She waves her hands in the air in front of her as if she's running through the entire memory in her head again. A tear slips from her glassy eye as she stares blankly into the distance.

"How did you know it was him with the paper scraps?" Charleigh asks.

"The security cameras caught him." She closes her eyes.

"He was wearing a mask, but I knew it was him. I just, I knew it was him. He must have paid the security guard to allow him access that late at night. I wouldn't put it past him to do some shit like that."

Julianna's story leaves all of us confused. I've never seen her this worked up.

"I mean"—London shrugs, scrunching her nose—"leaving tiny scraps of paper all over your office doesn't sound terrible. More annoying if anything."

"You don't understand." Another tear slips from Jules's eye, then she looks up, shattered. It's the only way I can describe the way she looks. Her bottom lip wobbles and her eyes are full of tears. The mask she constantly wears has completely disappeared. I've never seen Julianna this raw before.

"I was *so* angry with Rome," she grinds out.

"About scraps of paper?" Charleigh asks, eyebrows raised.

"Yes." Julianna's bottom lips quivers, pinning Charleigh with a look. "I was so angry that I didn't even think when I submitted the article to Holt's magazine."

"So, is the story of his sex parties even true?" London asks.

"No," she admits meekly.

"Does Holt know?" I finally ask.

I've been silent up until now, overcome with emotion from my best friend's confession. But I also can't help thinking of Holt. He's been consumed by this lawsuit, and I've seen the weight of it he's been carrying around with him. My heart breaks for them both.

Julianna shakes her head.

"You need to tell him," I tell her. I can't help it.

"I am," Julianna admits. "I will. I tried the day after the auction. I met him at his office, but we got into an argument about something else and I couldn't do it. He didn't even want to talk to me anymore, so I couldn't tell him. We haven't talked since. But I do still plan on telling him."

"It's been a week, Jules," I say softly, wincing.

"I know." She nods, her shoulders raising as she inhales. "I've spent all week trying to reach out to Rome to fix it."

"Is that why you've been quiet all week?" Charleigh asks.

"Yeah." Julianna's tears have dried in streaks on her cheeks. She wipes her fingers under her eyes, brushing away what's left. "Since Holt shut me out, I wanted to try to and mend things with Rome so I could go back to him with it fixed. I was hoping Rome would be willing to meet up or call a truce, then he'd drop the lawsuit. But he won't answer my calls or texts. He's stonewalling me in every way possible. He's probably blocked my number, too. If he has, I don't understand it because I don't even think he knows it was me who wrote the article. I'm guessing it's because he's sued Holt and doesn't have the balls to face me." She plants her hands on her hips and looks up at the ceiling. "Shit, I'm so stupid. I let this prank rivalry bullshit between us go too far, and now it's destroying my brother. What the hell was I thinking? Rome knows exactly how to get under my skin, and when he does, I don't know how to explain it. I just see red. I can't think straight. You know?" Breathing hard, she covers her face with her hands and groans. "What am I going to do?"

"It'll be okay, Jules." I stand from the couch and wrap my arms around her. She quickly wraps her arms around me, too, burying her face in my neck.

I soothe the back of her head. "You'll figure something out."

"I don't know how."

"You will."

She nods against me, then pulls away. "Thank you, Selene."

Her softened gaze causes an ache to echo inside me, because she isn't the only one who needs to make a confession.

I open my mouth to tell her about Holt but stop when she inhales a cleansing breath, then steps back, eyeing the drink London left on the table. "Maybe I will take that drink."

Charleigh and London giggle as Julianna takes a large gulp.

Guilt eats me from the inside out. Julianna has kept her secret about Rome the past week, and I've kept mine about Holt.

It shouldn't be a big deal that I've spent time with Holt. We've been in the same social circle for years. But I've never spent time with him alone before. I've never felt the feelings I've been having since he kissed me a week ago. Although I'm still working on diffusing the electricity inside me from his touch, remembering it's supposed to be fake, I know I need to tell Julianna.

"I have a confession to make as well."

My announcement causes all three girls to go quiet. Julianna lowers her glass and slowly sits on the edge of the large, wooden coffee table behind her. I follow suit and sit back down on the couch, directly across from her.

"I, um." I run my palms across the top of my legs. "I went on a date with Holt."

Julianna's perfectly micro bladed eyebrows pull together, and her mouth falls slack. Her neck visibly moves as she swallows thickly. "Wait, like the date he won from the auction?"

I don't know why her question stings a little. It shouldn't but it does. I brush the feeling off, chalking it up to the confusion I've felt ever since I agreed to go out with Holt.

"Yes." I nod once, then scoot forward, bringing my knees close enough to touch Julianna's. I take her hands in mine. "I'm so sorry, Jules. I should have told you sooner."

"Oh, Selene. Don't worry about it." She gives me a gentle smile. "When did you go on this date?"

Blinking, I try to wrap my mind around her reaction. I don't know what I was expecting, but it wasn't this. "A few nights ago. Like I said, I should have told you sooner. I shouldn't have kept this from you."

"Selene. You don't owe me an explanation. You're both adults. What business do I have telling you or him who to date?"

I'm both relieved and caught off guard. Relieved she isn't angry with me, yet surprised by her lack of anger. It isn't like her to be so calm, especially when it comes to the matter of her best friend and brother.

"I'm surprised at your reaction, Jules," Charleigh cuts in, as if she's reading my thoughts. "You've always been pretty vocal about your friends getting close to Holt."

"Old habits die hard I guess." Julianna works her mouth, chewing on the inside of her cheek, her gaze glazing over again. "Growing up, friends of mine used to pine over Holt all the time and I guess I just had this fear it would ruin what we had. My relationship with him. Mine with my friends. But honestly, you're both adults. I have no right to tell you what to do. Besides, I don't really have a leg to stand on, do I? I'm fucking up his life already." She sniffs, running her hand under her nose and shaking her head. "You know, I love you though, right Selene?"

"Of course I do." I give her a smile Running my fingers through her brown hair, I tuck it behind her ear, making sure she knows I'm there for her.

"Does this mean you and Holt are dating now?" London asks, sitting forward in her spot on the couch, her elbows resting on her knees. "Are you planning on seeing him again?"

I shake my head, my reflexes kicking in. "No. I don't think so. You know I don't date."

"But you dated Adam," London persists, hope lighting her up. "Maybe Holt is different."

"I don't think so," I mutter too quietly. "He asked me to go out with him again, but only because of the publicity it's given him ever since the lawsuit went public. Apparently, me being seen with him improves his image and serves as a distraction."

I tell them how all eyes were on us at the restaurant all night, and how Holt proposed the idea of fake dating me. I leave out the part where, after he'd received a text, he'd rushed us out of there only to finger fuck me in the elevator, or how I haven't stopped thinking about it since.

The fact that I haven't and that I'm wishing we'd gone further is terrifying.

"His publicist is probably encouraging it." Julianna leans back on one of her hands, crossing one leg over the other. "Treena's number one job is damage control, so it doesn't surprise me. But also, it wouldn't be out of character for Holt to go along with this. The man never dates seriously. Ever."

A tiny bit of disappointment stabs my chest, right in the center. I already knew this about Holt. None of this information is new. But for some reason, it's as if I'm hearing this all for the very first time.

"What are you thinking?" London asks, sensing my retreat from the conversation.

I never opened up to London about my belief that dating and love were never for me, but I can tell she already knows with one single look. We may not share the same blood, but it's never mattered. London can know exactly what I'm thinking and feeling without me ever needing to speak it into existence. Words are never needed when it comes to us.

"I don't know." *Lie.* "I guess it doesn't really matter to me whether Holt would date me for fake reasons or not." *Another lie.*

Memories of Holt's voice in my ear, telling me he wants to fake date me for show, ring in my ears. His words said one thing, his hands another.

My neck heats at the thought. I shake my head and wrap my hand over the heat under my straightened hair.

"Well, whatever you decide, I don't see the harm in going through with it," Julianna points out, straightening her back. "If he wants to date you for show, and you have no intentions of dating seriously, then it might work out. No feelings involved for either of you. Less messy, right?"

"Yeah." I blink, shaking my head and agreeing, shoving the feeling down in the places I've created to protect myself. "You're right." I chew on my bottom lip and nod.

I'm on a roll with these lies. Am I trying to convince my best friends or myself?

The problem is that feelings are already involved. Julianna and the girls think we had a simple dinner date; they don't know the details of how we took it a step further. They don't know how I've been haunted by the memory of his teeth sinking into the flesh of my ear and his fingers blazing down around my hips. They don't know how I've fantasized about how it felt to have my ass grind against his full, hardened cock.

"I changed my mind." Julianna bounces to her feet. "Let's go out tonight."

The dramatic pendulum swing from Julianna's confession to mine has caused a dark cloud to hang over our signature girls' night. One the four of us have prided ourselves in keeping up over these past few months. They're an escape. A chance for us to share in everything. We're sisters. Family.

Now, though, it seems Julianna's managed to change that by a simple clap of her hands and a grin I haven't seen her crack all night.

"Are you sure?" Charleigh asks, looking around. "We figured we'd check out that new movie on Netflix. We were okay with staying in."

London nods her agreement, but Julianna is quick to wave them off.

She spins to pick up her half-finished drink. She takes a sip, swallows, then says, "No, I think a night out is exactly what we need. I'm tired of throwing myself a pity party. It's depressing. Plus, if I sit around here all I'll do is lose my mind over this shit with Rome." Julianna turns to me. "Right, Selene?"

I surprise myself by saying, "Yeah, I definitely think we should go out."

Both London and Charleigh's eyebrows rise so high I think they might fly off their foreheads. My sudden agreement has them shocked.

Join the club.

But staying here will only make me think of Holt. I'd rather spend the night with my girls, dancing my ass off than sit in the dark, pretending to watch a movie, when the only one I'll be paying attention to is the one of Holt playing over and over in my mind.

Maybe going out will get him out of my system.

"Okay." Charleigh chuckles, pinching her sweatpants. "But we're not exactly dressed for a night out."

"Oh." Julianna moves around the table and picks up the dozen shopping bags she brought in. She holds them up. "Problem solved."

"Fine." London sighs, taking a few bags from Julianna.

Charleigh does the same, and they start to head back to Julianna's bedroom.

We're halfway there when Charleigh shouts over her shoulder, "I guess it's safe to say we aren't going to Club Verona!"

"Fuck, no." Julianna snorts behind me. "Not making that mistake again. After last time, I made sure to do my research. I took note of every club Rome owns within the five boroughs."

I laugh with the rest of the girls as I grip my phone, aware of

Holt's unanswered text still sitting there. I know I need to decide, and I know I'm only fooling myself if I say I won't even consider it.

It's the fact I'm even considering it in the first place that has me not responding. Maybe I'll just spend the rest of my life haunted by the memory of our one date. It would already be more than I'd bargained for, considering I've committed myself to remaining single for the rest of my life.

Maybe I could do this with Holt, though. Julianna's right. I don't fall in love with anyone. Fake dating him should be easy. After all, I'd be doing him a favor by actively rehabilitating his image as it's crumbling.

I've already begun to convince myself to let loose tonight, forgetting all thoughts of Holt and this fake dating scheme. I can figure this out another night.

We've made it just outside the threshold to Julianna's room when she grabs my hand. "Hey, Selene?"

I stop and spin around.

I've admired Julianna's beauty for years. She's stunning with her chestnut brown hair and cobalt blue eyes, but this time is different than any other time. I look at her, and immediately, my mind swings back to Holt.

Intense yet kind. It's in the Capuletis' DNA.

"Yeah?"

"Please don't tell Holt it was me."

"Jules." My shoulders drop, a sense of dread rushing through my veins.

"*Please?*" she begs, sliding her hand down my arm to squeeze my hand. "I know you said you don't know if you're going to keep seeing him, and I know it isn't right for me to ask you to keep this from him, but if you do, please don't tell him. I promise that I will soon. I need to be the one who tells him. He needs to hear it from me. I own this one."

I swallow, nodding in understanding. It needs to come from her. It should.

I may be considering dating Holt Capuleti—well, sort of—but first and foremost, I'm Julianna's best friend.

"I promise."

"Thank you." She breathes a sigh of relief, and so do I.

Then Julianna hooks her arm in mine, ushering me into her room, but the sudden realization that getting Holt off my mind tonight will be next to impossible when I'm spending it with his sister hits me at once.

Even if I weren't spending the night with Julianna, though, I still wouldn't be able to stop thinking about Holt. As much as I can't stop thinking about him, I don't want to. I fear, in the end, I'll crash and burn.

SIXTEEN

HOLT

This fucking woman.

She's all I'm thinking about. She's everywhere I look. She's in every breath I draw. My lungs burn and my hands twitch. How is it possible to have fallen this fucking hard?

I thought I'd hit rock bottom all these years, watching Selene from a distance. But now? Now, I'm royally fucked.

Every day, I wake up disappointed to turn over and not see her shining green eyes. How can I miss her in my bed when she's never even been in it?

Waking up frustrated, once again, I cancelled all my morning meetings and hit the gym, then headed back to my place to check in with Cory to make sure he and Macy were safe. After he assured me they were, I ignored another message from Treena, asking when I was seeing Selene again. Over the past few days, all she's done is remind me of needing to keep the gossip columns intrigued. She needs fresh pictures of us together, growing closer.

A message from my father, reminding Julianna and me of our monthly visit to our mother's gravesite was the final straw. I couldn't fucking take it, and if I receive another message from anyone other than Selene, I'm going to scream. So instead, I head back to my personal gym.

Her silence is killing me.

I'm wound the fuck up.

Restraint has never been my strong suit, and the past few days have only exasperated the situation. I've given her space to digest our first date. I've given her the time to think about my proposal of fake dating. I know it's all a mask for my true feelings. There's no amount of pressure from Treena or this fucking lawsuit that will convince me to pretend with Selene, but I know how quick Selene is to put up her walls. She's placed a rule against herself when it comes to dating, especially after Adam. It's probably naïve, but I'm hoping if she agrees to fake date me she'll see me for who I really am and maybe fall for me the way I have for her.

Because living this way, feeling this way, alone, is fucking torture.

I look down at my time on the treadmill: eighty-seven minutes.

Eighty-seven fucking minutes. I've officially gone insane.

What's even more insane is how none of this has done anything to loosen the tension in my body. I haven't felt this wound up, well... I don't think ever.

What the hell is wrong with me?

Sweat drips down my face, and my feet ache. Once I hit the ninety-minute mark, I slap my palm against the stop button and jump off. I plant my hands on my hips and pace in a circle, catching my breath.

"Watch the World Burn" by Falling in Reverse blasts through my earbuds. Still pacing, I grip my head in my hands, feeling as if I'm going to explode.

I've backed off on my surveillance of Selene over the past few days. I've only asked Knox to update me once a day, usually at the end, to know she's made it home safely. I don't want to tip Selene off to me watching her, and I won't deny the bit of guilt that is eating away at me. It feels wrong to watch her so closely when she's still processing and hasn't officially said she'll date me.

I try to have faith that she feels the same way I did. First when we kissed, then in the elevator. Her body reacted to me in the way I always hoped it would. I can't get her heated breaths out of my head. But the longer her silence goes on, the more I wonder if I made all this shit up. Am I imagining things? The mind can't be trusted.

I learned this fact over the years of my father telling me that the men I saw kill my mother weren't, in fact, the ones I saw. I've been raised to question my own memory. Maybe that's what I'm doing with Selene now.

Fuuuuuck.

I may just have to check myself into the psych ward at this rate.

Before completely losing my mind all together, I leave the gym and hop into the shower. When I step out, my phone rings, and my heart drops into my stomach. Then it jumps back into its rightful place when I read the name on my screen.

My thumb shakes as I swipe the green button and slap my phone to my ear.

"Selene?"

"Holt." Selene giggles. "You answered quickly."

"Of course, I did." Keeping the phone pressed between my shoulder and cheek, I slip into a fresh pair of lounge shorts. Without pulling my cell away, I manage to scramble into a plain black T-shirt.

The sound of footsteps on her end fills the silence.

"Where are you?" I ask her.

"I'm outside my apartment." Her voice is light and playful.

Different than usual. "My weather app says it's forty-five degrees, but I'm thinking it could be wrong. I feel fine."

"You're just standing outside?" I ask her, pulling the phone from my ear. I put her on speaker and scroll through my messages with Knox.

Knox: Wallflower is home and secure.

"Well, I was inside," she slurs. "But I wanted fresh air, so I came back outside. I also wanted to tell you something."

"You're by yourself?"

"Yep," she hiccups. "I mean, I haven't been completely alone. It was girls' night. Julianna's driver dropped me off a little while ago."

"But you're alone now?"

She giggles again, and I can't get over how different she sounds. She must have had more to drink than usual.

"Yes, silly. I just told you I was."

"Go back inside, Selene."

I'm already slipping into my shoes and swiping my car keys from my end table; a mixture of adrenaline and dread coursing through me. I'm sure Selene is safe outside her apartment, but the thought of her being alone when the threat of Rhys is still a possibility scares the fuck out of me. I hate that this is what I'm feeling, but I can't stop the wheels that have already been put in motion. This is my new reality.

"So, bossy." Selene's playful voice drops. I picture her bottom lip sticking out as she pouts. I'd kiss it right off her mouth if she were in front of me.

"I'm not bossy," I argue back. "It just isn't safe for you to be outside alone. I can tell you've been drinking."

"I'm fine. I only had, like..." She pauses. "I can't remember how many drinks I've had, but I know it was more than one."

"Go back inside, Wallflower."

"You using my sexy little nickname isn't going to make me listen any better, Holt Capuleti."

She thinks my nickname for her is sexy?

I flex my hand, stretching my fingers out fully. This woman has me unraveling so fucking quick. The urge to spank her until she screams my name consumes me.

"You know what your problem is?" She doesn't even give me a chance to answer. "You're so uptight all the time."

"Me?" I slip into my car, press the start button, and the engine roars to life. "I am not uptight, Wallflower." My phone connects to the car system and then I'm peeling out of the garage, heading straight for Selene's apartment.

"You are." Her voice vibrates through my car. "Everything you do is with a businesslike state of mind. When have you ever done something that didn't serve you financially or for the magazine?"

I grind my jaw and shake my head. *Oh, how wrong you are Wallflower.*

"A few nights ago in the elevator," I state boldly.

I race through the streets of the city, silently thanking the universe that she doesn't live terribly far. If there were somewhere to land close to Selene's place, I would have taken my helicopter, but there isn't, and I needed the quickest way to get to her.

My Porsche.

Selene hasn't responded to my comment about our date the other night by the time I'm pulling onto her street, and before I know it, I'm parking alongside the curb in front of her apartment building. I don't know how I got here in the time that I did. Weaving in and out of traffic and swerving around every corner must have made a difference. I drove on autopilot, knowing I just needed to get to her.

When I put the car in park, she stops on the sidewalk and leans forward, narrowing her eyes. Unsteady on her feet, she stumbles. Her heel scrapes against the pavement, and her ankle rolls. The glittery dress wrapped around her curvy frame shimmers beneath the streetlight.

"Is that *you?*" she squeaks.

I hang up the phone and practically jump out of my car.

She still has her phone pressed to her ear as I grow closer to her.

She takes a step back. "Either you're really standing in front of me, or those six shots of tequila were spiked with something that's causing me to hallucinate."

When I reach her, I fight the urge to scoop her into my arms. I slowly pull her phone from her ear.

"I'm really here," I tell her, handing it back to her. "And I thought you said you couldn't remember how many drinks you had."

Her eyes shift to my car before they're back on me. I haven't seen her in a few days. She may be drunk, but she's still as stunning as ever. I can literally feel the air leaving my lungs just looking at her.

"Did you seriously drive all the way over here from your place, or were you already out and just happened to be in the neighborhood?" She stumbles back again, catching herself on the wrought iron stair railing behind her. "Because seeing you here is insane." Her glassy eyes rake over my body. "Actually, seeing you in a T-shirt and shorts is what's insane."

"What, you think I only wear suits?"

"Yes." She pauses and blinks. "Yes, I... did." Swaying, she catches herself on the end of the railing.

I step forward, holding my hand out, just in case she might need it.

"Don't." She points to my outstretched hand with hooded eyes. "I can take care of myself."

"Of course you can."

"Really?" Her eyebrows pull together; both hands gripping the rail. "Because you driving all the way here means you trust me to take care of myself? I didn't call you to come over here. I didn't ask you to. I don't need anyone, and I certainly don't need a man to save me."

"You don't need saving, Wallflower. But you did call me."

"I did." She nods once.

We simply stare at one another. No words need to be said. I wish I could tell her everything. My feelings. All of it. But even if I wanted to right now, I can't. All she needs right now is an aspirin and some sleep.

"I'm going inside," she mumbles, turning to climb the five steps to her front door. She waves her hand behind her. "You can go home now."

I follow closely, not listening to a word she says.

I hold the door open for her, and she allows me to. She moves past me and straight for the stairs, taking the first few steps safely, but once she hits the first landing, she isn't as smooth. I catch her before she falls to the side, wrapping my arm around her waist. She's warm against my side, and I breathe a tiny sigh of relief.

There's the first hit, giving me the fix I desperately needed. She feels like heaven.

I hold her against me while helping her walk up the steps.

"So, why did you call me, Wallflower?" I clear my throat. "It's been days."

She smiles and looks up with those gorgeous, hooded, mossy eyes. "The place we went to had coconut cake on their dessert menu."

I chuckle. "That's what you wanted to tell me?"

She pauses and stares at her feet as she takes the last few steps. We stand in front of her door. "Made me think of you."

"Did you order it?"

"No." She frowns. "Maybe next time." The corner of her mouth lifts as she looks up and smiles. Silver glittery eyeshadow is spread out across her lids, matching her dress. She's a shimmering disco ball. She looks drastically different than she did on our first date days ago. I can tell Julianna had a hand in her outfit and makeup tonight.

"I haven't stopped thinking about you, Selene." My confession spills out of me, and I have no regrets once it does.

Not even when her smile fades.

My heart pounds as she sticks her key into the knob.

Rejection knocks the air from my lungs. I try not to let the disappointment ebb its way back in the way it has the past few days. I'm tired of living in it.

Selene's door squeals as it opens, and I stand in the open entryway, staring at her place. I've never been inside. It's a small apartment, and I immediately take note of how every piece of furniture and decoration screams Selene. The muted beige and white fabrics, with subtle hints of sage green. But then I start to notice the large crack in the ceiling, the dripping kitchen faucet, and the worn-out carpet.

Selene steps inside, tosses her key into the bowl beside us, then stops once she's on the other side. She spins to face me, swaying as if she's standing on the deck of a rocking boat. Tipping her chin higher, her eyes rake over my face. She lingers on my mouth, then looks me straight in the eye.

"I have something else I want to tell you." Her voice is barely a whisper.

She falls forward, landing weakly against me. Her eyes don't stay open for long. She says she's had six shots of tequila, but I'm wondering how much she's really had. I have a feeling she's going to pass out any second.

I grip onto the back of both of her arms as she presses her hands to my chest.

"You were right," she whispers.

I could hold her like this forever.

"Right about what?" I swallow my nerves. I'm on fucking fire. I allow the feeling to burn me from the inside out. If this is what it feels like to completely surrender yourself to falling in love with someone, I'll welcome this feeling for the rest of my life.

She smooths her palms slowly up along my neck. My breathing is quick and shallow. She's never touched me like this. It's impossible to not want to kiss her or allow my hands to roam, but I can't. I won't. I only want her when she's fully conscious and sober.

A thunderbolt vibrates through my body, electricity crackling through my veins when she drags her finger across my bottom lip.

"Your kiss did light something inside me." She stares me directly in the eye. "I've wanted to do it again, just to make sure I really did feel it. That it was real."

I blow out a heavy breath, emptying my lungs. I swear to God, I'm no longer anchored to this earth. I'm floating away, being hurled into another galaxy.

"Oh, Wallflower. I have, too." She's cracked open my chest and wrapped her hands around my heart, claiming it for herself.

I drag my finger down the side of her face, admiring her. She's the most beautiful woman I've ever seen. Then she's sinking against me. I catch her just as her knees buckle. In one swift movement, I pick her up, scooping her up into my arms. She places her head against me, tucking her hand between my beating heart and her cheek. She closes her eyes.

"But she said the same," she mumbles. "And look how well that turned out."

I have no clue what she means or who she's talking about. I stand there holding her, listening to her deepening breaths and the dripping faucet. Watching her sleep against me does something to me. I've never seen her this peaceful, this calm and out of her own thoughts.

I take one more glance around her apartment and then I don't waste any more time. I swipe her key from the bowl, lock the front door, and take her home.

SEVENTEEN

SELENE

When I wake up, it feels as if I've slammed my head against a brick wall. Repeatedly.

My mind is alive, but my world is black. It takes me several seconds and all the strength I have to crack my eyes open.

A sharp hiss passes between my teeth when I do. Bright, obnoxious rays of sunshine beam through the large, glass window I'm facing. A shadowy figure sits in front of it. He's draped in sunshine, surrounded by yellow and white. I lift my hand and block it out on a groan.

"Morning, Wallflower." Holt's gravelly voice breaks the silence.

"Where am I?" I ask, rolling onto my back and covering my eyes with my hand.

"My bed."

"Seriously?" I ask, rolling my head back to face him. That motion alone makes me feel sick again. I hold back a gag.

"Here. Take this." Holt sits up from the chair he's sitting in and hands me a glass of ice water and two white pills.

"How did I get here?" I ask after the pills make their way

down my throat. I'm afraid I might throw them back up unless I get some food in my system soon. "What happened?"

"You don't remember?" The bed sinks as he sits on the edge beside me.

I sit up until my back rests against the headboard. Fragments of last night come crashing into my hungover brain.

Slipping into Julianna's newly-bought, sparkly dress. Going to the bar. Refusing to think about Holt. Telling the girls I would only have one drink. Seeing the coconut cake on the dessert menu. Ordering six shots of tequila. Downing them back to back. Julianna's driver taking me home. Stumbling into my apartment, then suddenly feeling alone. Walking back outside to call Holt. Him showing up at my front step.

"I remember parts," I mutter, my cheeks reddening. I look him in the eye. "I remember you were standing inside my apartment with me."

My stomach growls loudly. Fuck. Could I be any more embarrassing?

"Not for long," Holt says, the corner of his mouth lifting. He leans forward and grabs a small plate of toast from the nightstand. He picks up the top triangle and holds it in front of my mouth. "Eat."

I swallow loudly. Heat burns across my body. It could be from the intense sun. We are closer to it, after all, with how tall Holt's building is. Or it could be the look in his blue eyes, telling me that if I don't take a bite of the toast he's offering, he might finally use that punishment he promised me.

Leaning forward, I take a bite.

He watches me intensely, his mouth parting as my teeth sink into the crusty wheat slice. It feels good to sit back and chew it, letting it soak up whatever alcohol remains in my body.

"You passed out on me," he says, watching me take another

bite. "I decided to bring you here so I could watch over you better. I'm glad I did because..."

Then it hits me. The shame. The embarrassment. For some reason, the memories of after I passed out against Holt in my apartment aren't as clear. My neck prickles with the thought of what could have happened.

Frantically, I look around, catching the shimmering sequins of my dress on the end of the bed. As if my mind is finally catching up to my situation, I look down at my body. I'm wearing an oversized, black T-shirt.

"Oh, God." I slap my hands to my cheeks, then my forehead. I can't even look at Holt. "Did we have sex?"

Holt chuckles, pulling my hand away from my face. "No, Wallflower. I'm not down with necrophilia. I prefer my women conscious, sober, and consenting."

"Oh." I sigh, then I see the hurt flash across his face. His eyes soften and his tiny smirk disappears. I wrap my hand over his. "Not that I thought you ever would. I'm just confused." I look down at his shirt. "How did I...?"

"Take another bite," he orders, shoving the half-eaten slice toward me again.

I do as he says, staring into his eyes the entire time. I'm working it over in my mouth when he continues.

"When I brought you home, I was going to lay you down here, but you stirred in my arms, and when I realized you were on the verge of throwing up, I tried to run to the bathroom but didn't make it in time. You got some on your dress." He places the plate on the nightstand, scooting noticeably closer to me. He tucks my hair behind my ear. "I didn't think you'd want to sleep in your vomit-covered dress."

"No," I chuckle, resting my head in my hand. "I wouldn't have. Thank you."

"Of course."

"But that means you saw…" Now my cheeks are hot. In fact, my entire face is on fire.

"Yes." His eyes darken. "Saw your little white lacy number with the embroidered flowers?"

"Oh, God," I groan, hanging my head in shame.

Holt's fingers hook under my chin, luring me back up to face him. "I didn't touch, but I won't lie and say it wasn't impossible to look away. I only let my eyes linger for a half second before slipping my T-shirt over your head."

"Thank you for being kind and helping me." I tilt my head to the side, this conversation confusing me further. "Although, I should probably get home and brush my teeth. I feel disgusting." I start to shift under the blanket. "I've caused you enough trouble as it is."

He quickly catches my hand. "You aren't trouble, Selene."

I sigh, dropping my shoulders. "You drove all the way to my place, then you had to carry me home, and I was a mess."

He places his finger to my mouth, stopping me from talking. Electric jolts crack across my lips at his touch. "I didn't *have* to do anything."

It's difficult to breathe when he's touching me this way. I'm a mess. A complete mess. The way I look on the outside is exactly how I feel on the inside. I'm almost certain my hair looks like a fucking rat's nest and my breath smells of a lovely concoction of vomit and tequila, but I can't ignore the way Holt's looking at me like I'm the only person he wants to look at for the rest of his days. It's insane. I must be delusional.

"Why are you so resistant to receiving help?" he asks. "Do you find it hard to believe that I care about you and your wellbeing?"

"No, it isn't that." I'm lying. It is hard to believe anyone would care about me. Love is for the fucking birds.

"Listen, Wallflower," he whispers, leaning forward. "Keep up with the lies, and I may just punish you after all."

He brings his mouth close to mine, and I snap my lips together. I can't kiss him when I can still taste last night on my tongue. At least let me brush my teeth first.

I swallow, naively believing it will help. "What type of punishment? You've said this before."

"Every time I catch you in a lie, I'll take you over my knee and spank that perfect, round ass of yours."

A sharp breath of air hits the back of my throat. "You wouldn't."

"Oh, I would." His voice deepens, tearing down the walls I've built for myself. "Don't tell me you've never been spanked before, Wallflower."

"No," I clip out. "I haven't."

He grins. He can tell it isn't a lie. "We might just have to change that then. With your permission, of course."

"I don't think I could. Spanking seems ridiculous."

He scoots impossibly closer, placing a hand on the other side of my leg. He's taking up all the space between us. "We'll see if you're saying that afterward. You'll be surprised what a spanking can do."

"We'll see about that." I can't stop looking at him.

"Fine." He pops a brow. "But I'll tell you this: just say the word and we'll put us both out of this misery of pretending."

"Pretending what?"

"Pretending we don't want each other."

He's gorgeous in this morning sun. I want to grab his face and slam his lips to mine. I want to tell him a ridiculous lie—one he will recognize in an instant. Like how the sky is green and the grass is blue just to see what it would feel to have his hand cracking across the sensitive skin on my ass, but I don't. My breath is absolutely criminal at this point.

He must read my mind when he says, "I have an extra tooth-brush in the bathroom cabinet."

"I have a perfectly good toothbrush at home," I whisper, cursing my breath brushing across his lips.

"Stay." One word. It's the only word needed to make the blood drain to my toes.

"I can't."

"Do you have work today?"

"No."

"Writing?"

"No."

His eyes trail from my mouth to my eyes. "We'll let that first lie slide of you saying you can't since you haven't given the go ahead yet on letting me spank you. But please stay, Wallflower."

"I... shouldn't."

I've spent years telling myself feelings weren't for me. Falling for someone isn't worth the risk that comes with it. The heartbreak. The betrayal. The death. What is there to show for it if in the end it turns out to all be a lie? Is the risk truly worth the reward? But Holt has managed to tear down every single one of my beliefs on falling in love. He's testing me, making me believe my heart isn't completely dead.

Logic tells me not to stay. To go home full of shame and pretend the time with him hasn't meant anything. But that would be the biggest lie I've ever told myself.

"Stay here today," he says, bringing his mouth dangerously close to mine. I've never wanted to kiss anyone as much as I do him. "You can shower. You can get whatever clothes you need afterward. Then I want to take you out tonight."

One brick from the wall Holt has torn down has managed to fall back into place. I crash back down to earth with that last statement. He wants to take me out to create fresh media content.

"You want to take me out." I nod, pulling back slightly. I fall back against the headboard again. "I'm guessing the headlines are starving for another Holt Capuleti dating story, huh?"

"They are." His fingers pinch the front of his shirt I'm wearing, and he pulls me forward. I sit up as he tugs me back toward him. "But that's not why I'm wanting to take you out, Selene."

"Why are you, then?" I ask, breathless.

"Because I don't want you to go. I want to know what it feels like to come home from work and see you here."

"Bold of you to assume I would want the same thing."

His blue eyes flash. "Tell me you don't."

I breathe. Count to three. Then I breathe again.

"Consider your answer, Wallflower." His voice wraps around me, heating my inner thighs. "I may just start collecting your little white lies for later."

"Oh, yeah?" I ask, having no doubt he means it.

"Yeah." He nods, cracking another smile.

Then I go against everything I've ever told myself since I was eighteen. "Where's this toothbrush?"

EIGHTEEN

After I've showered and brushed my teeth, I step back out into Holt's bedroom. Standing in the threshold between the bathroom and bedroom, I finally take it all in. I was too hungover and conscious of my terrible breath earlier for it to truly hit me where I am. Holt's towels feel like they are made of one hundred percent cashmere. Everything here is decked out in gray stone and gold tones. Shit, even the bathroom floor is heated.

My headache has faded, but the memory of Holt's words before he left for work echo across my body. I'm humming with excitement. It's terrifying. I remind myself not to fall too hard. There's still a piece of me that doesn't believe in this, despite his promise of spanking me when I give the go ahead, and my obsessive need to kiss him again. I've seen love's deception before, and I refuse to fall for it the way they all did.

I press my hand to my bare chest. Shit, what am I going to do about clothes? My dress from last night is no longer on the edge of the bed. Instead, there's a plain gray T-shirt and a pair of sweatpants. On top of them sits my apartment key. But it's what else is there that catches me by surprise. Next to them sits a black card resting on top of a handwritten note.

My pulse is racing as I tip toe across the warm tile, my hair still dripping wet when I run my fingers along the shirt and pants before picking up the card.

Holt L Capuleti

I reread the name on the card before picking up the note left beneath it.

> Wallflower,
>
> These clothes are for you to wear so you can run home and grab your own. Howard will take you. He'll also take you wherever else you want to go. Use this card to buy whatever you want today, but I have only one condition... pick something to wear for tonight. Anything you want. I won't tell you where we're going, but I'll give you a hint. Make sure to wear a dress. Pick something that gives you that spark and the fire I know that's inside of you. Something... you.
>
> See you tonight - Holt

After reading the note, I drop it down beside the card.

I stare at it the entire time while I slip on Holt's shirt and pants. They're swimming on me, but I remind myself I'm only wearing them until I get back to my place. Shamelessly, I lift the collar of the shirt and bring it to my nose. It smells like him.

I pick up my apartment key and hold it in the palm of my hand. He said he didn't want me to leave, but he's giving me the chance. I could take my key and stay home all day, hiding from the rush he gives me.

I'm almost lost in the thought when realization hits.

Holt saw my place last night. Sure he's been there before, *out*side, but he's never stepped inside. But last night, he did.

Without him even in the room, I feel embarrassed. Adam was right the day we broke up. Our worlds are completely different. I will never fit into this one.

I close my hand around my key and slowly walk over to Holt's closet. It's strange walking through here without him knowing it, but he did leave me here by myself. Well, Howard is here, but I need a moment to think.

As soon as I step inside the closet, overhead lights illuminate. One by one, they shine a dim light over each shelf and rack. It takes my breath away. I'm almost certain his closet is the same size as his bedroom. I step farther inside, breathing in what I can only describe as Holt's scent. Everything in here smells like him. Or it could be me. I used his shampoo and body wash, after all.

My hand moves along the rows of suits in his closet. Almost all of them are Armani, with some brands I've never heard of. All of them black. I start to add up the numbers in my head, remembering the price of the suit Holt told me he was wearing the day he crashed my yoga class. If these suits are at least the same price as he gave me that day, they would have paid for my college tuition countless times over.

Eventually, I come to a shelf with rolled ties. Again, all black. I can't explain it but being in here makes me feel closer to Holt. Closer than we've ever been before. Like I'm seeing a part of him only few have ever seen.

I take a deep breath, send a silent fuck you to Adam, then leave Holt's closet to go find Howard.

I went with the long, dark blue gown.

After running home and changing into my own clothes, I asked Howard to take me to a designer dress shop. I didn't know of a single one, but he took me to the one he knew of because of Julianna. I'd thought about asking her for her advice on where to start but wanted to keep this for myself. She was always my go to when it came to fitting into this world—the side Adam claimed I didn't fit into—but I wanted to do this one on my own. I wanted to own this feeling Holt had given me without the influence of my best friend, his sister.

I've told myself all day that spending the day with him like this is momentary. I'll only allow myself a little taste of it, knowing this feeling will never last. Nothing is permanent, no matter how tempted I am when it comes to Holt. This is all for show.

So, despite my reassurances, I picked the dress I thought spoke to me. A long, royal-blue gown, made of soft fabric, with a low neckline and a high slit. I picked diamond-studded, strappy heels, too that I'm almost certain cost more than a year's salary, plus a matching bracelet and necklace. It felt strange using Holt's credit card, and I felt nauseous when I saw the prices. Before I handed his card to the attendant at the designer dress store, I almost stopped myself. Until I received a text from Holt.

Apparently, he'd been anxious all day to finish his meetings so he could see me in what I'd picked out. He was also quick to point out that he hadn't seen a charge on his card yet, worried I'd flaked out on our date. I swallowed my pride and let the attendant swipe Holt's too-heavy, black charge card. Within seconds, I received a text that read: **Good girl**.

I wanted to slap him. Or maybe have him slap my ass.

Hours later, I was finishing cleaning up the kitchen after

making lunch for myself when Holt came home from work. The face-splitting grin he'd had when he saw me immediately dropped when he'd seen me cleaning. He told me he had a personal chef and a housekeeper, but I scoffed at him and simply shook my head, telling him I was fully capable of making a sandwich and loading the plate into the dishwasher myself.

I could tell he'd wanted to spank me for that comment by the way he flexed his hand as he headed toward his bathroom to take a shower.

Now, as the sun begins to set, I'm staring at my reflection in the mirror mounted in Holt's hallway, when he emerges from his bedroom wearing one of the hundreds of black Armani suits I saw this morning.

He stops on the threshold, freezing. Then, with one hand, he slaps his chest, catching himself from falling over with the other. His long fingers grip the doorframe.

"Fuck, Wallflower." He rubs his hand over his mouth. His silhouette is shadowed by the long hallway, but I feel his intense gaze raking over me. It burns, spreading to the places I've been aching to have him touch.

"It isn't too much, is it?" I ask, looking down. "Or maybe it's too little. I know it isn't as flashy as my dress last night but…" I run my hands along the front of my dress, hoping I didn't take it too far.

"Fuck, no," he breathes. "It's perfect."

When I look up, he's already marching down the hallway toward me. He steals my breath when he wraps his arm around me and his hand falls to the small of my back, holding me against him. It's the first time he's touched me all day.

"You're stunning." His eyes remind me of the night on the auction stage, wild and unyielding. "You took my instruction well. This dress is *very* you."

"I'm glad you like it." I smile, reminding my heart to calm down.

Don't fall for Holt Capuleti. This is for publicity.

Don't be a fool. Don't fall for Holt Capuleti.

He jerks me forward, pressing his body against mine. He's solid and strong, molding me to him. My mind fogs the same way it always does when he's this close. I try to focus on his gaze searing into mine, but all I want to do is kiss him. I want him to sink between my thighs. I want his cock to fill me so deeply, so fast, so hard. I want him to finally pull me over the edge of the cliff I've been toeing for days. In fact, I want him to hurl me over it.

But then my past rears its ugly head, and when I look into Holt's eyes, I see all my fears. Fear of loss. Fear of getting too close. Fear of this feeling I can no longer deny.

He leans forward, brushing the tip of his nose to mine. "You brushed your teeth."

I want to laugh. I want to crash my mouth to his.

"I want to kiss you," he confesses, his eyes darkening. "I take that back. I want to do more. I want to tear this dress off you and fuck you until your screaming my name."

The wind is knocked from my lungs. Every second Holt grows more confident.

My body is humming with anticipation. "I thought we were saving this for the cameras, Holt Capuleti," I whisper before clearing my throat.

The light doesn't die in his eyes as I expect it to. If anything, it grows. "Cameras or not, I don't give a shit. I'd do it all with you."

I inhale a sharp breath, a shiver slinking down my spine. "We should go."

He pauses, blinking. The pressure of his hand on the small of my back lightens. "Okay, Wallflower."

I suspect Holt has pulled back out of respect, but I can tell he hasn't let up on his comments. I'd be lying if I didn't say I was feeling the same, too. I already know by the time we leave wherever we're going, I'm going to spend the entire night fighting the urge to follow through on what we're both feeling.

Thirty minutes later, Holt is escorting me into the New York City Opera House, which is opulent, decorated in gold leaf detail and rich, deep maroon drapery. I can't stop staring at the auditorium in complete and utter awe. The eyes and whispers of some don't go unnoticed. It's only seconds before some are pulling out their phones to snap pictures of the two of us together.

I feel a million light years away from my cracked ceiling and the leaky faucet in my kitchen. But somehow, I feel comfortable here. Maybe it's the dress I've picked out, or how Holt hasn't stopped finding a way to touch me since we left. Cameras or not, he's held my hand the entire night.

The valet leads us to the private balcony facing the stage that Holt reserved for us. Holt holds his arm out as I take our seat. Just like I've seen in the movies, there are two pairs of gold binoculars laid out for us.

He sits beside me on the plush, velvety sofa. Our booth is private. There's one single door for entry and exit. Thick, long, velvet curtains line the sides of the booth, giving us a small semblance of privacy, but a piece of privacy, nonetheless.

"I'll be your private server tonight, Mr. and Mrs. Capuleti. If you'll be requiring anything, please don't hesitate to let me know." The young man dressed like a butler is bent at the waist, covered in shadows. The show hasn't even started and it's still dark in here. Once it begins, I can only imagine how difficult it will be to see.

I open my mouth to correct him on his assumption that we're married, but Holt stops me.

"We'd like a single bottle of champagne and two glasses, then we won't be requiring your services for the rest of the night."

"Yes, sir." The server nods once in acknowledgement and disappears.

I cross my legs, and the slit in my dress widens, revealing the smooth skin to my upper thigh. I don't fix it. Holt's hand immediately lands on my exposed skin, and there's the crackling of electricity again. I almost sigh with relief.

Fuck, I definitely won't be able to hold back tonight. Especially not at this rate.

"What show are we seeing?" I whisper, not tearing my eyes away from the stage. I've been too focused on ignoring the constant stares to pay attention to why we are here in the first place.

"Romeo and Juliet," he says not nearly as quietly as me.

I finally break my attention from the stage to look at him. He's handsome in the dim lighting. Freshly shaved and clean cut, he's every bit of the Holt Capuleti I've known for years. But being with him like this is different. He's giving me tiny pieces of who he is at his core.

"This ballet has been playing Romeo and Juliet for decades." His fingers slip between my pressed thighs. "Our parents used to bring Julianna and me when we were kids. Being here reminds me of when life felt perfect."

"I get what you mean." I glance around the auditorium with a warm smile. "My parents used to take us to Coney Island every summer."

"What is your favorite memory? Of Coney Island?"

"The bumper cars," I'm quick to answer. "Our parents would join London and me, and the competition was fierce but fun. I don't think I'd ever seen them laugh as hard as they did then. They were happy."

The memory cracks open a part of me I've kept stitched up for years. But why was it so easy for me to share it with Holt?

"But then again, nothing is as it seems," I admit, softly. Tears threaten to burn behind my eyes, but I refuse to let my parent's deceitful nature steal this from me.

"I agree," Holt whispers, still leaning in. He squeezes my thigh, his eyes glistening in the diluted light. "This place is my Coney Island."

It's difficult to breathe. I can't look away from Holt, his eyes becoming the windows to his soul. My heart breaks for him, knowing the struggle he's going through with this lawsuit. He hides it well behind his calm demeanor, always buried in his work, but I can tell being here with me is giving him a bit of peace from the chaos that surrounds him.

I understand it, too.

The secret I'm keeping for Julianna sits between us. I've been able to put it out of my mind until he brought her up just now. I inhale a deep breath, hoping Julianna doesn't take too long to tell her brother the truth. The last thing I want is to get between them.

The lights in the auditorium dim as our server returns with the bottle of champagne. It rests in an all-too-fancy bucket of ice. Holt pours me a glass, and I down half of it before the last audience member takes their seat below and the stage curtains open.

We sit in silence, but all I can think about is Holt's hand pressed firmly between my thighs. My body is screaming for his touch. I want more. I need more.

His silence is agonizing in the best way.

With my heart racing a million miles a minute, I'm all too aware of Holt's presence. We're both pretending to pay attention to the ballet, but all I can think about is him, and I know he feels the same way every time he squeezes my thigh just a little.

I'm already soaking wet, begging for the orgasm I've been denied for days.

I uncross my legs, and Holt lets out an audible hiss.

Romeo and Juliet continue to dance delicately across the stage, the longing on their faces evident from where we're sitting. The show is beautiful and moving. There's something about the forbidden nature of their love, the longing glances. All of it is overwhelming. I tuck my bottom lip under my teeth, realizing I haven't felt this way ever.

Between the ballet and Holt's touch, I feel everything now. I feel it all.

I hiccup on a breath as Holt's hand slides up my thigh. I sigh, my eyes fluttering. Then he leans close to my ear, his hot breath brushing across it as he whispers, "It's killing me, I mean absolutely *killing* me, not being able to kiss you right now, Wallflower."

My eyes snap open, and I place my hand over his, dragging it up the rest of my thigh, pressing his fingers firmly against my throbbing pussy.

Wide eyed, I turn to face him. "Then, kiss me."

Hungry and wanting, he doesn't waste time. He closes the gap between us, pressing his mouth starvingly against mine. It's strong yet soft, and he groans as his lips mold to mine.

I'm gasping for air, a jolt of electricity jump starting my heart. He reaches across, gripping the side of my face. His fingers get lost in my long, wavy hair, pulling me impossibly closer.

I grip his arm, letting my hand slide over the soft, silken fabric of his black suit. The orchestrated music in the background booms and vibrates through the auditorium. It's amazing how we're in a room filled with people but are somehow still in our own bubble.

The hand he has pressed against my pussy moves to my hip,

pulling me up out of my seat and onto his lap. My dress parts, bunching at the waist. As soon as I'm sitting in Holt's lap, I feel his length against my wetness. My barely-there, thin lace thong is soaked as I rock my hips against his stone-hard cock. I know I'm destroying his insanely expensive suit, but Holt must not care because he moves his hand under my dress, around the curve of my ass, to the small of my back, encouraging me to grind against him harder.

His mouth hasn't broken away from mine when he bites my lip, grunting as I roll my hips. I moan against his mouth, gasping as my clit brushes against his zipper.

"I want you, Holt," I breathe, tilting my head up to give him access to my neck. I try to quiet my mewls, instead focusing on the heat coursing through my body. It's as if I've been drowning in an endless ocean, finally coming up for air.

"Tell me how badly you want me." He reaches between us, shoving my thong aside and pressing his fingers to my swollen, aching clit.

I gasp, arching my back.

"Consider your lies, Wallflower," he warns softly. "You have no idea how badly I want to spank you right now."

His other hand slips down to the full curve of my ass cheek. He palms it, jerking me forward. I'm caught between both his hands, and although we're in our own private area, we're still in public. I'm almost certain if I allowed myself to fully cry out, the entire opera house would be able to hear me.

He trails his mouth down my neck and along my collarbone.

"I haven't given you the word yet," I tell him, grinding against his hand. My body is humming and vibrating. It feels even better than the time in the elevator. "Even if I did, we couldn't. Not here."

"So, you're saying it's a possibility?" He slips his fingers down my slit before plunging them inside me.

My mouth falls open and I don't think. I lose all hesitation and give him a coy smile. "Maybe."

His gaze softens as his fingers work inside me, tugging on the part of me I've left dormant for so long. "You have no idea what you do to me. What you've done to me all this time. I've dreamed endlessly of this. Of you."

"Please," I beg, shamelessly. I look down at Holt, pressing my hands around his gorgeous face. I kiss him once before looking him in the eye and confessing, "I want your cock to fill me. I want you to make me come harder than ever. I want you to fuck me, Holt. Fuck me like you've wanted to for the past six years."

His eyes darken, the blues in them sharpening in the pale light. His fingers pull out of me, and then he's scrambling to undo his belt and the zipper of his pants.

I don't believe giving in completely to your feelings. I've seen the devastation it can cause. No one can truly love someone else, not wholly. But I see Holt's truth in this moment. He meant it when he said he sees me. He's watched me for years, wanting this. Slipping down this rabbit hole with him, I surrender, telling myself it's only temporary. I'll feel this, then go back to pretending.

I lean down and press my lips to his jaw, then his neck. Being this close and feeling him this way is freeing. Terrifying and freeing. I know we're crossing a line. Being here, not in the view of the public, yet still in public, is the perfect metaphor for our situation. I'm asking Holt to relieve whatever this is between us without a single person glancing in our direction.

The other guests in their booths across the way can't see us. At least, I don't believe they can. They're too focused on the performance on stage, and we're covered in shadows.

I rise up slightly as Holt grips onto his cock, guiding me over him. Then he slams me down.

My teeth sink into my lip, stifling my cries as he fills me. I wish this stupid fucking dress wasn't between us. I need his hands on me. His mouth biting down on my peaked nipples that are aching to be touched. Still, though, this feeling consumes me.

I never once wanted to be touched by Adam but with one look, one whisper, I want Holt.

"Fuck, your pussy is so tight." He groans against my neck. "God, Wallflower..."

I move subtly, rocking my hips just enough to move along Holt's long, thick cock. It reaches deep inside me, and with every move it becomes more difficult not to cry out with pleasure. Difficult not to scream. Difficult not to want this to end but also not end at all.

"Holt... right there..." I whisper in his ear.

The orchestra plays another song, the chords and melodies striking louder and faster. Closing my eyes, I sink into this feeling building inside me. I'm wound tightly, like all the tension I've carried around me for years is on the verge of unraveling and spinning out of control. Like one of those wind-up toy cars, each thrust brings on another onslaught of explosions. Tiny bursts of electricity hum through my veins and across my skin. I'm still dressed, but Holt makes it a point to drag his mouth across every exposed inch of skin. My shoulders, the swell of my breasts, the base of my throat.

I comb my fingers through his hair before he's urging me to look down at him.

His blue eyes shine in the shadows.

We simply stare into each other's eyes as I move above him. He lifts his hips slightly, but he doesn't need to do much. My jaw falls, and I'm gasping for air, lungs burning.

Holt's sparkling eyes search my face as he reaches between

us again and presses his fingers to my clit. A new surge of adrenaline courses through me.

"Unravel for me, Wallflower."

With his other hand, he slams me down again before lifting his free hand to grip the side of my face and pulling me down to kiss him. His lips are soft yet commanding. I melt into them, and within seconds, I'm coming undone. I'm finally falling off the cliff, with Holt's touch surrounding me. His mouth is pressed to mine, and I slam myself back down, vibrating against him as I come undone.

My movements slow as I ride out my own orgasm, using our kiss to stifle my cries. He still has his hand pressed against my clit as I slide myself along his length several more times before he's coming, too. His cock pulses inside me, intensifying the rest of my orgasm as his cum fills me.

"Oh, fuck." He groans against my mouth, barely breaking our kiss. His body wracks beneath me, gripping onto me as his eyes squeeze shut.

His head tips back, resting it on the back of the velvet booth. Running my thumb along his jaw, I lean down and kiss his skin. It's rough and grating against my mouth, but it pulls me back down to reality.

I push down the feelings Holt has stirred inside me. He's awakened this part I've tried to hide from. Like flicking a lighter in a dark room. It's a tiny flame but it's unmistakable.

I'm coming down from my orgasm, staring at my hand pressed to Holt's chest, when I get an overwhelming sensation that I've crossed a line that I can't go back on. I've taken the path of no return. I've given parts of my myself, showed pieces of me, I was never able to show to Adam. Shit, or anyone else for that matter.

The song being played by the orchestra abruptly ends, and the audience bursts into applause. My back is turned to the auditorium, but I don't need to see them to know the show is over.

My hand is still cupping the side of Holt's face when he lifts his head. There's a dazed look in his eyes, and he cracks a smile. But I can't bring myself to smile back, because I fear I've caught myself in a tangled web. One I want to find a way out of yet surrender my fate to all at the same time.

"Don't let that light die out, Wallflower." He tucks my hair behind my ear, not moving me. His cock is still inside me, and I almost want to go again, but I know the lights are bound to turn back on any minute. We can't risk being brought into the spotlight like this.

"I'm not," I lie, denying his accusation.

He narrows his eyes at me.

I lean forward and press my mouth to the corner of his, then drag my nose across his cheek. "Appears you've caught me in another lie, Mr. Capuleti. Now, tell me, what are you going to do about it?"

I feel the growl rumble against my hand on his chest before he's lifting me off him. I don't even have time to clean myself up before he's zipping his pants and wrapping my hand around his to take us home.

NINETEEN

HOLT

We've barely made it through the front door when I'm tearing Selene's dress off her body. Now that I've buried myself inside her, she's all I want. Could ever want.

I've been obsessed with her for years, believing she was never within my reach. And although I'd convinced myself she was only doing this to play along for the media, because she simply doesn't do relationships, deep down, I know she feels differently now.

Or else she wouldn't be standing in my living room, about to be completely naked.

Her gasp tears through my apartment as I rip her dress from her body. It falls to a puddle at her feet. With her back toward me, she looks over her shoulder, and I nearly fall to my knees. Her green eyes shimmer in the dim lighting. She looks up at me through her dark lashes, resting her chin on her shoulder. "Are you going to stand there all night staring at me like you don't know what to do with me?"

"Oh, I know exactly what I'm going to do with you." I grab her hip, spin her around, and grip her ass to lift her up.

She squeals and wraps her legs around me.

I kiss her. I don't want to stop. I love the way she tastes and feels. I could do this forever. Bask in this feeling. Life can be complete and utter shit, but being with Selene makes me believe otherwise.

Keeping one arm under her, I move my other to her front and palm her breast. She tilts her head back as I flick my thumb over her nipple, and I grow painfully hard.

"Fuck, Holt." She closes her eyes as I carry her back to my bedroom. "I want to feel you inside me again. I need to." She wraps her fist around my tie, pulling me to her, as she studies me again. "Please," she begs against my mouth.

I give her a coy smile. "God, I love it when you beg."

She tugs on my tie again, raveling it around her fist. "Keep that up, and we'll see who gets the punishment."

"That wasn't a lie, Wallflower." I pinch her nipple again, squeezing her ass cheek in my hand other hand.

"I could still punish you." She sticks her tongue out and drags it across my bottom lip, tasting me. "I could tease you by refusing to give in to what you want."

"You'd be punishing us both then." I've made it to the edge of my bedroom when I move my hand from her breast to her aching clit. "Your cunt is soaking wet for me again. It's obvious what you want."

She leans forward and gently sinks her teeth into my lip. I hiss at the pleasure coursing through my body.

After biting me, she gently kisses the same spot. "Then, do something about it."

I take the few steps forward and drop her onto my bed. She sinks into it effortlessly. Fuck, she's gorgeous spread out for me. Her blonde hair is splayed out around her, and her skin glows from the city lights pouring through the windows.

She sits up on her elbows and bends one leg, dragging her

foot along the silk. With hooded eyes, she watches me as I undo my tie.

"Turn over," I order, lowering my voice.

She cocks a brow, the corner of her mouth lifting. "Please?"

"It wasn't a request." With my tie in one hand, I lean down and slide my hands up the length of her body. I'm inches above her as I crawl until my face is above her chest.

I stick my tongue out and flick it across the swollen, peaked bud, then I blow across it. A sweet moan climbs up Selene's throat, and she tilts her head back, exposing her neck. "Look at me."

She obeys.

"About what you said at the Opera House." I kiss her breast, all the while keeping my eyes pinned to hers. She's breathing heavily, caught in a trance. She's trying hard to keep it together, but so am I.

Selene's used to maintaining this image she's created for herself, but I love seeing her drop her walls for me.

"What did I say?" she pants.

I drag my teeth across her nipple then kiss her again. "About your lies."

"I... I don't remember," she stutters, squeezing her eyes shut.

I pull her nipple into my mouth and suck.

Her eyes pop open, and she wiggles beneath me.

My cock is throbbing, aching to be inside her.

I suck hard, puckering my lips before pulling back as her nipple pops from my mouth. "You're lying again."

She wraps a hand around the back of my head. Her nails scrape against my scalp. "I asked you what you were going to do about it."

I smirk. "That's my girl." I grip her breast and squeeze, pulling her nipple up again. I lap my tongue over it, swirling it around before wrapping my lips around it again. Then I come back up. "Is this you giving me permission to punish you?"

Her eyes soften and she pauses. I see the cracks in her armor. Her vulnerability.

"I... I, um... I don't know. I want to but..." She swallows and parts her lips. "I've just never done it before."

"Only when you give me the word," I reassure her.

"Okay."

She mews quietly as I work my hand down the length of her body, dragging it down her breast then her stomach before cupping her sweet pussy.

"Do you trust me?" I ask as she falls to the mattress and arches her back.

"Yes."

"Look me in the eye and tell me you trust me."

Her chin meets her chest, and her eyes meet mine. "I trust you."

"Good." I kiss her breast before settling myself between her legs. I part them with my knees, then press them into the mattress, towering over her. "Give me your wrists."

This time, she doesn't ask me to say please. She obeys with a heated gaze and a faint smile of anticipation.

I can practically feel her buzzing beneath me. Sitting up on my knees, I wrap my tie around her wrists, binding them together before lifting them over her head. Then I tie the other end to my bedframe. She's panting under me, her eyes following my handiwork.

Once I'm finished ensuring she's secure, I lower myself back down to her level. My hands press into the mattress at her sides as I lean down and kiss her on the mouth.

"You're so fucking beautiful," I say against her mouth before sliding my tongue against hers.

She pulls up to meet me, deepening our kiss.

My heart beats wildly. Normally, I detach my emotions when I'm with a woman, but it's impossible with Selene. I don't know where my body and heart begins or ends. It's all one with her. I can't be with her and not think about how I feel. It's debilitating, scary yet exhilarating all at once.

"Holt, I..." She tries to pull away, but I stop her by pressing my finger to her mouth.

"Shh." I clear my throat, my dick throbbing. "I know what you're going to say."

"No." She licks her lips, shaking her head. "I don't think you do."

"Actually, I do." I slip my fingers between her dripping wet slit and circle her clit before slipping them inside her. I hook my fingers, reaching up to the one spot that causes her back to arch and her neck to tighten as she gasps, throwing her head back. The tie pulls on her wrists as she tugs against them.

"I've thought about you for years," I confess. "I've watched you. You think I just showed up to your yoga class because Julianna told me about it once."

"You've been stalking me?" she asks, her voice cracking.

I chuckle, loving the way her body is reacting to my touch. "Stalking. Watching. Protecting. Call it what you want, but I've been obsessed."

"Then, why?" She rocks against my hand, clearly wanting more. "'Why didn't you say anything before?"

"Because, Wallflower." I drop my voice, my patience growing thin with every moment that passes where I'm not burying my cock inside her. "You're clearly out of my league. And I know you..." I press my mouth to the swell of her breast, looking up at her with hooded eyes. "But I intend to show you exactly how I feel about you so there's no mistaking it."

"Holt..." She pants, lifting her hips. "I can't make—"

Then I'm between her legs, dragging my tongue along her slit.

Her spine stiffens the moment my tongue meets her swollen clit. She arches her back, and I can hear the pull of my tie as it strains against the pressure.

I grin against her and flick my tongue over her clit. Back and forth. Up and down. Over and over. I keep my fingers inside her, pressing my hand flat against her lower belly to keep her still. She resists, but her moans quickly fill my bedroom.

"God, your cunt tastes so sweet," I tell her. "Just like you."

"I'm not sweet." She rolls her hips back and then up again. "Oh, fuck."

I let out a sardonic laugh. "There's another lie we're going to have to rectify later."

"I'm going to come, Holt." She moans. "Fuck, I want to touch you."

"Not yet," I tell her, then my mouth is back on her sweet cunt. I bite and suck and tease until her thighs are on either side of my head. "I want you coming all over my mouth. I want your pussy crying out for me, telling me you got my message."

"What message?"

I suck on her clit, pinching it between my teeth. She hisses, and, fuck, my resolve is waning. "That there isn't any question as to what I feel for you." I blow a tiny breath across her pussy.

She looks down at me.

"Now, come for me, Wallflower."

Her thighs press against my head the second I'm working her clit again. I drag my tongue up and down her slit while pumping my fingers in and out of her. I wrap my free hand over the top of her thigh, holding her down as she moans.

"Oh, God, Holt, I'm going to come."

"Do it," I growl.

She does as I command. Her body writhes against the bed.

The restraints are pulled taut as her chest quivers with her orgasm. Her thick thighs press against the side of my head as she cries out.

I keep working her, letting her cries tell me when she's coming down from her orgasm. I watch her in amazement, making sure to take in every detail. The way her hair shines in the lights above my bed. The way her fingers grip the tie. The way she tilts her head back, gasping for air.

My cock twitches, and I need her now. She's so fucking wet for me.

Heart racing, I pull my fingers out of her and sit up on my knees. "I want you to taste yourself." I place my fingers against her lips. "I want you to taste yourself and what I can make you do."

She obeys, licking my fingers. Her cheeks are flushed, and she's still trying to catch her breath, but there's a fire in her eyes. I can tell she wants more. Craves more.

"I love seeing this side of you, Wallflower. Keep showing it to me."

I slide back until my feet hit the floor, then I'm grabbing her ankles and flipping her over. She lets out a yelp as her front hits the mattress. I stare at her, admiring her backside in silence. She's panting, her head hanging between her tied arms.

The black ink along the length of her spine causes me to freeze. The words are permanently marked in Italian—a language I happen to know well.

Ma l'amore... è solo un'illusione

But love... it's only an illusion.

The phrase is etched in fine print. I've seen it before, revealed in the many open-back dresses and bathing suits I've seen her wear over the years, but I've never paid much attention to it before now. I've never been as close to it as I am right here. Not enough to fully comprehend the intricate Italian script.

I read her tattoo repeatedly in my head, wondering the meaning behind it and why Selene chose it, but I don't stay on the thought for long, because I've never wanted her more.

"I know I keep saying this, but I don't think I've ever meant it more than I do now." My eyes rake over her body, down to her perfect ass. "You're the most beautiful thing I've ever had the privilege of laying my eyes on."

I watch the muscles in her back and sides move as she swallows, catching her breath. Ten seconds pass before she's cutting through the silence.

"Please, Holt," she begs, then she's trying to speak over her shoulder. "Spank me."

I'm unbuttoning my shirt when I stop halfway through. "Are you sure?"

"Yes," her voice strains. "I want you to spank me. *Please.*"

I finish unbuckling my belt and unzip my pants before sliding them and my boxer briefs off, then press one knee into the mattress.

"Only if you're ready," I tell her, stroking my cock. I need relief, and I need it fast. I've imagined spanking Selene so many times. I need to make sure she wants this as much as I do.

"I'm ready," she says, still breathing hard. Maybe it's the anticipation of it all, but I know Selene wouldn't make the request unless she was absolutely certain this is what she wanted.

She shivers as I slide my palm along her spine and bend to kiss her round cheek before I'm lifting her to her knees. Her perfect round ass is on full display for me, directly in my face.

"Your cunt is still dripping for me." I slide my hand along the inside of her thighs, sweeping my fingers along the wetness coating her skin. I gently part her legs, urging her to separate them.

"Please, Holt."

Adrenaline courses through my veins as I slink closer to her. I center the tip off my cock against her backside and drag my crown along her slit, coating myself with her wetness.

She sighs, dipping her head. I tease her entrance, and she moans.

Then I pull my hand back and smack her ass.

Crack!

She yelps as her back arches before dropping her head in a pant.

A spark lights in my chest, and I pause, waiting for her reaction. A red imprint of my fingers blooms across her cheek and, fuck, I might just come right now before I'm even inside her.

"Are you okay, Wallflower?" I soothe my hand over the spot, worried she wasn't ready.

"Yes," she says confidently. She glances over her shoulder, blowing the hair away from her face. "Again. Do it again."

I give her a wicked grin, soothing my hand over her ass again. "As you wish, Wallflower. But not again until I sink myself into this pretty cunt of yours."

Pulling back, I drive myself inside her. She cries out, lifting her head, and pulling on the tie. I grip onto her hips, steadying her as I pull back and drive back in.

She feels so fucking good.

This is how I've always wanted her. I want to watch her come undone. I want to watch her bare and vulnerable just for me. Seeing her this way and being with her like this cracks open a piece of myself I've kept locked away. The piece that cares for another person, heart, body, and soul. I've pined over Selene Walker for years, but I never thought it would feel like this.

"You feel so fucking good," I tell her. "Slam that perfect ass into me, Selene. Take all of me, inch for inch."

She grunts as she obeys my request. I grow delirious, riding on a fucking high. Her tits bounce beneath her, and her hair falls around her shoulders as I fuck her from behind. With every thrust, I feel her getting closer.

"I'm going to come again..." she moans.

Her pussy tightens around me, and I feel the same. I take my opportunity and spank her again. This time, a little harder than the last.

"Fuck!" she cries out. "That feels good."

"It does, doesn't it?" Not wasting any more time. I spank her again.

Then I lose all self-control. I drive myself in and out of her until she's quivering against me. She screams my name, and I hold onto her, continuing to pump in and out of her as heat pools in my lower belly. My legs tingle and my arms hum with electricity. Her pussy walls contract, and that's all it takes before I'm coming inside her. I still, holding onto her tightly as I finish riding out my orgasm.

When I've finished, we're both left panting. Her head hangs lazily between her tied arms. Pulling out of her, I crawl up beside her, undo the tie, and let her lay against me on the bed. She rests her head on my chest, catching her breath. I stare at the ceiling, knowing we've crossed another line. Another path of no return.

Knowing Selene's mind, I press my fingers under her chin and pull her to look up at me.

"Selene," I whisper her name, my pulse racing.

Her soft eyes look tired but also satisfied.

"I didn't hurt you, did I?" I ask, my voice cracking. It feels incredible to be with her like this, but the thought of having hurt her in the process tears me up inside.

"No." She inches forward and rests her chin over her hand pressed to my chest as I brush loose strands of hair away from her sticky skin. "You didn't hurt me."

I smile and pull her up until I'm able to press a soft kiss to her mouth. "I'm glad because I don't think I could live with myself if I hurt you."

Her small grin fades, and her eyes soften, distancing.

"Hey..." I tell her, urging her to look back at me.

Her stomach grumbles, and then her cheeks redden even deeper. "Oh, my God." She groans, burying her face in her hands. "Could I be more embarrassing?"

"You need to eat." I chuckle, looking up at the ceiling before back to her.

She narrows her eyes. "You aren't going to feed me toast again, are you?"

I shift underneath her until I've gripped her ass and slapped it lightly before taking a handful of her flesh and pulling her against me. "What, you didn't like me feeding you toast?"

"Oh." Her grin reaches her sparkling green eyes. "You feeding me, I liked. The dry toast... not so much."

I laugh then grip the back of her head, bringing her deliciously gorgeous mouth to mine. "Better food, we can arrange, Wallflower. Whatever you want."

Fuck, I'm in Heaven.

TWENTY

There's been a shift between us. One I'm not certain I'm ready to face. I bury it down with the memory of my parents. I remind myself that nothing is permanent in this life. One day you're living the perfect dream, the next you're living a nightmare not even you could conjure up. Fear has gripped my soul since that day, and I've never wanted to break free from it.

Not until now.

Pressure builds behind my eyes, and I feel my insides twisting, transforming me into a person I don't recognize. I watch Holt sleep in fascination. He looks peaceful. I study his features, the curve of his lips, the slight crook to his nose. I picture his blue eyes shielded behind his soft lids.

Is this how she felt? Is this the illusion she fell for before it was all ripped away?

Questions eat away at me, and I want nothing more than to lose myself in Holt once again. I'm sore between my legs, and even though Holt washed me and gave me a bath, I want him again already. I need to know this isn't just a terrible dream I'm bound to wake up from.

"Holt?" I whisper in the dark of night that's draped all around us.

I almost regret interrupting his deep sleep, but it's too late when he says, "Wallflower?"

I simply breathe, remembering the techniques my therapist gave me to handle any situation that made me feel this way.

"What's going on?" he asks, cracking his eyes open. He shifts to his side, lying so he's facing me. He grabs the back of my knee, lifting my leg so it's draped over his side. I feel his cock swelling to life, poking me.

I want him inside me again. It's an insane thought and, again, something I'm not ready to face.

"Can't sleep," I confess.

He presses a kiss to my forehead.

I close my eyes and concentrate on every muscle and organ in my body.

It's amazing how one minute I'm reliving the splatter of blood, staring into my mother's life-drained eyes for the millionth, trillionth time, and the next, I'm looking at Holt lying beside me, grounded back in reality.

"Bad dream?" he asks.

I pause, tossing out the images that have forever been a stain on my memory. "Yeah."

"I have those sometimes, too." He sighs, resting his head on his pillow and shifting his attention to the ceiling.

"Do they have to do with the lawsuit?"

"I'm no stranger to lawsuits, Wallflower. Part of running your own major corporation."

"I don't doubt that. But it isn't every day the lawsuit comes from a family rivalry as intense as yours."

His chest inflates for a few seconds before he's releasing his breath. I sink along with him, my heart hurting for both him and my best friend.

"You're right. The fact the lawsuit is coming from Rome is a far deeper wound." He tips his chin to meet his chest as he looks down at me. "But that isn't why I have nightmares."

"What are they about?" I gently ask.

"My mom."

My brows pull together. I'm surprised by his answer. "You have bad dreams about your mom?"

"Only of her death," he answers solemnly. "I was twelve, and Julianna was ten."

His admission feels like a ten-pound lead weight dropping into the pit of my stomach. I flatten my hand, feeling his heartbeat beneath skin and bone. It beats at a steady pace, grounding me to this moment.

"We don't have to talk about it if you don't want to."

"No." His voice is light yet full of emotion. "I do. It's just... I haven't talked about it in a long time. In fact, I don't think I've ever talked about it. To anyone."

I nod once in understanding as my cheek brushes against his warm skin.

"We were at the subway station on our way home from Julianna's fifth grade play when it happened."

"Julianna was there?" I gasp, shifting to look up at his face covered in dark memories and shadows. He looks different than he did moments ago. As if he's caught up in it, the memory playing in his darkened blue eyes.

"We both were. Jules says she doesn't remember much, but I remember it all. I think she's mentally blocked it out. I don't hold it against her, though. We were young, and when you witness your mother's murder, it changes you."

"What happened?" I swallow thickly.

Fuck, Holt and I have more in common than I realized. We're both haunted by the same demons. Two sides of the same coin, never knowing how alike we are until now.

"Our father was stuck at some political fundraiser," he begins. "It was his very first campaign running for mayor, one month before the election. We didn't see him very much during that time of year, but our mother never held it against him. She understood and tried to fill his absence as best she could. He didn't have the security he does now. And, honestly, I don't think he ever thought he'd need it. At least not then."

His voice cracks, and so does my heart. I want to wrap myself around him, comforting Holt in a way I never thought I would. I see how fragile he is, how the memory still haunts him. I recognize it because I see myself when he looks down at me.

"We were waiting in the subway tunnel when these two masked men came up on us. Both were armed with pistols. One held one to me and Jules; the other was pointed at my mother." His voice breaks again. "The man pointing the gun at me and Jules pushed us back, tearing us away from our mother. We fell to the ground and..." He inhales a shaky, unsteady breath. "Everything happened so fast. One second, she's looking right at us, the next she's lying on the ground in a pool of her own blood."

My skin turns ice cold, and a shiver breaks out over my body. I try to shake it off, but I can't. The memory of my own mother on her bedroom floor comes roaring back to life.

Holt runs his fingers along my back, soothing me. I focus on his touch, letting it anchor me.

"They shot our mother, execution style, then left us. They ran away as if they didn't just kill a mother in front of her own kids. Security cameras caught the whole incident, and police made arrests, but..."

"But what?" Tears prick the corners of my eyes. One slips out, spilling down the bridge of my nose onto Holt's bare chest.

He sighs and presses his lips tightly together. Then he clears his throat. "I've never believed the people arrested were the ones who killed her. I think it was someone else."

"What makes you say that?"

"Before they shot her, the man recited some sort of poem or something. At the time, I didn't understand what it meant or what language it was, but over the years, I've never forgotten it. I also saw a tattoo on the back of his hand—a symbol I've never forgotten. A shamrock with two daggers piercing the petals." He sighs heavily. "I've searched for it all over the internet, unable to find it. But there's something else. As they were scrambling to get away, one shouted to the other a name I haven't been able to forget. I told the police, but they didn't believe me. They said I must have mistaken it because I'd just been through a traumatic event. My own father doesn't believe me even now."

"What was the name you heard?" I ask, my curiosity piqued.

His blue eyes cloud over, and his voice turns gravelly when he says, "O'Connell."

"Wait. I've heard that name before."

"Heath. West's brother mentioned his name the night he died."

"You're right." Unease flutters in my stomach. "You think it's the same O'Connell?"

"I don't know." He blows out another hefty breath. "That's what I'm trying to figure out. I can't explain it, but I just have this feeling they're connected."

"Holt..." Fear cripples me. I shouldn't let it, but I see the determination in him.

When Holt sets his mind to something, he goes for it. He hasn't stopped looking for his mother's killers, even when the world is telling him it's case closed. But I fear what will happen if he continues to travel down this path.

"I haven't figured it out yet, but I won't stop. As far as I'm concerned, I don't have a choice. I need to trust my own memory. But I think it's driven a wedge between Jules and me over the years. I used to talk with her about it. I would follow her down never ending rabbit holes, playing that night over and over, hoping for a clue. Eventually, though, I think it broke Julianna, hearing me replay that night repeatedly. I broke her even more than she already was, and she distanced herself from me. At least inside she has. I couldn't let it go when all she wanted was to move on. I've tried to live as normal a life for her sake, but everything I did only caused Julianna to doubt me when it came to anything."

I'm lost in the words he's speaking, completely under his spell. A mixture of sadness fills my gut for my best friend and for Holt. All this time, I thought they were close. We're in the same social circle, and I've seen them laugh and chat, but I guess they've been able to hide their wounds from the world.

Just like I have.

He drags his finger along my cheek as though he's memorizing me.

"Jules has lost trust in me," he whispers, the heartbreak evident in his eye. "Maybe that's why she doesn't believe I can ever love someone more than myself. She thinks I've been searching for our mother's killer out of selfishness, like I'm trying to do it to prove a point when it's the opposite. She doesn't know the lengths I'm willing to go to for those I care about. Love holds no bounds. It bears no restrictions. It has no red line or limits."

A lump builds in my throat, and it suddenly becomes harder to breathe. I blink the feeling away, refusing to let my thoughts overshadow this moment. Holt is being vulnerable with me—a side I know he doesn't show to just anyone.

"What?" He frowns, noting my silence.

"Nothing." I shake my head.

"You know, I can tell when you keep a secret." He nudges my back with his finger.

"You cannot." I play him off with a laugh of dismissal.

"Of course I can. You do this thing with the corner of your mouth." Lifting his hand, he draws an invisible line along the corner of my lip with the tip of his finger.

"What thing?"

"Your mouth does this little twitch."

"It does not, and no I don't."

"Yes, you do."

I should be laughing, but I'm not. It scares me how easily Holt can see me. Not just the parts others see walking down the street or at work, but the pieces of myself I swear I keep hidden. Somehow, he sees it all. Can he tell I've been keeping Julianna's secret from him? I hope not.

His hand effortlessly moves from my mouth to the back of my neck. His nose nudges mine gently. "Tell me your secrets, Wallflower."

His whisper sends shivers down to my toes. If he weren't holding me, I swear I'd be floating into orbit, getting lost amongst the moon and stars.

His eyes harden, the lights from outside catching his deep blue eyes.

I stare at him, knowing I've never believed anything as strongly as I do this. "I don't believe love is all encompassing."

His lips part with my declaration. I can tell he wasn't expecting those words to fall from my mouth. "How do you know?" he asks, his fingers working the base of my neck. They get tangled in my hair and make it hard to concentrate on the words coming out of my mouth.

"I've literally witnessed the unravelling of love and all its lies. I've seen how love has boundaries and limits."

"Hmm," he hums, his eyes dancing across my face, and for a

moment, I think I've scared him away. I'm surprised when he scoffs, following it up with a smirk. "Says the romance novelist."

"I'm not a romance novelist," I correct. "I haven't even published my book yet. And I wrote a love story because it's the only world in which true love exists. It's reliable. It doesn't lie in fairy tales."

"It's fiction, Selene," he argues. "Doesn't that make all romance novels lies?"

"Exactly," I agree proudly.

"Mmhmm." He hums again, amused with my comeback.

I give him a challenging stare, daring him to argue back. But he doesn't.

He steals the breath from my lungs when he smooths his hand over the curve of my ass. It's slightly sore from where he spanked me earlier, but I haven't stopped thinking about how it felt, how it intensified everything. Every nerve in me awakened, the blood in my veins raced, and the hairs on the back of my neck stood up. My arms and legs tingled, humming with life. It was as if the combination of his touch and the excitement from it brought light into a dark room.

Everything lit up and filled with warmth. I'm dying to feel that again.

I slide my hand over his smooth, rock-hard chest. The subtle planes of his abs contract beneath my touch while our conversation weighs heavy in the air, lingering and suffocating. I get this sudden sensation of losing control.

His hand is still gripping the back of my neck. He pulls me forward, pressing my mouth to his, and breathes me in, savoring our kiss, deepening it with every breath. A vibration hums across my body that I want to get rid of before it becomes too much. The anticipation of his mouth and his touch are almost too much.

"I want you again." My voice cracks against his mouth, and I move my hand over Holt's chest to his shoulder. I gently push him back onto the bed and climb over him. Straddling him, I drag my nails over his chest. I need a distraction from my own mind and the dark memories haunting me.

His hands wander from my thighs to my hips to my waist. I drop my head back and breathe a sigh of relief, closing my eyes to revel in this moment. His large hands roaming over my skin, like he's making a point to touch every inch.

"Before we go any further," he says, slipping his hand between us, "I need to make one final point."

I gasp as his hand slips inside me, rubbing my wetness all over myself.

"You wrote a book. Published or not. That makes you a romance novelist."

"What?" I pant, grating my nails across his chest. My entire body burns for him.

"Don't ever fucking dilute yourself for anyone else. Especially not me." He removes his hand, grips the base of his cock, then lifts me up. The crown of it teases my entrance. He slides it against me, coating himself with my wetness but doesn't yet give me the satisfaction of sinking into me. "Understood, Wallflower?"

My breathing is labored, heavy, passionate, and scorching. I stare into his heated gaze, feeling myself eating my own words from earlier. The vulnerability he offered up to me earlier, the story of his mother's terrible death, is gone. All that's left is desire. Same could be said for me. I think back to the secret I confessed about my belief in love, or lack of it. I'm thankful Holt didn't press me to reveal more to him. Perhaps he senses how deep my emotions run and how hiding them has become a literal skill. A skill of survival.

He does call me Wallflower, after all.

I try to sink lower, ready to lose myself in Holt, but he doesn't let me.

"*Understood*, Wallflower?" he grinds out, impatient with my non-answer. He slaps my ass, and my adrenaline kicks in.

"Yes." I swallow, breathless. "Understood."

He grips my hips and slams me down, filling me. "Good. Now, ride my cock until your sweet pussy is weeping for me."

HOLT

"These goddamn motherfuckers never learn," my father spits, his eyebrows slanted in anger. He brushes the dead leaves resting on top of our mother's headstone before taking a step back.

"It's fall, Dad. Leaves die. They fall. That's nature," Julianna mutters beside me. She sniffs, the brisk, fall air nipping at her nose, causing it to turn a faint shade of red.

"Well." He squares his jaw and shoves his hands in his pockets. "I pay a groundskeeper an insane amount of money to maintain your mother's gravesite. It's their sole job. It obviously hasn't been tended to since we visited last month." My father turns to his assistant-slash-bodyguard. "Fire the groundskeeper and hire another one. I don't care the price. Tess deserves the best."

I can't help the snort that comes out of me. My father snaps his head in my direction, shooting me a glare. So does Julianna. Admittedly, her glare hurts worse than my father's.

"Is there a problem, Holt?" he asks.

I frown and shrug. "No."

Not buying my answer, my father steps closer to me. The

late fall breeze blows through the cemetery. Dry, dead leaves tumble across the bright green grass, landing in a pile against my mother's headstone.

Tess Horan Capuleti
Beloved wife and mother

Emotion is thick in my throat. I hate that every time I come here and look at her name engraved into this godforsaken chunk of stone, all I hear is the sound of the gun as a bullet was put into my mother's head. And for what?

According to the police, there is no reason, but I'm not as easily convinced as them.

My father stands beside me, his anger evident in the way he hasn't stopped glaring at me. What the hell is up his ass today? Despite our disagreement over my mother's killer, we've had a great relationship. But with the way he's looking at me now, I barely recognize him.

"Say it," he says, curling his lip.

"Say what?"

"Say what's on your mind."

"Come on, you two," Julianna says softly, standing between us. "You know Mom wouldn't want you to do this today." She arches a brow, throwing his words back at him. "She deserves the best, right?"

"She does." My father sneers, not taking his eyes off me. "But I can tell Holt thinks otherwise."

"It isn't that I don't agree," I argue, a knot in my chest weaving tighter. "But I think it's ironic how you say what Mom deserves depending on the situation."

"What is that supposed to mean?" he grinds out, his salt and pepper-lined jaw tightening.

"If you genuinely cared, you'd want to find her true killer."

I watch the fire rise in his eyes. I swear, his head might

explode, but I don't regret the words coming out of my mouth. Steam is practically billowing out of his ears.

But I'm over the fucking nightmares. I'm tired of everyone pushing what I know to be true aside. I'm exhausted by it all.

"Her real killer is in jail," he barks. "When will you let this fucking go?"

"I won't." I raise my chin in the same way he has, defying him. "I truly believe Rhys O'Connell has something to do with it. I heard his name that night, and I heard it again—"

"Stop this! I'm through putting up with this bullshit!" He points his finger at my chest, his face beet red, and thick veins bulge from his neck. Even a large one appears in the middle of his forehead. "Drop it, Holt. I'm warning you, or else it'll fucking kill you."

The blood drains from my face and I squeeze my hand into a tight fist inside my pocket. I watch him leave us and walk back toward his car. He slips into the back seat, and within seconds, he's gone.

"We come here once a month to honor Mom," Julianna says beside me. "Is it really that hard for you to not press him about this when we're here?"

"Yes." I sigh, pinching the bridge of my nose.

"I just want you to let this go," she begs, her voice strained.

"I want to let this go, too. You know that right?"

There are tears in my sister's eyes. Her brown hair blows in the wind. It sticks to her cheeks, but she tucks the strands behind her ear. Tightening her coat, she wraps her arms around herself, then turns to face our mother's grave. She drags her toe gently across the ground, staring at it blankly.

"How's Selene?" she asks.

I'm shocked by her question.

She lifts her head up. "I talked with her about you last week. She told me about your date."

My stomach bubbles with nerves. I hate talking relationships with my sister because her trust in me has eroded over the years. I've shoved the sting of her distrust of me aside for so long. But with Selene, it's different. Everything about Selene is different. I haven't realized until this moment how much I long for my sister's approval. I usually couldn't give a shit about her opinion, but I know hers is the one that matters most.

If only Julianna knew how desperately I've wanted Selene over the years. How I've secretly pined over her in secret.

"Julianna..." I start, but she cuts me off.

Her once-frustrated gaze has now shifted to one of acceptance. Soft and kind eyes like our mother's stare up at me. "I gave her my approval if that's what you're worried about. Not that either of you need it. But she did tell me you're only dating her for the good publicity. I've seen the photos and videos of the two of you all over social media. It appears to be working, so great job."

I open my mouth to explain, but she stops me again.

"I know that isn't why you're doing this with her, though." Her bottom lip wobbles, and she inhales a deep breath.

It's been too long since I've talked to my sister since that day she was in my office. We argued then, and we've given each other space, but I still feel like there's this distance between us. We lost a piece of ourselves the night our mother died, and we've never gained it back. We haven't been the same, and I've been left longing for what we lost.

"I can tell there's more to what you feel for her. Did you propose the fake dating idea because Treena suggested it? Or did you do it because you know Selene doesn't date, and you thought it would bring you closer? It was a way for you to show her the man you can be without scaring her off, wasn't it?"

Her line of questioning practically knocks me off my feet.

My sister and I may not be as close as we used to be, but she still has the ability to see me in ways others don't.

"Tell me I'm wrong, Holt."

"I can't."

She nods, licking her lips. She avoids looking at me, coming to terms with my answer. "I knew it. But I'm telling you, Holt, Selene doesn't love easily. She's been through shit you can't understand. She may not ever be able to give you what you want. Just keep that in mind."

I think back to the other night when we were lying in my bed and she told me she couldn't sleep. She'd had a nightmare. I was never able to ask her why and haven't dared to ask her since. Selene is a walking vault full of secrets. But I know she only does it to guard that massive heart of hers. I'm hoping the more time we spend together, the more she'll open up to me. I often wonder what happened in her past to make her believe love isn't and can't be real.

There are times I see her softening, giving into the feelings she gets when we're together. She wouldn't have slept with me if she didn't feel at least the slightest fraction of *something* for me. But then in other moments, she's pulling away from me, slipping back into the role of being my fake girlfriend.

I can't find it in myself to give up on her or this thing we've built yet. I need more. More touches. More kisses. More of showing her the man I truly am, not the one the papers or media believes me to be.

"I can't help it. I'm falling for her, Jules." It's a relief being this honest, saying the words out loud. "Fuck, I take that back. I already have fallen for her. A long time ago."

"I believe you. It's hard for me to trust you but, somehow, I believe what you're saying." She tips her head to the side, narrowing her eyes. "Just... just be gentle with her."

"I'm sorry, I'm confused." I blink, thinking back to the night of the auction. "You told me to stay away from her, and I didn't listen, but instead of ripping me apart as usual, you're suddenly okay with it?"

Julianna turns her back on me, not answering my question. She stares at the city in the distance. We stand in silence.

I'm staring at my mother's headstone, thinking about Selene and what she told me last night. She doesn't believe in love. Not in the real world, anyway. But what do I do when I know I'm in love with her? How can I tell her without it making her want to run away?

I'm lost in my thoughts when Julianna finally turns back around.

Her eyes are wide. Tears well, lining her dark lashes. They spill over as her chin wobbles, and she worries her lip. There's heartbreak written all over her face.

What the fuck is going on?

"I need to tell you something, and I need you to listen to every word." She squeezes her eyes shut and shakes her head. "And don't do that thing you do where you cut me off and all that bullshit like you did last time."

I jerk back. "Last time?"

She sighs and cracks her eyes open. Her tears have spilled over, and now there's mascara streaming down her cheeks. "I just need you to hear me out."

"Okay." I feel like throwing up with how torn apart she looks. I can tell this is big.

She tightens her arms around her chest and huffs before pinning her eyes to mine. "I wrote the article."

"What article?" I pinch my brow.

She sighs, stamping a frustrated heel into the ground. "The article, Holt. The anonymous one in your magazine about Rome."

All the blood drains from my body. I feel lightheaded.

"What?" I breathe out, my lungs burning.

"I'm so sorry," she says weakly, stepping closer. "I didn't mean for this to happen."

"What the fuck, Jules?" I shout, anger quickly replacing my shock. "What do you mean, you didn't mean for this to happen?"

"I don't know," she sobs. "I was angry with Rome for what he did, and I thought it would be an easy way to get back at him. There's no way he could tell it was me."

"What did you think would happen?" I can't contain my anger. It bubbles over like a fucking volcano erupting. My skin is white hot and searing.

"I didn't mean for you to get hurt. I thought he'd be annoyed as usual and just move on. I didn't think he'd take this out on *you*."

My jaw drops, and it takes several seconds for me to draw in another breath as I come to terms with my sister's confession.

"This is fucking Rome Montgomery we're talking about. The same Rome Montogomery who made our lives miserable growing up. The same one who picked on you relentlessly as kids. The one who embarrassed you *any* chance he got!"

"Exactly." she fires back, her eyes full of hatred and pain. "But I'm not the one who has spent the past year trying to play at being his best friend."

"*Fuck!*" I scream, fisting my hair. I spin in a circle, forcing myself to catch my breath. "Do you understand what this has done? What you've done to me and the magazine?"

"I'm not the one suing you." She shakes her head "Rome is."

"Yeah, but he's suing *me* because of *you!*" I scold. "He wouldn't have any reason otherwise." I take a moment to catch my breath. My brain is fucking exploding. The entire empire I've built is crumbling because of my own sister. "Why are you just now telling me this? It's been weeks, and this has threatened to destroy *everything*, Julianna."

"I tried to tell you. That day in your office, after the auction, but I couldn't. You were angry with me for what I said about Selene, then you dismissed me. After that day, I tried to fix it on my own. I've called Rome, I've left messages at his office, but he won't return my calls. I don't think he knows it was me who wrote the article, but he must be ignoring me because of this lawsuit against you."

"I can't fucking believe this." I grind my teeth so fucking hard, I think they might crack. "How could you do this to me?"

"You don't understand," she cries, wrapping her arm around her stomach. Her face is slack, and her skin pale. "I didn't do this to hurt you. I promise, I didn't. I did it to hurt him. I wanted to hurt *him*." She bends over as if it's the only thing she can do to keep it together.

But then she collapses to the cold, hard ground, her arms wrapped around herself and her shoulders wracking with her sobs.

I flick my gaze to my mother's headstone, and my heart breaks. Breaks for my mother. Breaks for Julianna. Breaks for everything we've lost.

When I look back to my sister, I'm almost certain it breaks completely.

I close the distance between us and drop to my knees in front of her.

"Hey," I softly say, wrapping my hands around her face, pulling her up to look at me. "Hey, Jules."

"Holt," she whimpers, her eyes softening, full of sadness and regret. "I'm truly sorry. I didn't do this to hurt you. Rome has the ability to break me, and I couldn't let him do that. I couldn't let him win."

I have no fucking clue what she's talking about. I've

watched the two of them over the past year, in the times we've run into each other. I've seen the way they look at each other.

There's more there than meets the eye.

I cradle her face in my hands, wiping her tears away. She's my little sister and I will do anything to protect her. Seeing her this broken and distraught only confirms that our relationship isn't completely lost. We've just wandered a little too far from one another for now.

I couldn't protect my mother the day she died, but I will spend the rest of my life protecting those I love the best I can.

"I know, Jules," I whisper. "Please stop crying."

"But I hurt you. I hurt you and the magazine." She hiccups. "I promise, I'll make this right and then I'll cut Rome off completely. If he tries anything else, I'll ignore him. We need to move on from who we were—who we are."

I'm no longer angry, only heartbroken over my sister's pain.

I pull her toward me in the grass and hold her. I let her cry. I allow her to release it all, whatever it is that she has bottled up inside her.

Her cries grow quiet, and soon all I hear is her breathing.

"I'll tell him." She slowly lifts her head from my chest and wipes her drying tears from her cheeks. She almost looks the same as she usually does, strong as titanium, and beautiful like our mother. But the light she usually carries with her has dimmed.

"What do you mean, you'll tell him?"

"I'll find him." She sniffs. "I'll barge into his office and demand he hear me out. I'll tell him it was me who wrote that article."

I shake my head. "Jules, you can't do that."

"Yes, I can. If I tell him, then maybe he'll drop the lawsuit. Before, I was only wanting to convince him to drop it, but maybe if I actually confess and tell him it was me, it'll get him to listen."

"If you tell him, he'll smear your name and the Capuleti name. The headlines will be worse than they already are. You know he won't hesitate in dragging us through the dirt. He'll ruin our family, Julianna."

"I have to confess. This is my doing, and it's on me to fix it. Don't you understand?"

"I do understand." I breathe in and stare into my sister's eyes. "But don't you understand that I am your brother and I will always have your back? I won't let you replace my name with yours in the headlines."

"But what about the lawsuit?" she asks, her perfectly-manicured eyebrows pulling together. "What about Rome?"

"The lawsuit will play out." I crack a tiny smile. "Let me handle Rome Montgomery."

Julianna sighs, her shoulders dropping. We're still sitting in the grass. Our clothes covered in wet dirt. But we don't care.

We turn to look at our mother's headstone together, and from the corner of my eye, I see a single tear slip down Julianna's cheek.

"I know I haven't always trusted you, Holt." Her teary eyes find mine again. "I don't agree with your pursuit to finding Mom's killer. It's dangerous, and I often wonder if it's worth the risk. But I do believe you love Selene. For what it's worth, I think Mom would have liked her. In fact, I know she would have loved her."

That one statement from Julianna heals parts of me I didn't realize were as fractured as they are.

I've proven my love for my sister. Now, I just need to prove to Selene that love does exist, and it's mine she already has right in front of her.

TWENTY-TWO

SELENE

I told myself I was going to stay at my apartment tonight. Sleep in my own bed, cook my own dinner, and curl up on my couch to binge watch a new series on Netflix. Same as always.

It wasn't easy, but I did it. I had to. Holt is all I can think about.

I've reached the point of no return. I know I have, but I haven't been able to admit it out loud. I'm not a psychologist or anything, but I think I might be in the denial phase. Denial driven by fear.

Is that a stage reserved only for grief, though? Can grief be a stage for fear of falling for your best friend's brother?

The thought of pursuing anything with Holt seriously past whatever it is that we're doing is terrifying. Like diving off a cliff blindfolded. I just can't do it.

At the same time, I can't seem to stay away from him. Over the past days or weeks, however long it's been, my body hasn't stopped burning for him. Every inch is now overcome by the memory of Holt's touch. My nipples still remember the flick of his fingers. My pussy still remembers the feeling of his tongue lapping against it. My neck is haunted by the pleasant torture of his teeth sinking into my flesh.

The desire to keep going down this path with Holt is only made worse by me staying at his place. I need distance for now.

Being back home, in my own space, brings me back down to earth.

While sitting on my loveseat, I tuck my legs under myself. My laptop sits in the same position on the end table that it's been for the past several months since I finished my novel. I stare at it as if it's mocking me. Taunting me.

I tap my finger on my knee, my mind filtering through every single chapter. The way my characters started, the way they come together, pining and yearning over each other before they get their happily ever after. I feel so disconnected from them, it's hard for me to think about diving into their world again since I've been dipping into my pot of my feelings for Holt.

I bypass the laptop and pick up my phone instead. I flip through social media before typing Holt's name into a search engine. Every local news channel has at least one story about him and his new relationship with the woman, who he supposedly met at the auction. The woman he, quote, unquote, won. My stomach sours thinking that's how the world sees me. The woman who was *won* by the unattainable billionaire Holt Capuleti. Like I'm some piece of his property that can be bought.

I scroll through endless pictures of us walking in and out of his building. The night he took me to the ballet. Us at the market. Even some of me on my way to my shift at Charleigh's flower shop.

By myself.

An icy chill makes its way down my spine.

I close out the search results and toss my phone onto the

couch just as there's a knock on my door. Sitting upright, my heart races. No one ever comes to my apartment. Ever. Not even my sister.

I smooth my hair and bounce off the couch before opening the front door.

Holt is standing on the other side, looking good. Too good in his black suit and black tie. His eyes wander along my body before they drop to my mouth. Suddenly, I'm conscious of my appearance. I really should have taken a shower after yoga instead of vegging out on the sofa.

"Hey." I exhale sharply.

He stands at the threshold, gripping the doorframe, unmoving. I've barely furrowed my brow before he's claiming my mouth. He cradles my head in his hands and kisses me like he hasn't kissed me in days, weeks, even months.

He groans into our kiss, and I somehow step back, gripping the back of his arm.

"Holt." I search his eyes. "What are you doing here?"

"I missed you today."

I laugh but soon stop. I haven't forgotten how confusing this all is for someone who doesn't fall in love. For a woman like me who doesn't have those deep, visceral, life changing feelings for someone else.

"Wait," I say when he kisses me again. "Wait, wait, Holt." I gently push him away.

He reluctantly breaks our connection but keeps his hands wrapped around my face. My skin quickly grows cold the moment he does as I ask and drops them at his sides.

"What's wrong?" he asks, his eyes scanning my apartment.

Fuck, I just realized this is the first time he's been here since the night he showed up when I was drunk. This may be the second time he's been here ever, but this time is different. I'm sober and aware of how different it is from his place.

He looks back at me.

His eyes burn for me as he works to catch his breath.

"Nothing's wrong. I'm fine," I start, taking a nervous glance around. "It's just... you're here."

"I've been here before." He chuckles. "Remember?"

When I turn back to him, he's admiring me before he gently brushes his fingers along my cheek as he tucks my hair behind my ear. I'm still sticky and slightly sweaty from my yoga class earlier, and suddenly very conscious of the way I look.

"Yeah." I nod, agreeing. "But last time you were here, I was drunk, so I didn't care as much."

"Are you saying you care now?"

My stomach does that thing where it somersaults at least a thousand times when we're together.

"No." I laugh, playfully shoving his shoulder. "But I don't think I'll get over the shock of seeing you here."

He catches my hand before I'm able to pull it away.

My smile drops, and breathing becomes difficult. Especially when he presses his lips to my knuckles.

After he plants a kiss to every single one, he says, "I thought I'd find you at my place when I got home. Can I be honest?"

I swallow thickly. "I get the feeling you're going to be honest with me regardless of my answer."

He smirks. "I was disappointed when you weren't."

I inhale a deep breath as he lowers my hand. He holds onto it, just barely, keeping the tips of our fingers tethered.

"I needed some time to think in my own space," I tell him.

"Can I be honest again?"

I pop a brow, not giving him a verbal answer.

"I know you don't do feelings..."

I drop my hand, the fear from earlier creeping back in. I take a hesitant step back, but Holt doesn't relent. He maintains our distance, matching me step for step.

"Don't say it," I warn with a whisper.

"But I've caught them for you, Selene."

My breath catches in my throat, and I feel like running in the opposite direction. This doesn't feel the same as when Adam was standing in this same place covered in Dorito dust, telling me he wanted to marry me.

This time it's different. My feet feel like two lead weights. All the blood in my body has drained to them, and I feel light-headed. Panic sets in the longer I stare at Holt's gorgeous face. The way his brown hair rests just above his brow. The way his eyes won't stop staring at me. The way those eyes make me feel like my entire body is bursting into flames.

"No, you haven't." I shake my head. "You're only saying this because our fake relationship is doing so well in the media." I gesture toward my phone. "I've seen all the headlines."

"This was never for the headlines."

"I don't believe you."

"Why?" He continues stepping closer to me. "Why do you not believe me?"

We've somehow made it farther down the small hallway toward my bedroom. The floor creaks under my every step, reminding me of how my apartment is literally falling apart, and so am I.

"Because you're you." I gesture toward him with my hand. "And I'm me."

"That's exactly why you should believe me." He grabs my hand again and pulls me to his chest.

I relax against him, gasping with the electricity between us. It's as if we've completed a circuit, his touch coursing through my veins. "Holt, I've seen you with other women. You talk about me not wanting to be in a relationship, but you've never seemed to want to be in one either."

"Right." His nostrils flare as he takes a heated breath. I can tell I've hit a nerve, but it needed to be said. "Sounds exactly like what Julianna says to me."

"I'm sorry," I start. "I didn't mean to hurt you by saying that, but it's the truth. You're Holt Capuleti."

"I know." His eyes find mine again. This time, it's like I can see straight into his soul. "I may have jumped from woman to woman in the past, but what else was I going to do? You were my sister's best friend, and no one ever had faith in me to ever be loyal to anyone, especially not you. But the truth is, I never fell for any of them because I had already fallen for you a long time ago."

"Why are you telling me this right now?" I press my hand to my stomach, forcing myself to remain calm.

"Because I couldn't keep fake dating you with you thinking it has always been pretend. You honestly think that everything between us has been for show? If that were the case, I wouldn't be here, wanting you, kissing you. We wouldn't have done what we did in the elevator on our first date, or anywhere else after for that matter." He gestures around the room. "There's no one here. No cameras. Just us."

Tears swell behind my eyes. I refuse to let them spill, instead keeping them at bay by chewing on the inside of me cheek until it hurts. "I can't."

"It's okay, Wallflower." He presses his hand to my face, his thumb rests just below my eye, and his fingers thread through my disheveled hair. "You don't have to say anything right now. I don't know what happened to you to believe love only exists in romance novels, but I'm patient. I trust you'll tell me at some point. I just couldn't go another day without you knowing how I feel about you. Especially after today. Even if me telling you this only makes you want to run in the opposite direction or end whatever this is what we're doing. I'll take whatever you're willing to give me at this point."

I allow his words to sink in. I feel what I want to say inside of me, resting at the tip of my tongue, but I won't let those words out. They fill my mouth, both bitter and sweet.

"I don't want to end whatever this is, but I can't make you any promises, Holt." I blink the tears away and slip my hand under the coat of his suit, pressing my palm to his firm chest.

"I understand. But, when you're ready, I'll make sure you know exactly how deeply I've fallen for you, Wallflower. It's a promise."

I give him a small smile and rise to stand on my toes. His words sink in, hitting me in all the right places. Again, it's terrifying, but I'm grateful for Holt's honesty. It's difficult for someone like me to admit even the slightest bit of love I feel for him is real. I may not be able to tell Holt I'm falling for him, but I take the moment to tell him I don't want this to end in my own way when I press my lips to his quickly before pulling back to take in his face. I stare into his blue eyes and realize that, aside from his confession, there's something else weighing on his mind.

"What happened today?" I ask, holding onto his hand. "How did it go visiting your mother's grave?"

"Honestly?" He sighs, pulling back for the first time since he's been here. "It was a shitshow."

He spins around and shoves his hair back, but it slowly falls back over his eyes when he turns back to face me with his hands on his hips.

"What happened? Did your dad say something to you?" I think back to what he said about the contention between them over his mother's true killer. I hate knowing there's a wedge between them over this. I wish Holt's father would hear him out.

"My dad." Holt wafts his hand through the air. "Julianna."

"Julianna?" I ask, stepping forward. "Are you two okay?"

"We talked about the lawsuit from Rome."

I stop. "Oh."

My stomach twists with anxiety at the look on his face. The heartache there that can only have come from one thing...

"She told me something," he says solemnly.

"What... what did she say?"

"That she was the one who wrote the article about Rome." He holds my gaze. "She was the one who submitted it to my magazine."

It feels like the air has been sucked out of me. I freeze, unable to think of a single thing to say or do. Keeping Julianna's secret is one thing, but knowing Holt knows the truth now is another.

Relief washes over me because I'm thankful Julianna finally told her brother the truth. I didn't realize until now the weight of carrying a secret this big inside me.

Guilt slams into me like a gut punch.

Lost for what to stay, I simply stand in the hallway staring at Holt, when his expression shifts. His jaw hardens and his hand flexes at his side. "You already knew, didn't you?"

His question breaks something inside of me. Something that must show on my face as he takes me in, his brows creasing together with hurt. Hurt I've caused by keeping a secret that wasn't mine to share from him.

"Don't bother lying, Wallflower." He inches closer. "You already did that thing with your lip."

I suck in a sharp breath. Fuck. "Holt..."

"Tell me the truth. Did you know Julianna wrote the article in my magazine?"

I square my shoulders and grind my jaws, telling myself not

to fall apart. That's what you do when you're in love. You let the other person affect you.

I won't let that happen with Holt.

"Yes," I answer. "I knew." I can't explain it, I feel guilty for keeping Julianna's secret from him, but fear quickly creeps up to overshadow it.

Fear Holt is going to leave.

I try to prepare myself for it. Is that what my mother did before she was taken? The feeling inside me is wretched. I want to rid myself of it before I have the chance to get my heart broken. But it's useless. I'm already there.

My eyes water, and I try my best to hold back the tears.

Holt's cheeks redden and his fingers stretch by his side. "You kept this from me?" he asks, his voice cracking.

"Julianna is my *best* friend. She asked me not to tell you, so I didn't." The tears continue to build in my eyes, and I curse them, hating how they're revealing the way I feel inside. I've spent years hiding my true feelings from everyone, but here I am in front of Holt, showing him that while I was happy to keep my best friend's secret, I hate that it hurt him in the process.

He doesn't respond. His only answer is heart-shattering silence as his eyes roam over my face. I feel like I'm about to combust. Everything in me is wound tightly. I hurt, the pressure building in every single nerve.

If I lose Holt because I kept this secret, all my convictions will have proven true. It doesn't matter how hard you fall for someone, it never lasts.

The only one you can ever count on not betraying you is yourself.

"I kept my word as your sister's best friend. If that costs us this"—I wave my hands between us—"then, so be it. I'm sorry if it hurt you, but my loyalty to my best friend matters. She wanted to be the one who told you, and I respected her for that.

I agreed. So, if you want to leave over that, then you're free. You can go. You're off the hook."

Holt's face flashes. His shock turns to fury. His eyebrows slant under the ends of his dark hair before his flexed hand wraps around the base of my neck. He tilts my head up to look at him and spins me until my back lands against the wall in the hallway. I'm working to catch my breath as he presses his knee between my legs and his hips against me. I'm still wearing a sports bra and yoga pants. They're tight, clinging to my skin, and I feel everything. Every single point of connection between us.

But despite the adrenaline Holt gives me, a tear breaks free. My bottom lip quivers as it spills down my cheek and onto his arm.

"You want me to leave?" he asks darkly.

"I kept a major secret from you."

"I'm not leaving, Selene."

"I wouldn't blame you if you did."

I don't want him to leave. I hope he doesn't leave. But, dammit, hope is for fools.

He scoffs and shakes his head. "Why would I leave?"

"I'm just your fake girlfriend. And you've had a million other real girlfriends you've broken things off with for far less."

Clicking his tongue, he leans forward and licks my cheek. He drags his tongue across my skin, cleaning up my tear. I shiver, pleasure shooting straight between my thighs because his every move is intimate. Gentle. Butterflies flutter in my lower stomach. I've never felt anything like this. It's a rush.

Breathing heavily, I attempt to hold back my sob. I'm falling apart at the thought of him ending this—of him walking away.

"It appears you have short term memory, Wallflower," he whispers, staring directly into my eyes. "You think this newfound revelation erases the entire conversation we had before this?"

The tears break. I can't hold them back anymore. I'm almost certain Holt can feel my heart beating against his chest. My hands are pressed flat to the wall, and I try to steady myself as a hiccup rises up my throat.

"I just told you I've known it was your sister and kept it from you." Another tear falls. "I've betrayed you."

He hisses, inhaling a sharp breath. "I don't know how many times I'll need to tell you, but I won't stop, not even when hearing something like this." He wraps his hands around my face. "I know you feel something for me or else you wouldn't be crying right now. You're crying because you hurt me. While you were being loyal to your best friend, it was killing you to keep this from me, wasn't it? But I'll tell you something right now, Selene, you telling me to leave will only hurt me more. I would be broken, because there's no turning back after what we've done. I could never go back to being just your best friend's brother, existing around each other's orbit without actually being in yours. Understood?"

All that comes out of me is a sob. I'm broken but healed at the same time. The thought of watching Holt walk out the door and never coming back tears me from the inside out. A true nightmare. He's right. We can't go back.

But I want to take away his pain too. I want to kiss it away, offer up my body as a remedy. But what would that mean if I did?

"I know you're falling for me, Wallflower." His thumbs soak up the tears streaming down my face. "So, why don't you let me wipe up these tears and show you exactly how I feel about you keeping this secret from me?"

I grip onto his lapels and tip my chin to bring my mouth close to his.

Fuck it. If this is how it feels to be in love, or close to it, the pain will be worth it. Considering the alternative, I don't think I have a choice. At this point, I agree with Holt. Losing him would hurt worse than going back to the way we were, and that sounds like a miserable fucking way to live.

"Heal me, Holt," I breathe, the weight I've carried for years finally lifting. "Put me out of my misery."

TWENTY-THREE

SELENE

I fully expect Holt to tear my leggings and bra from my body, but he moves excruciatingly slow. He laps his tongue again, licking another tear from my cheek, making me shiver as I tilt my head against the wall. I'm delirious with pleasure, aching to have him inside me. I want him to take this pain away, to rid me of the fear that's crippled me for ten years.

Holt falls to his knees in front of me. His hands rest at my hips as I cradle his face, pulling him to look up at me. His blue eyes have softened, and it feels like I've crashed down to earth from the heavens.

"I'm so sorry, Holt," I whisper with labored breathing. "I do hate that I hurt you."

"Don't, Wallflower." He leans forward and presses his lips to my lower stomach as he wraps his fingers around the waist of my leggings and starts to slowly peel them away. "Don't apologize for holding your word to your best friend. You keeping this secret only shows me how deep your loyalty runs. You have a big heart, Selene. You shouldn't be afraid of it."

"Holt," I breathe, tears still forming in my eyes. "I need to tell you—"

"No," he cuts me off, pulling my leggings down and over the curve of my ass, then down my legs. "Now's not the time for words. Let me worship you in other ways. We can talk later."

My back arches from the wall the second his tongue slips between my folds, finding my clit. His arms stretch up to palm my breasts while my hands fly to the back of his head, gripping his hair. I tug and pull, reveling in the assault of his mouth on me.

My toes curl against the carpet, and I can't help rolling my hips with Holt's mouth. He works me roughly, then gently, never once using his hands to move inside me. There's only his mouth, tasting and teasing me. He bites on my swollen, aching clit, then soothes it with his soft, unrelenting tongue.

"Fuck, Holt," I moan, squeezing my eyes shut.

His hands work over my breasts, his thumbs flicking over my peaked nipples poking through my bra. His tongue works furiously against me, allowing me to reach my orgasm. I crest over the edge, crying out his name as tiny bursts of electricity explode all over my body.

Once I've slowed my breathing enough to catch it, Holt is pulling himself to a stand. "I need your mouth, Wallflower."

With more fevered measure, he grips the back of my head and crashes his mouth to mine. His tongue moves furiously, as if he's using every ounce of what he can give to let me know exactly how he feels. My tears may have begun to dry, but the feelings inside me multiply. It's a terrifying, exhilarating sensation, and I realize this is the moment I'm truly in love with Holt Capuleti, and I have been for a long time.

"I need more than just your mouth," he rasps. "Fuck, Wallflower. You're a masterpiece. I need you." His lips moves across my jaw, down the length of my neck. He nips and kisses, dragging his teeth across my skin. We're both panting, skin hot, and desperate for relief.

"I need *you*, Holt." I pull his face up.

He blows out a sharp breath and then I'm scrambling to shove his suit jacket over his shoulders. I untuck his shirt and unbuckle his belt. Keeping our mouths locked, he shoves the rest of his pants down and steps out of them, his rock-hard cock springing free.

I lift my bra over my head and toss it with the rest of our clothes.

I've barely caught my breath when he's gripping the back of my knee and lifting my leg over his hip, opening me up. Then he's driving himself so hard and so deep, I'm left gasping. My mouth falls open, and my head drops back against the wall.

Gripping the back of my knee, he continues to thrust himself in and out of me, burying his face into my chest, wrapping his lips around my nipple. I thread my fingers through his hair, tugging on the ends as he pounds into me harder and faster.

He grunts and groans, sweat building on his skin. I moan, feeling myself reaching another orgasm. This one is more powerful than the one from just his tongue. It's full on, unyielding pleasure. The kind I can't ignore. Bigger than any other I've had.

"Right there, Holt." I moan, heat pooling in my lower stomach. "Oh, God, yes. Don't stop." I tighten my leg over Holt's waist, pinning him to me. I feel my walls contracting around his length as he slides in and out of me. Three more thrusts, and I'm coming again.

Only a few more, and he's freezing, his body twitching against me. His head falls to my shoulder as his hand grips onto my waist, keeping me in place.

I'm still panting and catching my breath when he lifts his head and kisses me.

Before it's even hit me, I find myself smiling against Holt's mouth. I lower my leg from around his waist.

"What is it?" He pulls away, his now sweat-slicked brow drawing together.

"It's nothing." I giggle. "I just thought you'd give me a few spankings, considering the secret I kept from you."

He gives me a devilish grin. "There's still time for that."

"Good," I practically sing. "I could use a shower first, though."

"I think we could *both* use a shower."

I laugh against his mouth and drape my arms over his shoulder. "But with how long it takes the shower to heat up, we may not have to wait until we're finished for me to get that spanking."

"I'm loving this new side of you, Wallflower," he muses, kissing me. "Keep it coming."

HOLT

I fall asleep with my fingers woven through Selene's wet hair while her head rests on my stomach. She's lying between my legs, and for the first thirty minutes of the movie she put on, it was difficult for me to concentrate on anything but the raging hard on I had, as if I hadn't just orgasmed multiple times in a row. First, in the hallway with Selene pressed against the wall. Second, when I'd taken Selene over to her bed and spanked her for keeping my sister's secret from me while we waited for the shower water to heat. Then again when I took my time with her, worshipping her body for the stunning masterpiece it is.

My head is pressed against her small throw pillow, and my neck aches, but it doesn't matter. I'm just happy to be here with Selene.

Thankfully, she still had the clothes I let her borrow the day after she'd gotten drunk for her girls' night. I changed into my sweatpants and T-shirt while Selene slipped into an oversized sleep shirt, wearing nothing underneath.

I crack my eyes open to a vision of blue and black, the flickering lights of the movie still playing flashes across Selene's tiny apartment. The sound is muted, the only noise coming from the rickety ceiling fan above us. Turning away from the screen, I look up at the ceiling and focus on the crack stretching across it while the blades of the ceiling fan spin lazily below it. My heart aches thinking back to the tears she shed earlier in the hallway. So much of Selene's life is kept in secret.

Her apartment. Her book. Her *pain.*

I don't know when or if she'll ever open up to me fully, but I find peace in knowing I've done my part. I laid it all out there for her. She knows how I feel about her now, and, honestly, it felt good to get it out. It felt good to tell her how obsessed I've been with her for years. She still may not know how deep that obsession runs to the point where I've appointed a security guard to monitor her and keep her safe, but I'm hoping if she ever finds out about that, she will understand.

After witnessing my mother's death, watching in horror as a bullet took her from me, I'll never stop protecting the ones I love.

Instead of the pain and fear I saw in Selene's mossy-green eyes earlier, I try to think of the ones she laid on me on her bed or in the shower. Her flower-scented shampoo and body wash is filtering in the air. I breathe it in and close my eyes.

"Holt?" Selene's voice is barely a whisper.

I snap my head up but keep my fingers threaded inside her damp hair. "I'm awake."

There's ten seconds of silence before she says, "I watched my father kill my mother before turning the gun on himself."

My breath catches in my throat, and I freeze. The blood drains to my toes. It's a prickling stinging sensation—one I don't feel until the dizziness hits.

I clear my throat, working her words over in my brain.

She inhales a deep breath then turns onto her stomach between my legs. The blue and white lights from the TV screen flash across her face, capturing the light in her eyes. Those sad, green eyes I love. She folds her hands over my stomach and rests her chin on them, looking up at me.

"I, um. I…" I run my finger across her temple. "Fuck, I hate when people would say this to me about my mother, but I don't know what else to say other than I'm so sorry, Wallflower."

Fresh tears line her gorgeous eyes and, fuck, seeing them again makes me unravel. I hate seeing her in pain.

A single tear slips from the corner when she blinks. "I came home from school and heard them arguing upstairs. I shouldn't have gone up there, but they never argued." She looks past me, her eyes distancing with the memory. "At least not that London and I were aware of."

She pauses, and I allow the silence to settle. I don't need to speak, only listen. I want nothing more than to soothe Selene's wounds, but I know it isn't possible. She's known for staying in the shadows, out of the spotlight. Now, she's opening the door and inviting me into a space no one else has ever been invited. I allow her to continue, all the while, keeping my fingers to the side of her face, hoping she'll use my touch as an anchor to pull her through.

"My parents were childhood friends turned lovers. They grew up next door to each other. My grandfather—my mom's father—was an alcoholic, and so were both my grandparents on my father's side. My mom's mother was the only anchor in my parents' lives, and she always attributed that to keeping them together when the others lost themselves in their addictions. Both my father's parents died in a drunk driving accident, and my mom's father died of alcohol poisoning." She inhales a shaky, unstable breath before finally shifting her tear-soaked gaze to me. "My parents were each other's first for everything. My father worshipped the ground my mother walked on. My childhood was full of love and warmth. I never second guessed if they would ever be there for my school play or dance recital. They struggled to have another child after me and were so excited when they were able to adopt London. She was the same age as me, and as luck would have it, we had similar personalities. Our family felt complete."

Her voice finally breaks, and her eyes widen as a small hiccup breaks free. She's clearly replaying the memory over in her mind, shattering when she squeezes her eyes shut.

I inhale a deep breath, fighting back my own tears. I need to stay strong for Selene.

She buries her face against my stomach, resting her forehead on her folded hands. I press my hand on the back of her head, smoothing her hair. Her shoulders wrack with sobs, then she looks up.

"I can't..." Her words break as she tries to continue. "I can't even tell you what they were arguing about that day. I heard their shouts after I'd come home, so I raced up the stairs and barged into their bedroom. He had the gun pointed straight at her, directly between her eyes. He didn't flinch, not even when I entered the room, but my mother did. Her attention shifted to me, and I don't think I'll ever forget the look in her eyes. They were bloodshot and broken, and mascara stained her cheeks in black streaks. She was shaking as she looked back at him. Her last words before he pulled the trigger were, *'You were the love of my life, Sean. You still are. Even now, I promise.'* Then she was gone." She weeps, her voice lifting with every word. "Her limp body barely made it to the floor before he'd turned the gun on himself. But not before he said..."

She squeezes her eyes shut again, and I realize a tear has slipped from the corner of my eye, too. I feel its warmth slide down the side of my face as I press my fingers gently against Selene's cheekbone.

"He said"—she swallows, her mouth turning down in a frown—"and you, mine."

"Selene." Her name falls from my mouth like a plea, and my heart shatters when she opens her eyes and stares into mine.

She's shaking as her sobs grow, and her body rattles with every cry of pain. I lift her gently and scoot backward until my spine is resting against the throw pillow. Then I'm pulling her to me. She curls up between my legs, tucking hers to her chest. She wraps both her arms around them as I wrap my arms around her.

"Oh, Wallflower." I sigh, cradling her gorgeous face in my hands.

I want to kiss away her pain, but I know I can't. Nothing could take this from her. It's a pain I know will stay with her the rest of her life. Same as mine.

"They were supposed to love each other, Holt." Her swollen, red-lined eyes frantically dance across my face. "Their type of love was written in the moon and stars. That's what my mother said to me my whole life. Then he murdered her before killing himself. And the worst part is, I'll never truly know why."

My brows pull tightly together. I swear, it feels like I'm being ripped apart seeing her in this much pain. I think about witnessing my own mother's death. Selene has been through the same, but it wasn't a stranger that took her. It was her own father. The one person who was supposed to love and protect them.

"Love..." She sobs, her eyes hardening. "Love isn't real. There's no such thing as true, unconditional love. It's all a lie. He took her and then he took himself from us. He didn't even care what he destroyed, the ruin he left behind. I was right there, and he didn't even care."

"Selene, it wasn't right what he did. I wish you hadn't had to go through that." I move my hand over her cheek, willing her pain to evaporate as if it ever could.

"It's why I've never truly opened myself up to others. After their deaths, I only stayed close to my sister and my grandmother. I kept everyone else at a distance—one that was safe and reliable. My grandmother raised us for a year before London and I went off to college. Witnessing what happened that day changed me. It's why I swore off dating. Adam was the first relationship I'd had in years, and when he pulled the shit he did, I realized why I hadn't. I didn't care enough about him, but then he proposed in an odd sort of way, and I just couldn't. I guess you could also say that's why I wrote a romance novel. I wrote a world in which love isn't capable of betrayal. I tried to rewrite the story, change the ending, but the ending can't change."

It all makes sense now, the way she's resisted me, the hesitation and the need to keep me at a distance. But I see her love for me in her eyes. She hasn't expressed it yet, but I know it's there.

"Selene." I swipe my thumb across one of her tears again. "You may never know why your father did what he did, but love *can* exist. It does."

Her eyes turn down as she leans into my touch. "I know it does. Because I'm in love with you, Holt Capuleti, and that scares the ever-living shit out of me. I can't stop it. I've tried."

"Fuck, Selene." I scoot impossibly closer to her and grab her face with both hands again. I pull her close, vibrating with excitement. "I'm in love with you, too. I've loved you for years. I've loved you in the shadows, I've loved you in the spotlight, I've..." I struggle to breathe. "I've loved you for so long."

She sobs, and I swear her mouth lifts into a relieved smile ,but then it's gone as she inhales a shaky breath. "The thing is, he said he loved her, too."

"Listen to me, Wallflower." I brush my nose against hers. "I won't lie and say loving someone comes without risk. You will never know whether someone will eventually change their mind. But what you feel inside, that fire and spark you can't deny, that's what makes love worth the risk. You give me that fire. I will do whatever I can to tell you every day that you are loved, because if you're left broken, there will be nothing left for me. You deserve to love and be loved."

She grabs onto my arms, wringing her fingers over the corded muscles of my forearms, using me as an anchor. Her tear-filled, green eyes stare into mine. "Promise you won't break me, Holt Capuleti."

I blow out a breath and pull her close before kissing her deeply, only pulling away only long enough to say, "You're it for me, Wallflower. You have been ever since we met." Her mouth brushes against mine when I whisper, "I promise."

TWENTY-FIVE

SELENE

I watched my best friend Charleigh fall in love. Then London, and I saw how that love pulled her back to West.

Despite seeing those closest to me find happiness, though, I never believed it for myself.

Until Holt. I guess that makes me, like the rest of them, a fool, too.

I read over my text chain in the girls' chat, scrolling through their messages of encouragement for the day.

Charleigh: Good Luck! You've got this.

London: I have no doubt. You're going to kill it!

Julianna: I can't wait to watch this later. We love you both so much!

I grin, re-reading Julianna's message again. Her support means the world. Over the past six weeks, Holt and I have existed happily in our bubble together. We may have kept our confessions of love to ourselves, but that doesn't mean we haven't taken the time to hang out with our friends together. I just haven't brought up the fact that we're no longer playing pretend. Our relationship is raw, real, and full of love.

"I can't believe I agreed to do this," I mutter, smoothing my hands over my blue and cream plaid mini skirt while sitting on the large, leather sofa in Holt's office. I've paired the skirt with a simple, navy-blue knit turtleneck and chunky ankle boots. While I never took much stock in picking out my own outfits before now, Holt has pushed me to embrace my own style. At first, after we confessed our love for one another, I handed his black charge card back to him. I didn't want to keep using his money for things that weren't important. But I don't think I'll ever forget the offensive expression he wore when the cold metal hit the palm of his hand. He'd barely held onto it for longer than a minute before stuffing it back into my purse, telling me to use it whenever I felt I needed to.

Since then, I've only used it once: to buy this outfit.

I felt guilty for using his money. I've fought against the tiny nagging sensation in the back of my head, reminding me of what Adam accused me of when we broke up. But this is different than when Julianna would lend me her clothes. These are mine. I picked them out, and I own them, knowing I don't need to give them back.

The best part is remembering how, after they're washed, they'll settle back into their home in the space Holt has carved out for me in his closet.

I relax into the sofa, keeping my hands resting on my wool skirt, and take a deep breath.

"Are you regretting saying yes?" Holt asks.

My stomach turns as I glance over the growing crowd in Holt's office. Suddenly, I feel nauseous. Sick, even. Perhaps it was the sushi I had for lunch.

"No." I swallow around the lump in my throat, swearing I can still taste a slight hint of the dragon roll I devoured. "At least, I don't think I do. But I may be second guessing my reasoning now. I'm not entirely sure why I agreed to this. You know I hate anything that makes me the center of attention." I give him a nervous chuckle.

"You agreed to this because you love me, Wallflower." Holt leans in, half turning beside me, sliding his hand down my thigh before he grips my knee. He leans into me, burying his nose in the crook of my neck. "And I love you."

My skin prickles from his mouth at the shell of my ear.

The lights, the cameras, Treena… everything fades into the background. The only thing I see is Holt sitting in front of me in a crisp, black suit. I grip the knot of his tie and pull his mouth to mine, kissing him deeply before I inch back to stare into his eyes.

"I love you, too." I crack a smile. I can't help it. I'll never tire of hearing this, hearing him say he loves me, and me saying it back.

A glint flickers in his eyes. "After this interview is over, I fully intend on bending you over my desk, shoving that tantalizing little skirt over that delicious ass of yours, and fucking you senseless."

I smirk, heat spreading across my entire body. "Why do you think I opted out of wearing tights with this outfit?"

"That's my girl." He growls, his eyes darkening. "I fucking love you, Wallflower."

I can't believe Holt and I are saying I love you. I'm still terrified as fuck. I'm terrified I'll wake up from this dream, or that one day Holt will just disappear. It's been weeks since we talked in my apartment, since I shared the history of my parents' deaths and how it shaped my view on life and love. Despite my convictions, Holt has challenged them every step of the way, making it impossible not to surrender to them.

I mean, how could I when he touches me like this or looks at me like that?

He pulls away just enough to stare into my eyes.

"You should have done this weeks ago, honestly," Treena chimes in from across the room. She uncrosses her legs and rests her elbows on her knees. Her eyes shift to the cameraman standing several feet from us, who's adjusting his tripod before setting his camera on top of it.

"It's fine, Treena," Holt mumbles, clearly annoyed with her comment. "I wasn't going to agree to a public interview unless it was okay with Selene first. The important thing is we're doing it now."

"Right." She presses her lips together and sighs through her nose, unable to look at us for long. "I just wish you'd agreed to have Vanessa here as well. Considering your court date with Rome Montgomery is approaching, you need to watch what you say. He could use this against you."

"We aren't going to say anything that will jeopardize my case. We aren't here to talk about the case, anyway." Holt clears his throat. "Besides, I still think there's a possibility we'll be able to settle this through mediation or in a settlement."

Treena's jaw drops. "A settlement?" She scoffs. "It's admirable you think this can go away quietly."

"Shouldn't we hope for that?" I offer her a weak smile. "Isn't that what we should all want?"

Treena's cheeks blush as she gives me a weak, unconvincing smile in return.

Holt squeezes my knee, letting me know he believes we can. At least his hope is as strong as mine. He doesn't want this to go all the way to court. Especially not now, knowing it was Julianna who wrote the anonymous article about him in Scribe. We want this to go away with as little damage as possible, but the uncertainty of it all still leaves me on edge.

"The media has been clamoring for more of mine and Selene's relationship," Holt explains to Treena. "This interview will give them a little more of what they're already seeing, and we're hoping it will deliver more of an impact than just those pictures and videos of us from afar. An interview is personal."

"I agree." Treena sighs, but I'm not totally convinced with her understanding. She still looks apprehensive, though I guess you could say I feel the same. I still hate being in the public eye, but I try telling myself this is different. Holt is with me, and he loves me. Because of that, I have the strength to sit through an interview.

It helps that we're agreeing to this interview because it's through Holt's magazine. The transcript will be published both in print and online, accompanied by a video.

Cory, one of Holt's editors, enters the room and sits in the chair on the opposite end of the sofa Holt and I are sitting on. I've run into him a few times over the past few weeks when visiting Holt's office. Cory is young and kind. I can tell Holt has a special relationship with him, compared to the others on his editing team.

Cory shoves his hair off his forehead and adjusts in his chair. The bright spotlight coming from the light behind the camera is nearly blinding. "Man." He blows out a heavy breath while adjusting his necktie. "I don't think I've done a formal interview like this since college."

"You're going to do great, man." Holt drapes his arm over my shoulders, pulling me closer. "If you hadn't agreed to stay on as part of my staff, I don't know what I would have done. You're the only one I trust."

I offer Cory a closed-mouth smile of reassurance.

Holt told me about Cory's affair with another staff member. He'd given him an ultimatum, a choice, of whether to keep his affair going or stay on at Scribe. He must have chosen to give up on his fling with Macy, but by the tan line on his bare ring finger, something tells me it didn't come without a price.

"I appreciate that, Mr. Capuleti." He nods and looks down at his phone, which is opened up to a list of interview questions. "Especially considering what happened before."

Holt's gaze shifts nervously to Treena before he's lowering his chin and voice. "You haven't received any more threats, have you?" Holt whispers.

"No," Cory whispers back, trading glances between the two of us. "Thankfully, they've stopped ever since that day they left the photos."

"Good." Holt nods once, his jaw clenched. I can tell he's nervous, and I get the sense he isn't totally convinced they've let him and everyone else off the hook.

"We're all set whenever you three are ready." The cameraman gives a thumbs up before settling into his position behind the camera.

My nerves have completely taken over, and I can't get the taste of that damn sushi out of my mouth.

"Okay." Cory crosses one leg over the other, resting his ankle on his knee as he nods toward the cameraman. "Ready."

The cameraman holds his hand up, counting down with his fingers until there are two remaining. Then he points at Cory to begin.

"Hello, New York. My name is Cory, staff writer and editor for Scribe Magazine. I'm here today for a short, rare interview with my boss, CEO, and owner of Scribe Magazine, Holt Capuleti. Plus, a special guest who has managed to capture the eyes, ears, and hearts of our fellow New Yorkers." Cory smiles for the camera before shifting to Holt and me. "Welcome, Mr. Capuleti and Ms. Walker."

"Please." Holt gestures toward Cory and chuckles. "For this interview, you can call me Holt, Cory."

Cory laughs, relaxing a bit. "Okay."

"You can call me Selene." I press my hand to my chest. "And thank you for having me."

"Of course." Cory's grin widens. He glances down at his phone before looking back up. "Now we've established that, I guess we should start with what everyone wants to know about: the story of you two. You and Selene have been quite the topic of conversation this fall and winter. I understand most of the conversation has been surrounded by your legal battle with Rome Montgomery, and I won't get into that, with it still being an open case. But let's talk about the night of the auction at the Omni Plaza Hotel instead. Was that the first time you and Selene had met?"

I nervously glance at Holt. He removes his arm from around my back and rests his hand back on my leg. His fingers gently press into my flesh while his gaze rises to meet mine. I fall in love with him even more.

Finally, he tears his eyes from mine and looks back at Cory. "No. Selene and I have been in the same friendship group for years. She's my sister's best friend."

"Wow." Cory blinks. "So, if you two have been friends for years, what made you want to bid on Selene? Since winning meant you won a date with her, were you concerned you were crossing from friendzone territory into dangerous, uncharted waters?"

"The expected answer would be yes." Holt smiles, leaning forward and resting his elbow on his leg. He massages his chin in thought. "But, no, I wasn't concerned."

"Oh?"

"The truth is, I've been secretly pining after Selene for years. I guess I saw an opportunity and took it."

Cory nods, then shifts his attention toward me. "What about you, Selene? What was going through your mind when you were up on that stage and you realized your best friend's brother was the winning bidder? Did you feel the same way about Holt as he had always done for you?"

I want to melt into a puddle. My hands are clammy and my neck prickles with anxiety. I focus on Holt's hand on my leg, anchoring me to my reality. I ignore the camera, the bright lights, and look directly at Cory.

"If I'm honest, no," I say quietly, quickly wincing when Holt looks at me. I place my hand over his, giving it a gentle squeeze. "I never thought of him as anything more until he'd taken me on the date he won. I will say, he didn't have to do much for me to fall for him, though. I guess some things are always directly in front of us, but sometimes we're too blind to see them."

"I love that," Cory says.

"I do think, even if I hadn't felt those feelings for him on that first date, he wouldn't have given up. If anyone knows Holt" —I gesture toward Cory—"which you do, you'll know he's very ambitious. He was just as ambitious in pursuing me than he is with his career."

"I agree." Cory nods, then turns his attention to Holt. "You *are* a very ambitious man, Holt. Would you attribute that to your father, our former mayor of New York City?"

A heavy, obvious pause settles in the silence. Sensing the shift, I nervously shift my eyes to Treena, where she's sitting against the far wall. She hasn't moved, and there's no expression on her face. She's simply waiting.

I squeeze Holt's hand, reminding him I'm still here, urging him to answer Cory's question.

"Um." Holt clears his throat. "Not entirely. I owe a lot of my drive to my mother."

Cory's shoulders drop as he offers him a sympathetic frown. "Your mother passed away when you were young, correct?"

Chills slither their way down my arms. This interview has

taken an unexpected turn, and I want to stop it. I want to pull Holt back, but I can't. Not when the cameras are rolling and everyone's eyes are on him. I bite the tip of my tongue, hoping Holt's answer will be short and to the point. But knowing how haunted Holt remains over his mother's death, I'm afraid he won't be.

"Murdered, yes," Holt answers.

"I'll admit, I read a few articles covering the story when I was considering working here," Cory tells him. "I'm so sorry for her passing. I don't know if this helps, but I'm hoping that knowing the ones who committed this heinous crime were caught has given you and your family a sense of justice."

Holt's grip on my knee tightens.

I open my mouth to speak, to stop this before Holt has another chance to continue this conversation, but he's too quick.

"I don't believe they caught the killers."

The air is sucked out of the room.

"You don't?" Cory's eyes widen.

"No. I never have," Holt declares. "I was there the night she was killed. I remember everything I heard and saw that night, and I haven't given up in my search. I'll never give up."

Cory's face pales, and he gulps. His eyes nervously dart between Holt and me.

I give him a subtle shake of the head, hoping he understands what message I'm trying to send him. *Shift the topic.* My stomach turns, thinking about how this is going to be posted out to the public later. Bile rises in my throat, but I force it down.

"I don't doubt your vigilance and commitment," Cory says before looking down at his phone. "Speaking of commitment, Scribe Magazine's annual masquerade ball was originally set for this weekend." Cory eyes us both before continuing. "Considering how you started the annual masquerade ball when you announced your anonymous column, and with everything going on regarding *that*, is it still on?"

"Of course it is. The annual masquerade ball has become a corner stone for the magazine. Recent events won't change that."

"Right." Cory's mouth twitches with a tiny smile. "Normally, all of New York's top celebrities and personalities would be there. Is it safe to say you two will be attending together, officially?"

Holt glances over his shoulder, wink at me in a way that makes me fucking weak in the knees. I'm grateful for Cory's swift shift in topic, lightening the mood. I can even sense the tension dissolving from Treena across the room.

"Is that a serious question, Cory?" Holt muses, returning to his usual lightheartedness. "Selene is it for me. She's the only one you'll ever see me walking beside."

Cory coughs into a closed fist, hiding his smile.

"Are you okay?" I ask Cory, unable to drop my smile.

"Yeah." He nods. "It's just strange hearing my boss talk this way."

"What?" I nudge Holt's shoulder with mine. "You mean he doesn't always talk like this?"

"No." Cory shakes his head and laughs. "No, he doesn't."

I hum in amusement, still unable to wipe the grin from my face. My cheeks are sore, but seeing the difference in Holt makes my heart flutter with excitement. I still can't ignore my instinct to second guess everything, but the instant I even get close to letting that show, Holt pulls me right back.

He quickly turns my way before whispering in my ear, "I love you, Wallflower."

Goosebumps spread across my skin, and for the rest of the interview, I don't let my smile drop. How can I when Holt

Capuleti basically just announced to the entire world that he's in love with me?

TWENTY-SIX

HOLT

"We only have five minutes left before everyone is expecting us to be there."

"They can wait," I breathe, grabbing her hip and pulling her onto my lap.

Her black, sequined gown parts, allowing her bare thighs to wrap around mine. My dick wakes right the fuck up, hardening the second she rocks and rolls her hips, rubbing her sweet pussy along my length.

"Howard can hear everything, Holt." She wraps her hands around my neck as I gaze up at her.

"Howard can't hear anything."

"Yes, he can." She giggles, glancing over her shoulder.

Howard's eyes lift to the rearview mirror before he's flipping on the blinker, waiting for the light to turn green.

Selene looks back at me. "He's inches away from us."

I lift my mouth into a devilish smirk. "Howard can't hear anything, Wallflower." I raise my voice. "Can you, Howard?"

Howard doesn't look in the rearview this time.

"See?" I tease.

"Oh, my God, Holt. You're the worst." She taps my shoulder, but she hasn't stopped shifting over me. My naughty girl cares just as much about Howard being inches away as I do.

I shove her curled hair aside as I stare up into her black, sparkly-dusted eyes. They're surrounded by an intricately detailed matching black mask. Everything about her is dark and mysterious, like night and day when compared to her usual light-colored clothes.

"You're really beautiful tonight, Wallflower." I drag my thumb across her bottom lip.

"Thank you." She traces her finger along the bottom of my midnight blue mask. "I love this color on you. Brings out your eyes." Her mouth pulls into a delicate smile.

I wrap my arm around her waist and pull her closer. With my other hand, I grip the back of her head and pull her down to kiss me before I pull back slightly.

"Are you feeling better than you were earlier?"

"Yeah." She swallows. "I think that nausea medicine after dinner helped."

"Good." I growl, slipping my hand between us. "That means I can do this."

I'm quick to find her clit. She tilts her head back, her jaw dropping on a gasp.

"I love you, Holt," she breathes, rubbing herself over my fingers.

"I love you, Wallflower." I work her clit until she comes undone.

She bites her lip, stifling her tiny moans and breaths. I'm fully aware she's conscious of Howard sitting in the driver seat and that we're only minutes from the event venue, but I have no patience. I can't keep my hands off my girl.

She lowers her head and buries her face in my neck. She smells like flowers and sunshine, even though she looks like a storm cloud ready to make her presence known.

"You're absolutely diabolical for this," she pants. "I hope you know."

"Come for me," I breathe into her ear. Heat pools in my lower stomach, and although there are several layers between us, my dick revels in the way she's sliding against me.

She turns her mouth to my ear. "If I'm going to come, so are you."

Tiny bursts of electricity shoot across my skin the moment she lowers herself onto my length. She grinds her sweet pussy harder, dragging herself across my rock-hard cock.

"Wallflower." I growl, digging my fingers into her hips. I want her to stop, because the last thing I need is to come in my fucking pants, but I also *don't* want her to stop. I can't stop. She feels too fucking good.

Dammit, I feel like a fucking teenager.

"If I'm going down"—she presses her lips to shell of my ear—"you're going down with me." She moans, and my cock is throbbing, on the verge of release.

Frantic, I move my hand from her hip to her face, pulling her toward me. I kiss her hard, catching her breath with mine. The windows in my blacked-out Bentley quickly fog over with a thin coat of steam. Our skin is sweating, and I hate the thought of ruining both of our outfits, but I have no self-control. Not when it comes to Selene.

I press my fingers harder against her clit, and every time I do, she matches me thrust for thrust. Blood shoots straight for my dick, and she grinds herself over me twice more before I'm coming. Fisting Selene's hair, I grip the back of her neck and still her movements as I come.

"Fuck." I groan, stifling what noise I can against Selene's neck.

I haven't moved my hand as she grinds the last few times

before she's coming herself. She shudders against me, vibrating as she comes.

Lifting my head, I try to catch my breath while staring into her mossy-green eyes surrounded by diluted light. My sinfully dark wallflower. I love seeing this side of her.

But then it hits me. I just fucking came in my pants, and we're almost at the masquerade ball.

Selene must realize it, too. Her cheeks turn an even darker shade of red, and her eyes widen. "Oh, my God." She slaps a hand over her mouth, then slowly lowers it. "I'm so sorry, Holt. I didn't mean—"

I chuckle under my breath and run my hand over her hair, tucking it behind her ear. "Yes, you did, but it's okay."

"No, it's not. I shouldn't have done that."

"I like it when you show this side of yourself to me." I kiss her nose. "I love it because it's a side no one else gets to see but me."

Her expression transforms into one of happiness, and I melt with her smile.

"Howard!" I shout, not taking my eyes off Selene. "Take us back home. I need to change."

"Yes, sir," Howard answers, immediately making a U-turn.

"Oh, no." Selene groans, burying her head. "Now we're going to be late."

"I don't care." I hook my fingers under her chin, pulling her to look up. "If this is the reason we're late, it was worth it. You're always worth it."

***

After quickly changing into a clean suit, Selene and I eventually show up to the masquerade ball over an hour past our original arrival time.

We make the rounds, greeting every single celebrity and guest in attendance in support of Scribe Magazine and my team in the anonymous article department. Photographers and reporters clamor for interviews with Selene and me. We answer a few questions, avoiding the most prying, but thankfully, Treena and Vanessa are in attendance, immediately pulling us away when there is any hint of a mention of Rome Montgomery.

Every year, my event team throws our annual masquerade ball at an old estate outside the city on lavish grounds in what looks like an old castle built out of pale gray stone, as though it's plucked straight out of the English countryside.

It's my favorite event of the year, mostly because it's a nice break from the hustle and bustle of city life, fitting in with the romantic tones that come standard with a masked ball.

After making our initial greetings, I wander around to chat with some of my colleagues while Selene leaves to find our friendship group. We stopped to talk to them at the start of the ball but have barely spent any time with them since. Charleigh and Asher were inseparable, as usual, unable to keep their hands off one another. West and London were practically the same, too busy losing themselves in one another to notice the rest of us, or at least participate in much of the conversation. Which led us to making the rounds around the ornately deco- rated ballroom covered in silver and black roses. They slither along the walls like ivy while the floor is decked out in mirrored glass.

The event coordinating team at the magazine has outdone themselves this year.

Julianna, thankfully, didn't coordinate this event, so she hasn't been overrun with a million tasks. She's been able to spend her time here relaxed, not worrying about keeping the guests entertained or failing to meet their expectations.

Once I'm finished talking with a group of investment bankers, I immediately begin searching for Selene among the shadowed crowd. We haven't even had a chance to dance yet tonight, and my hands are itching to touch her.

I find West standing at the back of the estate, overlooking the expansive garden grounds. He's leaning against the large, stone pillar, scrolling through his phone. The blueish-white light from his phone screen illuminates his masked face.

He looks up when he sees me approaching.

"Hey, man." He grins, dropping his phone into his pocket. "London and I were wondering where you and Selene have been. Charleigh and Asher left a few minutes ago—something about Charleigh's mom needing help with putting her new bed frame together." He sighs. "Anyway, we were about to head out ourselves."

"Oh." I glance around the garden. "Is Selene not with London?"

"No." He shakes his head. "She went inside to grab her coat from the valet. I stayed back to see if I ran into you so we could say goodbye." He grins. "Looks like I ran into you."

"Yeah." I give him a weak smile, hoping I find Selene. I slap him on his arm. "Thanks for coming, man."

"Of course." His mouth lifts into an uneasy smile. "You okay?"

I nod, waving him off. "I'm fine. Just want to find Selene."

"I know that feeling." He chuckles. "We never stop searching for them, do we? We don't feel complete."

I laugh before shrugging my shoulder. "Guilty."

"See you later, Holt." He slaps me on the arm and heads back inside the estate.

I pull out my phone and try texting Selene again, but my last sent message still sits unread. I turn my attention back to the backyard.

Not seeing Selene from my vantage point, I walk farther down the grounds. The full moon shines brightly in the clear night sky, illuminating the entire party. I take the cobblestone staircase down to the expansive garden leading to the small labyrinth that's existed here for centuries. According to historical records, anyway.

The farther I go, the fewer guests I encounter. The heads of the ones I do see move on a swivel as they follow me, gossiping as if seeing me here is a shock to them. But I don't give a shit. I only want to find Selene. I know for certain she isn't inside, so this is the last logical place she could be.

I follow the rose-covered terrace wall but stop in my tracks when I see the two men standing at the opposite end.

With black hair, a black mask, an unmistakable bird tattoo on his neck peeking out from the top of his black suit, Rome Montgomery stands at the opening to the labyrinth maze.

I take a step forward, white-hot anger boiling in my veins. My hands immediately curl into tight fists, and all I can think about is what it would feel like to drive it straight into his face.

I would say I'm surprised to see him here, but I'm not. Rome Montgomery doesn't shy away from taking the chance to make himself the center of attention, even if he does have a lawsuit against me. The fucker.

But it's the man he's talking to that distracts me from my anger at Rome. I don't recognize him, mostly because half of his face is hidden by the intricately gold and green mask he's wearing. A small, X-shaped scar stretches across his chin, then I see the tattoo on the back of his hand. Even among the shadows of the night, I recognize it.

A clover with two piercing daggers.

He and Rome are caught up in conversation, but I don't give a shit. My vision turns red, and I'm quick to march forward.

Both men snap their heads in my direction on hearing my footsteps.

"Hey, motherfucker!" I shout.

"Capuleti." Rome's voice drips with venom on a sneer, thinking I'm talking to him.

The man snaps his head toward Rome, his eyes wide. Then he looks at me. I'm still at least twenty feet away, somehow resisting the urge to sprint toward him. Instead, I walk slowly, not to raise alarm. I tread carefully and stick my arm out, pointing to the man.

"Who are you?" I dart my eyes to Rome. "Who the fuck is that, Rome? *Tell me.*"

Neither of them answer me. I imagine driving my fist into this fucker's face, standing over him, demanding answers as to who he is. I don't think I've ever been this close to discovering my mother's true killer before. For all I know, this could be the man who pulled the trigger. Adrenaline pumps through my veins. I feel like I'm going to explode. Spontaneously combust into a million little pieces on this perfectly manicured lawn.

The sound of my mother's last gasping breath echoes in my ears, drowning out the orchestra playing closer to the estate building. Pressure builds behind my eyes, my anger fueling me to keep going.

I've nearly reached the stranger when I hear someone vomiting into the bushes between the two men and me. I abruptly turn to find Julianna running up to Selene, who is bent over in front of the bushes.

My anger dissolves immediately.

"Selene," my sister says, jogging to catch up to her. She places her hand gently on her back. "Are you okay?"

"Jules!" I announce, catching her attention.

Julianna looks up, her eyes meeting mine before they drift to my left, where they narrow in obvious anger, even from behind her mask.

Selene is still bent over, hurling into the bushes.

"Wallflower?" I call out, my feet already carrying me in her direction, until I fall into a jog.

My only focus shifts to Selene and taking care of her.

Once I've reached her, I start gathering her hair, pulling it away from her face.

"I've got her, Jules," I tell my sister.

She takes a step back, nods once, then looks over her shoulder to where Rome is still standing. I follow her gaze, looking over my own shoulder. The man he was standing with has quickly disappeared.

"Holt?" Selene's voice quivers, pulling my attention back to her. A string of spit dangles from her mouth, and she sniffs as her back racks with a sob.

"I'm here, Wallflower. What happened?" I continue to gather any loose strands of hair and tuck a few behind her ear, away from her face.

"I don't know." She spits on the ground before turning her head to look up at me. Tears line her eyes. "I grabbed a glass of champagne, came out here to look for you, and I started to feel sick again. I couldn't hold it down."

She turns back to face the ground. One hand is perched on her knee, her other wrapped around her middle. An empty champagne glass rests at her feet.

"How many glasses have you had?" I ask her.

She slowly turns her head again. Her worried eyes search mine. "That was my first glass."

I draw my eyebrows together.

"Oh, no. It's happening again." Her cheeks swell, and her body roils, then she's vomiting again.

Some of her hair falls from my grip but I'm quick to gather it back up. I rub my hand over her back, hating that she's feeling like this.

"I'm certain being an asshole is the only thing you're capable of." My sister's raised voice in the distance cuts through Selene's vomiting. "Seriously, you should add that title to all of your company letterheads."

With one hand wrapped around Selene's hair, I use the other to rub circles over her back while I listen to what's going on between Rome and Julianna.

"Oh, God." Selene groans, lifting her hand to wipe the back of it across her mouth.

"Tell me, Lark," Rome announces raising his arms in the air. "Lay it on me. Release me from this torture."

"Oh." Julianna snorts. "Now, you want to listen to me?"

"If it'll get you to stop chasing me like a sad, pathetic, lost little kitten, then yes. Anything to get you to stop talking."

A pause, then, "Now I remember why I hate you."

"Feeling's mutual, Lark."

"Stop calling me that!" she shouts.

Rome exhales sharply and stuffs his hands into his pockets as he looks away dismissively. "What have you been chasing me all night to tell me? Let's get this over with so I can go home in peace."

"You're the one who slithered your way in here like the serpent I've always known you to be," Julianna lashes out. "I take that back. You aren't a serpent, you're a coward. Sneaking into the one place no one will be able to recognize you under that mask. You have no reason to be here."

"Very original, Lark." Rome scoffs, unamused. "Why don't you try coming up with new insults to hurl at me? It would make our interactions a little more worthwhile."

"What's happening?" Selene asks with a shaky voice, still bent over.

"I don't know," I mutter, not tearing my eyes away from my sister and Rome.

Selene vomits again.

"I've been trying to reach you for weeks," Julianna seethes angrily.

"I'm aware," Rome replies dryly.

"Great." Julianna plants her hands on her hips. "Well, since you've asked so kindly as to why I've been trying to talk to you, I'll tell you. I was hoping I could convince you to drop this lawsuit against Holt."

"Why should I? He knowingly published an article that was clearly defamatory. Do you understand the damage this has caused? Although, I do have to give him credit where credit is due. Took balls for Holt to do it, considering our family history."

"Holt wasn't aware of the article."

"How do you know?"

"Because I just do," Julianna clips.

"So, what are you saying?" Rome takes a small, measured step closer to Julianna. "You *were* aware of it?"

A long, torturous pause.

Selene sniffs and pulls herself to stand upright. I reach inside my front pocket and grip the bottom of her chin, using my pocket square to clean up her face. I stare into her eyes, worried she hasn't been feeling well lately. First, the day of the interview with Cory, then earlier, after dinner. Now, the champagne.

"Yes," Julianna states loudly.

Selene's and my attention to each other breaks, shifting to Rome and Julianna.

"And how would you know that if your brother didn't?" Rome asks.

"Because it was *me!*" Julianna's cries are clear. "I wrote the article."

Rome's amused expression falls, completely disappearing under the moonlight.

"Of course you did." He lifts his chin in defiance, curling his lip. His eyes darken beneath his mask.

I'm several dozen feet from Julianna and Rome, but distance doesn't matter when it comes to recognizing my sister's expression. Her chin wobbles, and her entire upper body stiffens.

"Drop the lawsuit against Holt," she grinds out. "This war ends now."

Rome's silence is deafening. He simply stands a few feet away from her, unmoving. Julianna doesn't waste another second before she's spinning on her heel. She gathers the length of her dress in her hands and marches back toward the party with her head hanging low.

By the time I look back to see Rome, he's gone, disappearing like a ghost.

"What the hell was that?" Selene asks.

I shake my head, too stunned with what just unfolded.

Then I look at my girl.

"Are you okay?" I cradle Selene's face in my hands, massaging my fingers into her hair. "Do you need to go to the hospital?"

"No," she answers weakly with a small smile, her masked eyes searching my face. "Must have been the champagne. I just want to go home. Please take me home."

"I'll take you wherever you want to go, Wallflower." I bend to scoop her into my arms. "Where you go, I go."

She drapes her arms around my neck, and I'm pulled back to the night I took her home when she was drunk. But this time, she isn't looking at me with alcohol-soaked eyes.

Instead, she's looking at me with love.

TWENTY-SEVEN

ROME

Being with her is like drinking from a vial of poison. Deceptively sweet, quickly turning bitterly sour before you realize it's too late. The poison swims in your veins, consuming everything good left inside you until all that's left is darkness.

"Should be any minute, Mr. Montgomery." Marcus, my bodyguard, eyes me in the rearview before I tear mine away.

"Good."

I don't need him to talk me out of this. Again. I saw the hesitation in his eyes. A longtime friend and ally, Marcus has talked me out of some insane shit over the years that, to a person who didn't have the money and social standing I do, would have had them locked up for life.

But I do have money, and I do have social standing. Therefore, I can do batshit crazy things like this without worrying about charges being filed against me. Especially her.

However, I don't miss the resolve in Marcus's eyes before I look away. He knows there's no use in talking me out of this.

I'm staring at the back of Marcus's head from the back seat when he rolls it slightly to the left, eyeing the side mirror.

"Here she comes."

Three words are all it takes for my heart to jolt to life and the blood to drain to my toes. I snap my head to the left and spot her immediately. Her sharp heels click against the concrete as she stares at her phone cradled in her delicate hand. Long legs, barely covered by her fluffy, pink, feathered skirt move effortlessly through the parking garage. Her soft, plush lips part as she flicks her gaze up long enough to keep track of where she's walking before turning her attention back to her phone.

Sweet, innocent, obnoxiously oblivious.

Fuck, she's infuriating.

Hilarious considering her brother has assigned a security detail to her every move lately. But somehow, the asshole didn't think to cover the parking garage outside her apartment.

I spend a beat too long watching her. If I don't move quickly, I'll miss my chance. She's walking directly past my car, dangerously close.

I snap out of my hypnotic trance and swing the car door open, creating a wall that blocks her from taking another step. She screeches to a halt, rolling her ankle in the process. She hisses and curses, her hand flying out toward the door to catch herself before falling over. She shrieks when I reach out and wrap an arm around her waist, pulling her into the back of the car with me.

"What the fuck?" she screams, falling back against the back of my leather seat. Her wild eyes turn to me and, once they've registered who has kidnapped her, she scrambles to try and get out of the car.

But I'm too quick. My arm flies out to grab the handle of the door, slamming it shut. My entire body pins her down as I glance over my shoulder to Marcus in the front seat.

"Keep the child lock on," I tell him.

"I'm not a child!" she yells, slapping my shoulder, trying to shove me off her.

"Jury's out on that one," I mutter, my heart racing.

"Fuck you, Rome." she grunts angrily.

"Morning, Lark," I practically sing, deriving too much pleasure from feeling her squirming with hatred beneath me.

"Let me the fuck out," she demands.

I simply laugh. "Not going to happen."

Julianna's heated breath hits my neck as she pants and huffs. "Let me out, Marcus."

"Sorry, Ms. Capuleti," Marcus apologizes.

"Marcus doesn't take orders from you," I remind her. "He works for me."

My knee presses into the seat beside her, and I hate how her signature, intoxicating scent of patchouli and vanilla surrounds me.

Goddammit. I'm drinking from that fucking vial of poison.

I snap myself out of it, not wanting to travel down that road again.

"Let me out of here, Rome!" she yells even louder, shoving me even harder.

But I'm stone, unwilling to move above her.

She grunts and fights me, kicking her feet out. Her heels stab and scrape the back of Marcus's seat. She's destroying my fucking car, for Christ's sake.

"Let me out, or I will scream even louder."

"No one will hear you," I tell her, my nostrils flaring with impatience. "These windows are soundproof. Doesn't matter how loud you are. And we both know how loud you can be, Lark."

Her icy glare pins itself to me, the blues of her irises darkening. Pupils dilated, she stares at me for several breaths. "I fucking ha—"

"Hate me," I finish for her, rolling my eyes. "Yes, we know. If it's any consolation, the feeling is mutual."

"Happy to know nothing has changed," she grunts, pushing me again, albeit slightly less forcefully this time. "Now, let me out of the car, psycho."

"We haven't even touched the surface of why I pulled you in here yet."

"You kidnapped me... in the parking garage where I live, on my way to work. The only thing missing is the creepy, window-less white van." She balls her hands into fists at her sides. "I stand by what I said—you *are* a psycho. All Montgomerys are."

Her body still rolls beneath me while she catches her breath.

I give her a devilish smirk. "If I'm a psycho, you must be one too."

She stills, and I count her breaths in my head.

One. Two. Three. Four...

"Whatever." She groans, falling back against the seat with a defeated huff. "Can you get off me now?"

"Promise you'll have a calm, civilized conversation with me, and I'll move."

"I don't think you're capable of a calm, civilized conversation."

"Come on, Lark." I press my lips together. The silence swells, and I tighten my grip on the leather seat, forcing me to keep my hands to myself.

Stay away from the poison, Rome. Remember the reason you hate her.

"Fuck," she breathes, crossing her arms over her chest. "Fine, I promise."

"Good girl," I tease, taking one last jab at her for the fun of it.

She doesn't take the bait, though, now unwilling to even look me in the eye. She keeps her arms crossed over her chest as she stares blankly out the tinted window.

I sit back in my seat and adjust my tie, straightening out my suit before clearing my throat. "I dropped the lawsuit against Holt."

She lets out an audible gasp before snapping her head to the right.

Somehow, I pull myself together and gather the strength to look back at her.

"You did?" she asks.

"Yes."

"When?"

"My lawyer contacted his team this morning. I'm sure he'll have received the information by now."

Her eyes soften, the relief practically oozing out of her the moment she realizes I'm telling the truth. But it doesn't last long. Suspicion is written all over her face, as it should.

"Thank you for dropping the lawsuit." She swallows and unravels her arms. "Can I go now?"

"We aren't finished." I lower my voice.

Her eyes roam over my face, and I see it all there staring back at me.

The hatred.

The betrayal.

She's always been so easy to read. Perhaps it was our downfall.

And it continues to be.

"I should have known there was more," she says dryly. "This entire conversation could have been an email up until this point."

I shove down the sting that pricks my chest at that. "Yes, you should have known. You nearly destroyed my life with your silly, anonymous article."

She rests back against my seat and stares at me with those wide blue eyes I've seen up close too many times before.

I clear my throat and force myself to say what I came here to say. "I may have dropped the lawsuit against Holt, but let's not get this twisted. I didn't do this for your benefit."

I haven't been able to let go of the anger I have for Julianna. I would say it's lingered since she told me the truth three nights ago, at the masquerade ball, but it's been around long before that. I've held a hatred toward Julianna Rosaline Capuleti for as long as I can remember.

Her cheeks heat again, the color turning from pale pink to bright red. Her icy glare turns to fire. "I never thought for once you did do this for my benefit."

"I figured to save myself the trouble of going to court over defamation, there are better ways to spend my time getting revenge on the Capuletis."

She inhales sharply but stays silent.

"My revenge would be best served going straight to the source," I add.

"Me." The word falls from her disgustingly pretty mouth on a near whisper.

"Yes." I chuckle. "You honestly didn't believe your confession the other night would let you and your family off the hook, did you?"

Her delicate neck bobs as she gulps nervously. Then she quirks a brow. "What did you have in mind?"

"Oh, come on." I smooth my hands over my suit jacket. "You know me better than that, Lark. I never show my hand before the appropriate time."

She tucks her bottom lip between her teeth, and I think she's going to bite a chunk right out of it with the pressure she's applying.

She doesn't even need to say the words I know she's thinking. She hates me. Despises me.

Good. Because I feel the same.

"Timing is everything, Lark," I tell her, lingering on her gaze a second too long.

Then I nod toward Marcus, blinking at him once through the rearview mirror. The clicking sound of the child lock releasing echoes throughout the car. I lean forward, hovering over Julianna the same way I had when I dragged her in here.

"You'll be hearing from me."

"When?" She looks up at me with blue doe eyes.

Turning away from her, I pull on the door handle and push it open. It swings open, and the sounds of the city outside quickly return. We're no longer in our own world.

She surprises me when she doesn't immediately jump out of the car. Her hands rest on the tops of her legs, tangling the gentle delicate feathers of her skirt. Funny how even snakes can disguise themselves as gentle birds sometimes.

I slowly back away and settle back into my seat, where I wait.

She opens her mouth as if she's about to argue but doesn't. Instead, she snaps it shut, blinks several times, then turns her back on me. Once she's slid out of the backseat, I wait until she's taken a few feet away from the door before shutting it.

She spins around, turning her back to me, and simply stands beside my car. My lungs burn with every second that passes where she doesn't move.

Drop the vial of poison or drink every last drop?

"Go, Marcus," I order before I say or do something I'll inevitably regret.

"Sir?"

I squeeze my eyes shut and breathe through my nose before turning to shoot him a furious glare in the rearview mirror. "Get us the fuck out of here. Now!"

SELENE

Breathe in. Breathe through. Breathe deep. Then out.

The shrill sound of the three-minute timer on my phone shakes me to my core.

I can't decide if I'm queasy because I've felt nauseous every single day for the past several weeks, or if it's from the uncertainty of the stick of plastic resting on the edge of the bathroom sink.

I didn't set out to spend my day like this, but the signs were too great to ignore. So, when Holt told me he had to run out for an emergency work meeting, I took the opportunity.

I feel like I'm standing on the edge of a precipice or, fuck, even a fork in the road. Which direction will my life take me?

It all feels dramatic and life altering. Like at any moment, my life is going to implode.

Even after the timer goes off, I don't pick up the white plastic stick.

I'm terrified of the answer—an answer I'm already certain I know. It feels as if there's a taut string pulling me on the inside of my stomach. I gently place my hand over it and think about my mother.

It's hard to think of her as she was before the last time I saw her. The fear in her eyes. The love she had for me. Something in her gaze told me she knew it was the last time she'd be looking at me, too.

I chew on the inside of my cheek.

Falling in love with Holt wasn't expected. I did everything I could to prevent this from happening, to avoid falling into the same trap my mother had, where she believed my father would love her to the ends of the earth. I guess, in a way, he did. He couldn't allow her to live her life in this world, and he couldn't live in one where she didn't exist, either.

Love can be volatile, and it can't be trusted.

I want to believe every word Holt has told me over these past months. I want to believe he's pined after me, secretly yearning in the shadows. But isn't that what my mother believed?

Closing my eyes, I picture Holt. I imagine the way he looked at me this morning before he walked out the door. His gentle touch. His starving kiss. The love in his rich, blue eyes. He was looking at me as if I was the most precious person in the world. Will he do the same if the answer on the stick is yes?

For years, Holt has been a chronic bachelor, moving from one woman to the next, never sticking with one long enough to allow anyone to draw the conclusion he was in a long-term relationship. I think back to the last girl he'd been seen dating. They were together the same amount of time him and I have been together now.

Is Holt capable of commitment?

I pick up my phone to text my sister but quickly put it back down. I want to talk to her. I want to tell her about my hesitation in my career, my blossoming love for Holt, my fear that it will all slip away. I'm afraid the rug is going to get pulled out from under me at any moment. I want to tell her all these things, but I can't. This is between me and the piece of plastic sitting on the counter.

With sweaty palms and shaking fingers, I reach out for the stick.

I hold my breath until my lungs burn, then turn it over.

The plus sign fades, blurring with my tears. My heart swells then contracts. I feel like it's going to explode. I clamp my hand over my mouth and stifle my cries. Holt's penthouse is filled with his staff: housekeepers, chefs, security. Every single one would come racing in here if they heard me crying. I swiftly shut the bathroom door and press my back against it. Then I sink to the floor.

Placing my hand gently on my stomach again, I take a deep breath. Years of therapy have taught me to think analytically when it comes to overwhelming situations. I try to think logically, making a point to remember the things I know as fact.

I have blonde hair.

I love yoga.

I'm a strong woman.

I'm healthy.

I'm capable.

I'm in love with Holt Capuleti.

I snap my eyes open as soon as the last thought registers in my mind. The truth rests there, as positive as the test I have clenched in my hand.

Instinct tells me the uncertainty of Holt's reaction is inevitable. Normally, I would run, end things as soon as possible. I would let him go the same way I let Adam go. I would spend the rest of my life alone, because being alone is safer than sharing your life with someone. But if the feelings I have for Holt have taught me anything, it's life and love don't come without risk.

Loving Holt, like death, is an inevitable fact—one I can't escape.

I rise from the bathroom floor and wrap my hand around the pregnancy test before slipping it into my pocket. After a quick look in the mirror, I swipe my fingers under my eyes, then step out of the bathroom.

Two hours later, I'm shoving the same bit of scrambled egg and microgreens across my plate for the thousandth time. I've played out every possible scenario in my head, but the one that sticks out the most is imagining what Holt's reaction will be when he walks through the door.

I picture him wrapping his arms around me, telling me he's all in. But just when I'm convinced that'll be his reaction, I imagine another scenario that involves him backing away, telling me this isn't what he signed up for. Holt is an ambitious man, focused on his career and finding his mother's murderer. Not raising a child.

Then I think about what he told me the night I poured my heart out to him. The way he wrapped me up in his arms, promising over and over again how much he's in love with me.

I glance up at the clock, wondering when the moment will come.

I won't deny, fear has set in. Fear of losing everything I've gained over these past few months.

But he needs to know the truth, regardless of the outcome.

My breath catches in the back of my throat the second I hear the door open.

"Wallflower?" he announces from the end of the hallway.

My pulse races, and I inhale a deep breath, lifting my shoulders and wringing my fingers in my lap.

"In the kitchen!" I yell back, trying not to let my voice break.

"Hey," he sighs, a smile stretched across his mouth. It reaches his eyes, lighting him up. "You won't believe what I'm going to tell you." He crosses the room and moves around the kitchen island. Gripping the back of my head, he tilts me up until my lips meet his. He sinks into it, using every ounce of energy to hold me close.

I grip his suit jacket, moaning against his mouth. He's warmth and comfort, soothing the worried parts of my mind and soul.

I'm full of nervous energy, unable to quiet it.

"Holt," I pull away. "I need to—"

"Hang on, Wallflower," he cuts in. He's practically bouncing with excitement. I can tell something has happened. He rakes his hand through his hair, revealing his gleaming eyes. "Rome dropped the lawsuit."

"What?" I sit up out of my chair, and Holt sweeps me into his arms, then spins me around in a circle.

"Yeah," he laughs, gently placing me back down.

I'm dizzy and feel like vomiting, but his mood is contagious. Despite my inner struggle to come to terms with what I need to tell him, I'm now fully focused on Holt's news.

"H-How?" I stammer. "Why?"

"His lawyers sent word to mine this morning. They didn't give a reason, but I think it must be because of what we overheard the other night at the masquerade ball. Julianna asked him to drop it, and he must have done it for her."

I jerk my head back.

"What?" Holt asks, his eyebrows tugging together in concern. "This is a good thing, right?"

"No, of course, it is." I take a deep breath and look up at him. I softly chuckle. "I just don't know how much of this he did *for* Julianna. I can't imagine Rome wanting to do anything for her."

"You're right." Holt gives me a soft smile. "I don't know his reason, but I guess it doesn't matter. This gives me a chance to focus back on work and, maybe down the line, I can figure out who he was talking to that night. But as far as my reputation, my team assured me it's all taken care of now. My PR is managing the media coverage. It'll probably be in the cycle for a little while, but once the dust settles on that, we're in the clear."

"That's amazing." I grin, watching the stress melt away from his body. He's almost back to the man I knew before he was slapped with this lawsuit.

"I'm considering asking Rome who he was talking to the night of the masquerade ball."

My stomach turns. I understand Holt's drive, but I also hate the idea of him getting involved in something dangerous. Something tells me the man he saw talking to Rome won't be considered a friend.

"I just want you to be careful, Holt. If that man is connected to your mother's killer, are you thinking Rome is somehow connected, too?"

Holt pauses, considering my question. It's been one that's weighed on me ever since that night.

"No." Holt shakes his head. "Rome didn't look entirely friendly with him, and despite the hatred our families have toward one another, I don't think Rome is capable of murder. I'm not sure how much he knows, though. I'm hoping he can give me something to go on."

I nod as an icy chill slinks its way down the length of my spine. I shake it off and focus on the news I'm keeping locked inside me. "I don't think someone who has knowledge or had anything to do with your mother's death would drop the lawsuit the way Rome has."

"Point well made." Holt gives me a large grin, agreeing.

"I'm thankful he dropped the lawsuit." I wrap my arms around his waist and squeeze, holding him impossibly close.

"Same, Wallflower." He tilts his face down to kiss me, then

he starts to sway me back and forth, almost as if we're dancing. My hair dances across my back with how high my chin is lifted to stare into his eyes. His smile hasn't wavered.

"Does this mean our fake dating agreement is over?" I tease, scrunching my nose.

Holt abruptly stops dancing. His hand rests on my lower back while his other wraps around the side of my face. His thumb rests under my chin, keeping me looking up into his blue eyes. He makes sure I'm reading his thoughts loud and clear, leaving no room for any confusion.

"I thought I made that clear that night at your apartment. Our fake dating agreement was never real. You know that, right?"

I swallow the lump in my throat.

"I love you, Selene," he says, with more conviction than I've ever heard him speak before. "I've been obsessed with you for years. I'm at your mercy, and yours alone. You're the only one who has the ability to destroy me. You're also the only one I will ever love. None of this was ever fake."

Tears sting the backs of my eyes. I repeat Holt's words in my head, knowing he means them, because this isn't the first time I've heard them. Just when I think he's going to change his mind or take back what he says, he proves me wrong.

But that still doesn't take away the fear of what I need to tell him.

My lips part as I inhale a shaky breath.

Holt's expression shifts. His brows pull together, and three creases form between his eyes. His mouth turns into a frown, and he pulls back slightly.

"You have something to tell me."

His eyes drop to my mouth—a clear tell he knows I'm keeping a secret from him.

I must have done that fucking thing with my mouth again.

Shit.

I loosen my arms around Holt's waist and roll back onto my heels, heat blooming in my cheeks. My cold feet press into the cold tile, and I close my eyes.

"Tell me, Wallflower."

I'm dizzy, sick with fear. I picture my mother. My father. Then my grandmother. I cling to her memory and what she always used to tell me.

Nothing worthwhile doesn't come without risk.

I open my eyes and find Holt still looking down at me with concern.

"I, um," I whisper shakily. A tear slips from my eye, dripping down over my upper lip. "I'm pregnant."

Two words.

Two words that change everything.

I hold my breath, waiting for Holt's reaction.

His face pales, and his hand falls from my face. I miss his touch the second it's gone. I didn't realize how tightly I was clinging onto it, using it to keep my head above water.

"You're pregnant?" He gasps, clamping his mouth shut. He swallows, then shifts his gaze over my shoulder, looking vacantly off in the distance.

"Yes," I mutter, unable to bring my breath above a whisper. I stare at his chest, focusing on the intricate detail of his black silk tie. "I took a test earlier. I've been sick practically every day for the past several weeks and I couldn't understand why. At first, I thought it was this meal or that meal, but then it started to happen every time I went to eat. Then I couldn't hold the champagne down at the masquerade ball. I took the test, and the pink plus sign was unmistakable. I mean, you didn't ask for this, so I understand if you don't—"

My rambling is abruptly cut off by Holt's mouth.

He steals my breath, crashing his lips to mine. He pours

everything into our kiss, and I can't help the sob that escapes the corners of my mouth.

He grips the back of my head and pulls away long enough to look into my eyes. "Whatever you were about to let spill from that pretty mouth, don't." He searches my face, clearly still letting the news of my pregnancy sinking in. "You're pregnant?"

I gently nod.

"You're going to have my baby?" His blue eyes widen as the hand he has wrapped around my back moves to my front. He gently runs the back of it over my stomach.

"I am." My voice cracks. "And I'm sorry, Holt."

"Why? I'm not."

I blink. "We should have been more careful, and I don't want you thinking…"

"Are you kidding me?" He beams, the smile he walked in with returns. It reaches his eyes. "If there's anything I wanted more than you in this life, it was to *build* a life with you. That includes all of it: marriage, babies, old age. Whatever you can give me, I'll take. As long as it's with you, I want it."

I let his words sink in. He's happy. He isn't running. He isn't giving up.

He must read my thoughts because he falls to his knees in front of me. Tears stream down my cheeks as his hands slide across my hips. I reach down and run my fingers through his brown hair. Will our baby have his brown hair, or will they have my blonde? My mother's, too?

My stomach flutters at the thought.

Tears coat his dark lashes as he lifts the bottom of my small cotton tank to reveal my stomach. He stares at my stomach in amazement. My throat swells, and it's difficult to breathe. I've never had anyone look at me the way Holt does.

He presses his lips to my stomach. Then again. And again.

His mouth is soft and gentle, lighting a fire inside me. A fire I've never felt with anyone else. Only Holt.

"If this baby is going to be anything like you, Wallflower, I'm already obsessed with them." He plants another kiss to my stomach, then leans in to whisper against my skin. "I love you."

"Holt," I whisper, unable to hold back the tears.

He looks up at me as another tear slips from the corner of his eye. He's all long lashes, sexy hair, and vulnerability. Completely at my mercy. "I love you both."

"I love you, too." I cup the side of his face and urge him to stand.

When he does, he hungrily takes my mouth with his. His hand slides down my back, slipping under my cotton shorts. He cups my ass cheek and squeezes the flesh, pulling me toward him.

"But I won't lie," I tell him. "I'm scared. What if... what if..."

There isn't a single hint of fear or hesitation in his expression. "I know you're scared, Selene, but I'm not your father, and you aren't your mother."

"What if something happens?" My voice breaks. "When it was just you and me, there was less to lose. But now?" I swallow back the tears and sniff. "With a baby... I would understand if you didn't want this, Holt."

My outspoken fears have wounded him, but I need him to know he has options.

"Listen to me, Selene."

The way he's cradling me pulls out another sob. I cry for all of him. The way he fights for me at every turn, even when I'm not fighting for myself. His love for me radiates, sinking into every fiber of my soul.

"The greatest loves don't come without risk. But if I had to choose between living life without you both, just to be sure I'd never feel the pain of loss, then I wouldn't want it. I don't want it. I promised you I wasn't going anywhere, Wallflower, and I'm not. I'd travel to the ends of the Earth for you or sell my soul to the Devil before letting you go. I have my sister and my father, but when I lost my mother, I felt my whole world shift from under my feet. I never thought I would have a chance at a life with a family of my own making. You're that for me, Selene. I'll spend the rest of my life proving it to you, too. To the both of you."

I've lived a life with a fractured heart, and no amount of reassurance Holt tries to give me will ever erase the nagging sensation that, at some point, this all might disappear. But as he said, the greatest loves don't come without risk.

I drape my arms around his neck and roll back onto my toes, heat spreading between my thighs. Tilting my head to the side, I drag my nose along his, feeling every bit of the promise he's given me. "Prove it to me then."

TWENTY-NINE

HOLT

Obsession is in my nature. Or is it called hyper fixation now? Whatever it is, I'm the poster boy for it. I've spent most of my adolescence into my adulthood obsessing over finding my mother's murderer. Still am, by the way.

I've also been obsessive over my career. I've never backed down from taking my magazine to the next level, eager to stay relevant in a world of ever-changing media.

But my greatest obsession has been Selene Walker. With her shy nature, secret inner fire she reserves for only those she truly deems worthy, and her salacious green eyes, I can't seem to get enough. Simply thinking about her makes my heart hammer erratically and makes my dick painfully hard. And just when I didn't think I could be more insanely obsessed with her, she's going to have my baby.

There were moments in my life I never thought this was the direction it would take. I was too career focused. Too caught up in my grief. Too obsessed with my sister's best friend. But here I am, the luckiest fucking man on the planet.

Every minute, every single solitary second since she told me the news, three days ago, has been spent thinking about the two of them.

Sitting in hours-long board meetings? Selene and the baby.

Sprinting on the treadmill? Selene and the baby.

Drinks with West and Asher? Selene and the baby.

Love has turned me utterly crazy in the best way possible.

Selene and I agreed to keep the news of her pregnancy to ourselves until the doctor confirms it, which means we haven't told our friends or family. But that hasn't stopped us from wanting to celebrate.

The night sky is already pitch black from the view in my office. Cory steps out with a stack of paperwork tucked under his arm. Once he's gone, I'm switching off my computer when Selene's name flashes across my phone screen.

I pick it up and quickly swipe my thumb across the green button while I finish gathering the papers scattered across my desk. "I know I'm late for our date, Wallflower. I got caught up in my meeting with Cory."

"I figured that's what happened." She sighs heavily into the phone.

I stop what I'm doing, nearly dropping the papers on my desk. "Is everything okay?" Fuck, I need to calm down.

"Of course." Her voice lightens. "I've just been looking forward to this date all day. We haven't been on the yacht in months."

"I know. Not since our group got together that first time. I was playing poker, and you were wearing that sexy as fuck blue bikini."

"You remember that?" Her giggle sends a jolt of electricity through my veins.

"Of course, I do." I clear my throat. "I told you I've been obsessed with you since I met you."

"You know, I guess in a way you were a wallflower, too, huh?" she teases.

A smile slowly spreads across my mouth. God, this woman *owns* me.

"On second thought, I bet it would be faster for you to come up to my office than to meet me on the yacht."

"Holt. Howard is already driving me there. So, no, it wouldn't be faster. I'd be going in the opposite direction."

"Well, shit. I got my hopes up imagining bending you over my desk. You know it's one of my favorite views of you."

"Did I know that?" she teases again.

We laugh as I organize the rest of the paperwork for me to go over tomorrow.

"Of course I knew that, Holt," Selene adds, her laughter fading. "But there are other places I can bend over on your yacht."

My dick twitches, the thought of sinking myself into her with the sparkling water of the Hudson in the background waking it up.

I shut off my lamp and grab my suit jacket from the hook near the door of my office. "I'm on my way now."

"Good," Selene says proudly. "I'll be waiting." She ends the last word in a singsong voice that makes me want to take the fastest way possible to get to my girl.

I quickly utter an, "*I love you*," before ending the call and rushing out of my office.

HOLT

Once I reach my yacht, I make my way down the pier. Since I haven't come down here as much as I'd hoped, it's parked in the farthest spot away at the end. My hands are shaking in anticipation, craving to touch Selene.

It's amazing how I can touch her, sleep next to her, yet still ache for her the way I did before we started dating.

The cold, early winter breeze nips at my skin. A white cloud puffs out from my cold lips, reminding me this is the entirely wrong season to be here. When I grow closer to the yacht, all the lights are off apart from the one on the top floor, toward the bow.

"Selene?" I shout, heading straight for the small stairway, just inside the deck.

I only hired a few staff to run and manage the yacht during the summer months, so I'm not surprised to find it empty, aside from Selene being here.

But I can't help how the hairs on the back of my neck suddenly stand up the closer I get to the upper floor. It could be the colder temperatures coming up off the water, the cold settling in to my bones, or it could be the eerie, chilling silence.

"Wallflower?" I call out again once I reach the second deck. "You up here?"

I slowly walk down the side walkway, fully expecting to find Selene sitting inside the enclosed dining area.

Instead, when I round the corner to the back lounge area, I find her standing on the far side of the bench. Her bare feet sink into the cotton padding, and her dress clings to her entire body as the wind blows. My eyes travel up her body as I take in what the fuck I'm seeing.

The gravity of what's happening hits me with the clicking sound of a pistol and my name falling from Selene's mouth.

"Holt," she cries quietly, a tear slipping down her cheek.

Her hands are gently layered over her stomach, her eyes spread wide in panic.

My gaze moves to the man standing beside her, tightly gripping her arm with one hand while the other holds a pistol to the side of her head.

"Get the fuck away from her." I take several steps closer without thinking, but I'm stopped when two other men surround me, emerging from their guard positions. When they step closer, closing around me, I recognize the one on my right. Only this time, he isn't wearing a mask. But the X-shaped tattoo on his chin is clear.

He was the one I caught Rome talking to the night of the ball.

I send the man holding Selene a fiery glare. "Who the fuck are you?"

The question has barely left my mouth before I realize the answer. Sort of.

The clover and dagger tattoo on the back of the man's pistol-wielding hand is unmistakable.

"Name is Rhys O'Connell," he utters in a distinctive, unmistakable Irish accent. His eyes are dark and shadowed by the night sky, but something tells me even under the brightest light, this man has no soul.

I swallow, glancing between the three men, unsure of what to say or do. Between the gun pointed at Selene's head and how close she is to the edge of the yacht, I don't want to do anything that might give them reason to act. There are too many risks.

"Nice to meet you, Mr. O'Connell," Rhys mocks. "I'm Holt Capuleti, the fucker who's been tracking you down for years." He scoffs and shakes his head. "Italians always forget their manners."

He gives me a devilish smirk, and the silence that follows makes me want to fucking vomit.

My nostrils flare, and white-hot anger flows through my veins.

"You're the one who killed my mother," I state, the words falling from my mouth with a bitter taste I can't get rid of.

Rhys clicks his tongue in disapproval. "That's not exactly the proper way to start this conversation, now, is it? Like I said: *manners.*" He frowns and tosses his head to the side. "Now, let's start with the fact you maybe should have kept your security detail following this little viper for a little while longer. I did wonder, when my men told me they were no longer an obstacle, why you'd done it. What was your reason?"

I clamp my mouth shut and bite my cheek until the metallic taste hits my tongue. Pressure builds behind my eyes, and I look at Selene.

I keep my focus on her, even when Rhys continues.

"Did you know your boyfriend was conducting surveillance on you?" he asks Selene. "Sweet, really. But it would have been more of a grand, romantic gesture had he been consistent, no? Considering all the media attention you've been getting lately."

Selene doesn't answer him. She sobs, practically choking on

her own tears. Her hands continue to press against her stomach, and I can't imagine the fear she must be feeling.

"Moving on," Rhys abruptly cuts in. "Let's get to the real business of why we're here. Why you keep following me."

I huff and curl my hands into fists at my sides. "Let her go, and I'll talk."

"Not how this works, Capuleti. If you remember, I'm the one in charge here." He presses the gun harder to Selene's temple.

She whimpers, and I take a step forward.

"Familiar, no?" he asks, nodding toward his gun.

Bile rises in my throat.

"Answer me!" he shouts, veins bulging from his neck.

"Yes," I say weakly on an exhausted breath. "Just, please... you don't understand..."

"Here's how this will go." Rhys ignores my plea. "I'll give you the information you've been seeking—within reason, of course—and you'll make a promise in return. Then we'll let your precious little Wallflower go."

My stomach drops at his use of my nickname for Selene.

"If you can't make the promise," he continues, "I guess we'll just make history repeat itself."

"What information?" I ask.

"About your mother's untimely and unfortunate death."

Adrenaline pumps hard in my veins.

"That is what you've been searching for since you were, what, twelve years old?" His eyebrows rise on his smooth forehead. He can't be much older than me.

"How do you know all this?" I raise my chin.

"Which part?" he asks, cooly. "The part where I know all about your precious Wallflower here, or the part about your mother's brutal murder?"

I grind my teeth. "All of it."

"Promises first." He glowers.

"What promise will I be making?"

"I'll tell you the truth about your mother's death, and you'll stop searching for her killer. You'll stop this pursuit, and you'll never think of it again. You will let this go." He quirks a brow. "Do we have a deal?"

I clamp my mouth shut and shift my gaze to Selene. I think about my mother and all the years I've spent searching for answers. I have them here, right in front of me, but at what cost? If I make this promise to Rhys, I'll never be able to bring her killer to justice. But then I think about Selene. Her green eyes are spread wide with fear, her body shaking uncontrollably. She's silently pleading for me to find a way out of this, just like the night of the auction. Her bottom lip trembles with tacit fear and uncertainty. She mouths my name, subtly shaking her head as tears stream down her soft cheeks. I wish I could wrap her up in my arms and take her away from here. My entire world is standing before me with a loaded gun pointed in its direction.

Instinct tells me a promise made to Rhys O'Connell isn't one I would be wise to break. Especially one such as this.

I would sell the soul to the Devil himself if it meant Selene and my baby would live.

"We have a deal." I flick my gaze back to Rhys. "I promise."

"Good boy." Rhys snickers.

"Get on with it then," I grind out. "What do you know?"

He chuckles. "To answer your question about your girl first, I know about Selene, here, because your little circle has been easy to track. In fact, our family has kept an eye on yours for quite some time. Necessary, considering who your mother was."

"What do you mean?" My focus doesn't stray from Selene, even though I haven't taken my eyes off Rhys.

"You're aware your mother was my father's cousin?"

"What?"

"Oh, yes. Sweet Tessa Saoirse Horan." Rhys jeers. "According to my father, he and her were incredibly close growing up in Southern Ireland. Practically brother and sister." He frowns as anger flashes in his eyes. "That was until she escaped to New York City and betrayed our family by marrying that fucking asshole Italian father of yours."

I flash, jerking back, confusion building inside me. I try putting the pieces together but quickly get overwhelmed. If my mother was Rhys's father's cousin, that makes Rhys and I second cousins.

What the fuck?

I never knew much about my mother's past. She never lived long enough for her to tell me about her life before Julianna and I came around. She was stolen from us before she ever could.

"My parents loved each other." It's the only thing I can think to say.

"Do you truly think love conquers loyalty when it comes to the Irish mafia… or family?" Rhys quips, his mouth still turned up in a sneer.

I shake my head, squeezing my eyes shut before looking back at him. "Irish mafia?"

"Yes, fucker," he snaps.

Selene lets out a small whimper, and I think I may just die watching her this way. I need to end this conversation as quickly as possible. I'm afraid Rhys will change his mind at any moment and snap, pulling the trigger without another thought.

"I had no idea." I shake my head. "My mother never told me."

"Of course, she didn't." Rhys scoffs. "Why would she when she thought she was getting away from what was in her birthright?"

"What was in her birthright?"

"To marry an Irishman within the organization. Her leaving

put us all at risk of strengthening our alliances," Rhys explains. "In turn, her marrying your father was a betrayal of the highest standard."

"I don't understand how this plays into her death." I wet my lips. My mouth is dry and my throat burns, but I think I already know the answer before Rhys manages to say it out loud.

"Oh, come on, Capuleti." He laughs maniacally. "You're family. I think you already know where I'm going with this."

I swallow around the lump in my throat. "Your father had my mother killed because she married the enemy?"

"Exactly." He nods, unwilling to remove the gun from Selene's temple.

A chill seeps into my bones.

"But they'd already been married for years before she was murdered," I argue. "Doesn't make sense."

"That father of yours was about to become mayor of the largest fuckin' city in the world. Your mother was going to be in the spotlight, paraded around as the First Lady of New York City. He stole her from us, and he needed to be punished for it. They both did."

"But..." Intense pressure builds behind my eyes. "She was family."

"She was dead to the Horan and O'Connell line the second she left Ireland without uttering a single word to her family." He narrows his fiery gaze. "My father took matters into his own hands and made sure what needed to be done was done."

I curl my hands into tight fists at my sides. I don't understand the logic. Not completely.

The anger that overtakes me is debilitating.

"Your father killed my mother" It's a statement. A final nail in the coffin of what I've been trying to dig up for years.

The truth.

"Yes." He tightens his grip on Selene. "He needed to make a

statement to those in the family who might ever consider leaving. The price you'll pay for betraying one of your own."

I take a step forward, noticing how Rhys hasn't let up his hold on Selene. He's still keeping the gun pressed to her head. The fear in her expression has only deepened over my conversation with Rhys. She's silent, aside from her quiet sobs, but I see the panic in her eyes.

"I know the truth now." I hold my hand out. "You can let her go."

"Not so fast," Rhys spits out.

The two men flanking me grow closer.

"I need assurance that you'll let this go. You won't publish what I've told you in that stupid fucking magazine of yours. You'll call off your staff, coming down to the docks, asking questions."

"I..." I promised I would follow through on Rhys's request to let this all go, but that was before I found out his father was behind my mother's death. She was murdered in cold blood before my eyes because she fell in love with the enemy.

"You listen to me!" Rhys shouts, his anger suddenly consuming him. He shakes Selene and presses the gun harder against her temple. She winces, attempting to tilt her head away from it.

I'm going to be fucking sick.

"My father died years ago, along with the men who carried out his wishes that night at the subway station." His voice booms through the cold night air. "There's no one alive left to pursue ,but I guarantee you that if you expose the truth, I will be the one to pay the price. While I understand my father's convictions, that he did what needed to be done, I don't hold with killing family as he did." He glares at me, then turns his head to stare at Selene. He leans forward and breathes her in before slowly turning his head back to me. "But seeing how she isn't married to you yet, and she isn't family, I have no problem making a statement of my own. Fuck up my life, I'll fuck up yours."

I try to take another step forward. I imagine lunging at Rhys, taking him down. But then I imagine what could happen if I do. He'll pull the trigger. I'll witness the love of my life and my child being torn from me within a matter of seconds. I'll see the only future I've ever wanted gone. I'll see the life drain from Selene's mossy-green eyes, just like I did my mother's. Or perhaps he'll toss her overboard into the frigid water of the Hudson below us.

Her death would destroy me. It would be the end of me.

Panic overrides all logic. The two men at either side of me grip my arms, holding me back.

I open my mouth to shout at Rhys, but my gaze briefly moves to Selene. She's breathing heavily, with mascara staining her cheeks. Her hand moves over her stomach, caressing the life growing inside her. She's silently pleading with me again.

"*I love you,*" she mouths.

My mind flashes to the memory of her that night on stage. Then again to the night she opened up to me, revealing her darkest secret.

To the promise I made to her.

"Selene is family," I choke out as a tear slips from the corner of my eye. I inhale a deep breath. "She's carrying my child."

Rhys's eyes spread wide, and his eyebrows shoot high on his forehead before they pull together when he snaps his head in Selene's direction. His eyes drop to her hands on her stomach.

"You're lying," he says quietly, but there's still a darkness in his voice. He takes a step back on the bench, putting distance between himself and Selene. His arm stiffens as he pulls the gun away from her head, but he keeps it pointed at her. He cocks the gun again, staring at her down the length of his arm and the gun.

My mother's eyes flash in front of me. The heartbreak, knowing it was the last time she'd see Julianna and me.

"You're lying, Capuleti," Rhys repeats in a sinister tone that makes me feel as if my soul is leaving my body. I have no other way to convince him other than my words.

"I'm not." My voice breaks. I'm hollow and empty. Desperate. "We just found out the other day. She's pregnant... and she's the love of my life. So, please..." Another tear spills as Rhys looks up at me. "Please, Rhys. I'll do whatever you want, just, please... don't hurt her. She's my whole world."

It doesn't matter the promise I made to myself for all those years to pursue my mother's true killer. Rhys's father is dead, and I can't change the past.

Selene is my future, and I'll do whatever it takes to protect her. To keep her safe.

"Say I believe what you're telling me," he challenges, sticking out his chin, still skeptical. "You'll let this go?"

"Yes." I tear my arm out from one of the henchman's grip and slap my hand against my chest. "You have my word, as family, that I'll keep the truth to myself. I'll let go of the past."

Selene's shoulders wrack with heavy sobs. She wraps both arms around her stomach and hunches over. Rhys watches her in silence, then slowly looks up at me.

I hold my breath the entire time, not certain I'm going to survive.

That is until Rhys lowers his arm. He shoves his gun into the back of his black slacks, under his suit jacket. He darts his eyes to his left, sending Selene a silent acknowledgement that she's free.

Selene takes a breath and steps down from the bench before falling to her knees on the wooden deck. She presses one hand to the wooden planks, keeping the other wrapped around her stomach. Her blonde hair curtains her face as she sobs uncontrollably.

"I'll hold you to your word, Capuleti." Rhys glowers at me from under his thick, dark brow. "But don't think for a moment I don't have eyes and ears around this city. They won't hesitate to tell me if they have the slightest inclination of you lying about this or breaking your promise to me."

Rhys's men drop their hold on me. I curl my hands at my sides, itching to get to Selene. But I wait, just in case. Just in case Rhys decides to change his mind.

"You have my word." I steel my chest, holding my breath until I'm almost certain I'm going to faint.

Rhys shoves his black hair off his forehead, then casually buttons his jacket as if he wasn't just holding a gun to my pregnant girlfriend's head.

I stay frozen in place, aching to get to Selene. Rhys moves past me, stopping only long enough to grip my shoulder and lean in. "Congratulations, Capuleti. Enjoy fatherhood."

Then he disappears, with his two henchmen following quickly behind him.

Once Rhys's hand falls from my shoulder, I'm racing to Selene.

I sink to my knees in front of her. With shaking hands, I reach up and brush her hair away before lifting her face up. When I see her eyes, I fall apart. My heart is both shattered and pieced together. I feel relieved knowing her and the baby are safe and unharmed, but I'm left broken over the pain and trauma this has caused.

It's obvious the memories are playing out in her mind. The terror and fear of what she experienced the day she witnessed her parents' deaths.

"Holt. I... I t-thought..."

"I know," I soothe her, running my hands along the side of her face. "I know, Wallflower. You're okay. We're okay."

Tears flow from my eyes.

I can't hold it in any longer. "I'm so sorry, Selene."

My voice cracks. My entire world is sitting in front of me, and I nearly lost it.

Selene's wide, red-lined, green eyes stare up at me. She wraps her hands around my wrists. "Sorry for what?"

I frown, choking back my own tears. "Sorry for putting you in danger."

"You couldn't have known," she strains.

"The thought of losing you..." I start. "Fuck, I was terrified. I thought I was witnessing it all over again..."

"I know." She hiccups on a sob. "I felt the same way."

I close my eyes, but Selene implores me to open them.

"You saved us, Holt." She slides her shaking hand from my wrist to wrap it around my hand. She takes it in hers and guides it to her stomach. "Your promise saved us. You kept your word."

I tilt my head to the side, and my shoulders drop with relief. I feel drained and alive all at once. I cradle her head in my hand while keeping the other pressed to her stomach. "I told you I would, Wallflower."

Her lips press together as she inhales a shaky breath. She frantically nods as though the reality of the situation is catching up to her before wrapping her hand around the back of my head and pressing her forehead to mine. "You did, Holt. You did."

When she presses her lips to mine, I taste her, surrendering my entire body and soul into this one kiss. I wrap my arm around her and pull her close, promising over and over again that this is forever.

I leave the past behind, vowing to never let her go.

And I don't.

SELENE

Forever didn't exist until there was Holt.

And tonight, I almost lost forever.

Holt carries me all the way home. I keep my arms tightly around his neck and my head on his chest. He even holds me in the back seat of the car. I don't speak a word. Shivering uncontrollably, I can't decide if it's from the freezing cold or everything that happened tonight.

I keep my eyes squeezed shut until Holt lays me in our bed and covers me under the safety of the blanket. He tells me I need to eat, but I refuse. Not arguing, he climbs in after me, sidling up behind me.

He's removed his suit jacket and rolled his sleeves up to his elbows. What little skin exposed is warm as it wraps around me. His entire body molds to mine, his legs and back pressed tightly against me. I place my hand over his, weaving our fingers together.

Tilting my face into the pillow, I cry.

I cry for Holt. I cry for his mother. I cry for my parents. I cry for the baby growing inside me. I cry for myself.

Holt buries his nose in my hair and breathes me in. Deeply. The gesture creates a new wave of goosebumps. It's been hours since I was sitting on the bench of the upper deck on Holt's yacht, staring out at the water, when Rhys and his men suddenly showed up, pointing a gun directly at my face.

My tears haven't stopped, remembering the terror that consumed me from that moment on. Rhys ignored my pleas to tell me who he was or why he was there, insisting he would explain everything once Holt showed up.

And he did. But Rhys never let up on his threat to kill me. Not until Holt vowed his secrecy.

"Talk to me, Selene." His whispering voice forces my eyes open. "Tell me what's going on in that beautiful mind of yours."

I stare blankly at the slate-painted wall.

"I..." my voice breaks. "I don't think I can."

"I get it." He pulls me closer, soothing his hand over my stomach. "I just need to know I haven't completely lost you. With what happened tonight, with Rhys, I wouldn't blame you..."

I abruptly shift, rolling over to face Holt. His face is broken and weary. His bright blue eyes are swollen from crying.

"You haven't lost me, Holt." I press my hand to his cheek. "What made you think that?"

"You haven't talked since we left the yacht, and you're never silent when it comes to me." The corner of his mouth twitches. "You have a sharp tongue for me, Wallflower."

I frown. "Holt..."

"I know." He sighs, closing his eyes. "For everyone else, you're silent. Not for me." He moves his head just enough to lean against my touch as if he's memorizing it before it disappears.

"Right." I scoot closer to him, raising my leg to wrap around his hip. "For everyone else, but never for you." I dig my fingers into his hair, around to the base of his neck. My gaze drops to his lips. The same lips that have reassured me a million times he isn't going to disappear. The same lips delivering a million promises of forever, both in words and kisses.

His nostrils flare as he exhales heavily before cracking his eyes back open.

We've traded places. For the first time, it isn't me who's worried the promise of forever will end and I'll be the one watching as he walks away.

Holt's worried this has pushed me away for good. My silence is scaring him.

"Look at me, Holt."

He lifts his gaze, crippled with fear. His chest inflates but never settles.

"Tonight was terrifying. I don't even know where to begin." I blink rapidly, sorting through all the thoughts crowding my mind. "Whether it's the thought of my parents and their death, or the way this has reminded you of your own mother's death. Or the fact Rhys O'Connell, a high-ranking member of the Irish mafia, is your cousin and has been watching us for God knows how long." I draw in a breath. "It's a lot to process, and therapy has taught me to sort through my thoughts and feelings before reacting."

"I'm so sorry, Selene. I still can't get it out of my head, seeing you like that. And I can't shake the feeling I had. You felt so far away, even though you were only a few feet from me. I was helpless."

"I know." I swallow the bile threatening to spill out of me. "I felt helpless, too."

Holt wraps his arm over my side and presses his palm against the small of my back.

Having the tip of a gun pressed against the side of your head, knowing your life might be stripped from you by the simple pulling of a trigger changes you. My brain chemistry isn't the same as it was a few hours ago. It changed the day I watched my father do the same with my mother before turning it on himself. Now, it's changed again.

Death is an ugly, vile thing, taking a piece of you each time you're forced to witness it.

Even the possibility of death is enough to steal a piece of you.

But what it's never done is steal my love for Holt.

That it can never take away from me.

"I'm sorry if it made you think I was withdrawing the way I used to," I say, brushing away the dreadful knot growing in my chest. "Or that I was treating you like I do anyone else. But I love you, Holt. I've never loved anyone but you. You're the only one who has ever seen me for *me*."

He finally exhales, his body sinking into the mattress. I slide my hand from behind his head to grip his arm. I feel his corded muscle, down the length of his arm, before feathering it back up to his neck.

"You made me a promise, now it's my turn to do the same." I pull him close, bringing his mouth just in front of mine. "I never believed in forever. Until you. So... I promise you have my forever, Holt Capuleti. No matter what."

When I press my lips to his, I pour all my traumas, fears, hopes, and promises into this one kiss.

My kiss must heal the part of him that had him worried, because his grip on me tightens. The tips of his fingers sink into my back as he presses his lips harder against mine.

"I must admit though, Selene." He kisses me once before reluctantly pulling away. His eyes lock onto mine. "I don't know where we go from here."

"Did you mean what you told Rhys? Your promise to not tell the police the truth? I'd understand if you didn't."

"Shit, Selene." He sighs heavily, like he can't believe I'd even question his commitment to his promise. "I meant what I said. I fully intend on holding my promise to Rhys. I never thought there would come a day I would accept letting go of pursuing my mother's killer. But now that I know the truth, and now that I understand what it would mean if it got out, I don't think I've ever been more certain of anything. Because after all this, only one truth remains."

"What truth is that?"

"If it means a long, long future with you, I'm willing to let go of the past."

I give him a small smile, his declaration rocking me to the core. It's the kind I feel settling into my bones. In my DNA. That's what Holt is now. He's a part of my DNA. He is my future, and just like him, I'm willing to release the pain of the past in order to have a future with him.

Holt and our family.

We have done nothing but live in the ugliness of our pasts. It's easy to get swept up in the hurricane of it all, shadowed by the darkness of witnessing death, allowing it to blind us from the colors life and love have to offer.

And when I look into Holt's blue eyes, all I see is a life filled with a myriad of colors.

"I do have one question." I rub my feet against Holt's under the blanket. "It has to do with something Rhys said."

Holt's face pales. "What is it?"

"Rhys mentioned something about my security detail." I raise a brow. "Did you hire someone to follow and keep an eye on me?"

Color returns to his cheeks in the shade of red. His mouth pops open, but no words come out.

I jerk back, dropping my jaw, pretending to be appalled. I stab my finger to his chest. "You did!"

He tries to roll onto his back, quickly covering his eyes with his hand. It's amazing how his usual tough exterior fades away when it comes to me. There's a softness to Holt—one he only has for me.

That thought makes my heart explode.

He groans before rolling back to face me. "I can explain."

"You don't need to explain." I giggle, feeling light for the first time all night. "I get it."

"You do?"

"Yes, of course, I do." I grin, butterflies fluttering in my stomach. "You weren't lying when you said you were obsessed with me."

His delightful growl vibrates across my body as he slips his hands around me. He leans in and draws my mouth to his.

I kiss him when I get this sudden thought.

Holt was in love with me long before I even realized.

I drape my arms around his neck, and he digs his fingers into my waist.

Shifting onto his back, he pulls me with him. I lift my leg and move to straddle him. I'm still wearing the sage green dress I picked out for our date night. He slips the fabric up my thighs, then over my hips. After lifting my arms in the air, he removes my dress and tosses it aside. The warm air of Holt's apartment soothes the remaining parts of me still carrying the chill of the night.

I rock my hips, grinding against Holt's hardened muscles. Pressing my palms to his chest, I stare down at him, knowing I've never loved anyone the way I do him.

He sees me in a way no one ever has.

"I just realized something," I say in a low voice, unbuttoning his shirt.

"What's that?" he rasps. His vibrating hands run impatiently up and down my thighs, sending an electric jolt straight to my core.

I moan, quickly sticking my tongue out to swipe across my lips while gathering my bearings. I tuck my bottom lip under my teeth then bend forward. The little knot in my lower stomach tightens, knowing in just a few short weeks or months, I won't be able to bend over as easily as this.

I plant a kiss on his mouth before hovering my lips over the shell of his ear. His breath dances across my neck, and I fight for self-control when I whisper, "You kept a secret from me, and you know what happens when we keep secrets, Mr. Capuleti."

His heated breath brushes against my skin with more force when his hands move to cover both my ass cheeks. He squeezes them before I sit up. A yelp makes its way out of my throat when he tosses me back onto the bed and settles between my legs. With his knees bent, he begins unbuckling his belt and unzipping his pants. His blue eyes shine in the late-night city lights pouring through the window. Once he's freed his cock from his pants and boxer briefs, he falls forward, pressing one hand into the mattress beside my head. I raise my chin, craving him.

He places a soft, gentle kiss to the tip of my nose.

"We'll get to your punishment a little later, Wallflower," he drawls in a deep voice. "But right now... right now I intend on showing you just what you mean to me, and that I'm never letting you go."

"So," I tease. "What you're saying is that we're stuck with you forever?"

His devious grin fades only for a moment, noticing how I said *we* instead of just *me*. His smile quickly reappears, lighting me up from the inside out.

"Forever, Wallflower."

He sinks his cock inside me, and I arch my back, gasping as he fills me. I moan, never feeling more loved or worshipped than I do in this moment.

I guess I was wrong.

Love can be trusted.

THIRTY-TWO

HOLT

One month later

The scent of freshly brewed coffee hits my nose the second I open the door, and while I'm craving caffeine, I'm craving something else more.

I find her sitting in the corner near the bookshelf littered with old, worn leatherbound books. She's sitting in the aged, light brown, leather armchair, with her laptop resting on the edge of the round, wooden table in front of her. Her blonde hair is pulled into a high messy bun, and her pretty mouth is twisted in thought. She's resting one hand over her growing stomach. This sight of her makes me fucking weak in the knees. I place my hand over my heart, knowing if I was to die right now, I'd die happy knowing this was the last thing I'd get to see.

It's been one month since the encounter with Rhys on my yacht and, as promised, he's been silent. So have I. Nearly losing Selene put a lot of my priorities into perspective. At times, it's been difficult to wrap my head around the truth and how I'll never see justice served to Rhys's father. But the thought is only momentary.

In the end, I guess Rhys's father did get justice. He's dead and long forgotten. Even Rhys doesn't carry out the same desire for vengeance. At least not on the level of his father.

But knowing he's dead has made it easier to move on.

Selene's focus lifts from her laptop screen when she sees me approaching, and her mouth stretches into an effortless smile.

"Hey," she greets in a sing song voice. "About time you showed up."

"I'm so sorry, Wallflower." I bend to plant a kiss on her mouth, stealing her smile. I wrap my hand gently on her jaw, tilting her face up. "I got stuck in a meeting with the anonymous column staff."

"How's that going?" she asks, sitting back in her chair.

I sit in the chair across from her, with the small, wooden table and her open laptop between us.

"Fine." I sigh, pinching the bridge of my nose. "Now that I've hired a new copy editor whose sole job is to vet the articles submitted to be published."

"Smart man." Selene giggles.

I snort and toss her a smile. "Learned my lesson, Wallflower."

"Sounds like you could use a cup of coffee, then." She points to the service counter behind me. "Do you want to order one?"

I glance over my shoulder, eyeing the line of at least ten people waiting to place their order. I turn back to face Selene and rest both my arms on the chair and simply sit back and stare at my girl. My girl and our baby growing inside her. I still can't believe they're both mine.

Fuck, she owns me.

"Nah." I wave her off. "I'd rather not waste my time standing in line. There are other things I need more than caffeine at this point."

Her cheeks blush bright red. She knows exactly what I mean.

Selene's phone vibrates on the table. My sister's name pops up on the screen with a message, along with Charleigh and London's.

"Girl chat?" I ask.

"Yeah," she laughs, picking her phone up to read the message. "Ever since I showed them the ultrasound pictures yesterday, they haven't stopped gushing over the fact we're having a baby. Julianna is convinced it's a girl, even though it's impossible to know at this stage. At least not by that ultrasound picture."

"Of course, she is." I chuckle. "She's been sending me messages, too. I'm pretty sure she's already done a bunch of baby clothes shopping. She sent me a picture of some designer dress she picked up at a boutique. I didn't even know they made designer dresses for babies."

"Oh, my God." Selene groans and rolls her eyes. "What if it's a boy?"

"She'll probably end up saving them for when someone else in our group has a baby," I offer. "Then, if we find out we're having a boy, she'll go on a shopping spree for boy clothes."

She nods then stares at me with this unwavering grin.

"What?" I chuckle.

"Nothing. I was just thinking how much I love you."

My cheeks grow sore from how hard I'm smiling. "I love you, too."

"Okay." Selene sits forward, placing her hands gently on her knees. "I just need to finish up one more thing and then we can head out."

I toss my gaze to her laptop. "What are you working on?"

Puffing her chest and raising her chin, she gives me the largest grin I think I've ever seen her wear. She's fucking stunning, glowing with pride as she spins her laptop around to show me what's on her screen.

"I submitted my manuscript to that agency I was telling you about."

I read the email she just sent, along with her query letter.

My wide-eyed gaze bounces between the screen and Selene on the other side. "Holy shit, Wallflower." I stand and move around the table before bending to kiss her again. I cup the sides of her face and pull her close. "You're going to get it," I tell her, crashing my mouth to hers.

She laughs against my mouth, and it sends a delightful shiver across my body. My dick twitches, aching to show her just how proud I am to have her in my life.

"We'll see." She giggles between kisses. "I'm trying not to get my hopes up."

"You will," I tell her again before reclaiming my seat.

Her smile fades, and she looks off to the side, distance and uncertainty in her eyes. "I'm just glad I was able to gather the courage to put myself out there." Her gaze shifts back to me. "The romance market is flooded with incredible works that often go unnoticed. For a time, I thought I would go the self-publishing route, but I figure why not try this way first. If I don't hear back from the agency, I'll publish it myself."

"I think that's a smart way to go about it," I tell her, understanding the struggles of the publishing world. "Your story deserves to be told."

"Thank you. I've spent so much of my adult life with this story, and I think when I was finished with it, I got scared. Like, in a way, I was holding myself back from taking the risk. Much like everything else in my life."

"Selene..." I soften my voice.

"I know." She blinks the tears threatening to build in her eyes. "I'm not saying I wouldn't have ever gotten here on my own—I probably would have in my own time—but being with you has given me something I didn't have before."

"Oh?" I arch a brow, unable to hold back my smirk.

"A reason to be the best version of myself." She grins. "And you were right."

"About what?"

"The day you crashed my yoga class." She closes her laptop and slips it back into her bag. Slinging it over her shoulder, she moves around the table and grabs my hand. "You said your kiss lit something inside me. You were right."

No other woman has ever had this effect on me. I stand, keeping my hand wrapped around Selene's. I close the gap between us and bring my mouth to the shell of her ear, breathing deeply.

"I love it when you tell me I'm right," I whisper, my dick twitching, the thrill of playing this game of confessions with Selene reminding me that every bump along the way to get here has been worth it. "But I must tell you, Wallflower, you lit something inside me that day, too."

Her breath hitches as she leans into me. We're in a crowded café, but all we're focused on is each other. All the heartbreak and loss it took to get here has been worth it.

She looks me dead in the eye, her nose touching the tip of mine. "Why don't you show me then?"

I pop a brow and lower my voice. "You ready to go home?"

"Who said anything about going home?" She tugs on my hand and starts pulling me toward the darkened hallway near the back corner of the café.

I catch a glimpse of her sparkling green eyes once more before she's leading me into what appears to be a storage room.

I'd follow this woman anywhere.

Once we're out of sight from everyone inside the café, my hands and mouth are on her—the only woman they've ever belonged to, and the only one they will for the rest of my life.

It's a promise.

THIRTY-THREE

Two months later

Springtime in Paris is more beautiful than I ever could have imagined.

The girls and I have spent most of the day walking around the city, exploring the beautiful gardens. We took several breaks, since the aches in my ankles and lower back are growing with every week that I inch closer to my third trimester. I'm nearly there, and the thought of how different my life is going to be in less than four months is insane. When I think back to where I was just last year, it feels like a lifetime ago.

Now, here I am, heading home from having dinner in Paris with my best friends.

"Are we ready to head back to the hotel?" London asks, hooking her arm through mine while leading us down the streets of central Paris. The trees and buildings are decorated in twinkling lights, and I feel like I'm living a dream.

"No," Julianna groans, hooking her arm through Charleigh's. "I don't want to go back just yet. Can't we find a club or bar to go to?"

We continue walking down the street in the direction of our

hotel as she reaches up and adjusts Charleigh's bachelorette crown, decorated with delicate pink roses and a white toile veil cascading down the back.

This trip wasn't meant to be a bachelorette party, but Julianna can rope anyone into doing anything. Charleigh doesn't seem to mind because she hasn't stopped smiling ever since we touched down in Paris in Asher's plane.

Charleigh nods and glances down the row to London and me beside her. "What about you two? Do you want to go out with me and Jules?"

I laugh sardonically, then rest my hand on my stomach. "What am I going to do at a club? I can't even drink right now."

London gives me a small smile of reassurance. "They have mocktails, Selene. Besides, pregnant women can go to clubs."

I toss her a side-eye, then shake my head. "No, that's okay. I'm pretty exhausted, anyway."

"We understand," Charleigh says, reaching out and wrapping her hand around my arm.

"We do," Jules says, nodding sharply. "You and my baby nephew need rest."

"We're fine, Jules," I say, giving her a small smile. I love how she's already settled into the protective aunt role.

"Oh, that isn't coming from me." She tucks her brown, beach-wavy hair behind her ear. "That's coming from my overprotective, love-obsessed brother."

I blush at the thought of Holt telling Julianna to keep an eye on me.

"Of course, he would task you with making sure I'm not overdoing it." I smirk. "He's only messaged me about three times, making sure I'm staying hydrated and eating enough."

"He loves you," London coos, resting her head on my shoulder. "He's thousands of miles away. I'm sure it's eating him up that you're so far. It's sweet how obsessed he is with you."

Julianna fakes a gag, causing the four of us to break out in laughter.

Once we reach the end of the block before the hotel, Charleigh and Julianna point to a bar they spot around the corner. London reluctantly agrees to join them, but only after she insists on walking me back to my room.

I don't bother arguing with her, knowing she just wants to make sure I get there safely.

My phone pings in my purse. Before London and I break from the group, I pull it out, assuming it's a message from Holt. But my hand is flying to my mouth when I see an unread email notification waiting for me instead.

"What is it?" London asks.

With a shaking hand, I pull it away from my face and nervously click on the email, opening it. I frantically read the first few lines before swinging to my three best friends.

"They loved it!" I manage to choke out.

"Who loved what?" Charleigh asks.

"My book," I breathe. "I have an agent."

"Oh, shit!" Julianna shrieks.

London and Charleigh join in on the screaming when they start jumping up and down in a circle around me. Onlookers and passersby stare at us with confusion before continuing on their way.

"Congratulations, Sis." London wraps her arms around me, sobbing happy tears into my shoulder. The other girls join in.

When they pull away, I realize I'm crying as well. I smile at my best friends through watery eyes. "Oh, my God, I can't believe this." I sniff and read the email again just to make sure I read it correctly.

"We can." Charleigh squeezes my hand.

"Thank you." I melt, knowing I couldn't have gotten to this point without their support.

"Holt's going to freak when you tell him, you know that, right?" Julianna asks, her smile unwavering.

"He is." I laugh.

After the reality of what this means subsides, London walks me to the door of our shared hotel room before she heads back out to join Charleigh and Julianna. Honestly, I'm thankful I don't have to go, even after declining their invitation again after receiving the email from my new agency. My lower back is killing me, and I could use the sleep. Once I was out of the first trimester, my constant, chronic nausea transformed into constant fatigue. I swear, all I want to do is sleep.

But I'm anxiously awaiting Holt's reply to my text or a phone call. I'm staring at my phone when I enter my dark hotel room.

The air is stolen from my lungs when two arms wrap around me, spinning me until my back hits the wall.

Even in the darkness of my hotel room, I recognize his familiar brown hair hanging above his brow and those bright blue eyes staring straight at me.

"Hello, Wallflower." His voice is as smooth as velvet, hitting me in all the right places.

"Holt?" I'm still trying to catch my breath. "You scared the shit out of me."

"Sorry." He drags his finger along the side of my face. "I didn't mean to startle you."

"You're lurking and hiding out in the shadows of my hotel room like a fucking stalker. How did you expect me to react?"

The corners of his mouth curl into a devilish grin.

"What?" I ask, my shoulders deflating.

His chest rumbles. "I missed you, that's all. You and that smart mouth of yours. The one you only reserve for me."

"Well," I scoff, laughing. "You did scare me."

He hums before crashing his mouth against mine. I reach

up, threading my fingers through his hair. His tongue slips between my lips, tasting me.

I'm lost in his intoxicating kiss when reality hits me. I pull away, pressing my hands to his chest. "Wait." I catch my breath and swallow. "What are you doing here? How did you get into my hotel room?"

I'd almost forgotten I was in Paris and not at home.

"I have my ways, Wallflower." He smirks.

Very true. Holt apparently had a security detail following me for months without me knowing. Him finding a way to get into my hotel room doesn't surprise me and isn't completely out of character.

"Besides," he continues, still dragging his finger along my jaw, down my neck, and over the swell of my breasts. "I'm aware I'm crashing your girls' trip, but do you think I could just sit at home while you and my son were thousands of miles away with an ocean between us? It's been the purest form of torture."

I giggle, resting my head back against the wall to look up at Holt. I slide my hands down his chest before finding the buttons to his collared shirt. I start undoing them slowly, one by one. "You are *so* obsessed with me. With us."

His hands press against the wall at either side of my head. "I thought we already made that clear months ago."

I undo the last button and slip his shirt over his shoulders. I'm quick to work on his belt. "You did."

He pants, letting out a heavy breath. His eyes have darkened, taking on a hungrier gaze. Suddenly, I'm not so tired. I ache to have him inside me.

"You sent me a text a few minutes ago, telling me you had something important to tell me. What was it?"

I stop unbuttoning his pants, looking him directly in the eye. "The agency emailed me back. They want to sign with me."

A smile comes alive on his face. He's gloating, and the idea that he always knew I would get here sparks that light he's brought to life inside me. The one only he has been able to start.

"I knew it." He kisses me deeply.

I get lost in his kiss before he pulls away. I miss his mouth the second it leaves me.

"I truly did miss you both," he whispers deeply.

"We missed you, too."

His eyes soften in the dark. He's telling the truth. "I don't plan on staying long," he confesses.

I roll my eyes, shocked Holt is treating a day trip from New York to Paris like it's normal.

His eyes search mine, and there's an electric charge in the air. I feel it cackling between us, between the parts where we're connected. I cradle the side of his sculpted jaw in my palm. My hand slips away when he falls to his knees in front of me.

I hold my breath when he kisses my swollen belly, then he reaches in his pocket, pulling out a single ring. The rock is a large, blue gem, surrounded by little white diamonds. I gasp, clamping my hand over my mouth.

"I have one more question before I go."

A tear slips from the corner of my eye, sliding down my cheek.

"I know we don't need a ring for us to promise each other forever, Wallflower." His neck bobs as he swallows. "But I can't imagine spending my life with anyone else. I've been obsessed with you from the start, and I used to daydream what a life with you would look like. And when I pictured it, you were always there beside me, wearing my mother's ring. You're the best person I've ever known, and I've never been too afraid to admit what everyone knows to be true. I am obsessed with you. I want you for life."

"Holt..." I breathe. I've never been this deliriously happy.

"So..." He lowers his gaze, looking up through hooded yet focused eyes. "Wallflower, will you marr—"

"Yes," I cut him off. "Yes, I will marry you."

He lets out a heavy breath of relief before slipping the ring on my shaking ring finger. Then I'm pulling him up to kiss me.

I drape my arms around his neck in disbelief.

The woman who only ever believed this type of love existed in romance novels now has it all. Best friend's, billionaire, older brother falls for the woman whose sworn off love forever.

Okay, well, maybe not forever.

But Holt is just that. My forever.

<hr>

Want to read more of Holt and Selene? You can read an extra special bonus scene HERE - https://dl.bookfun nel.com/kfcfvr1ot7

PLUS There's more coming from the NYC Billionaires! Rome and Julianna's story is next and the final book in the series. This is an enemies to lovers romance you won't want to miss!

You can get your copy HERE! - http://mybook.to/frwh

PLAYLIST

- "Labyrinth" by Taylor Swift
- "Now That We Don't Talk" by Taylor Swift
- "On My Mind" by Alex Warren
- "How to disappear" by Lana Del Ray
- "Don't Blame Me" by Taylor Swift
- "The Only Exception" by Paramore
- "Nothing's Gonna Hurt You Baby" by Cigarettes After Sex
- "Watch The World Burn" by Falling In Reverse
- "Power Over Me" by Dermot Kennedy
- "Oh! Darling" by The Beatles

ACKNOWLEDGMENTS

And here's to another one...

Whew! In many ways, this book was probably the smoothest writing experience I've had. Holt and Selene were such a joy to write and I hope you had just as much fun reading them as I had writing them.

As always, the first person I'd love to thank is my husband, Brett. The love of my life. Sounds cheesy as fuck, but I still find myself looking at you, amazed I get to call you mine. You're my person through and through. Thank you for putting up with me. All versions of me.

To my readers. For falling in love with the NYC Billionaires. I see all of you and can't thank you enough for your messages and support. They are literally what keeps me on this train. Love to you all.

To my best friend and assistant, April. I'm pretty sure I added a list of titles in front of your name on the last book and they all still stand. I could probably add another slew of new titles for all you do for me, honestly. For the hours long video calls to schedule posts, discuss plot lines, and just overall stress of this career... I can't thank you enough. You understand all of my doubts, triumphs, disappointments. All the while never losing your doubt in me. I guess all there is left to say is... I love you, April!

To my cover designer, Amanda Shepard. Another one out of the ballpark. Love all you've done for this series.

Thank you to my editor, Vicki James. You are absolutely

incredible. The feedback and comments you left on this one gave me so much life!

My agent, Nikki Groom. For your continued support in all books I write. Thank you!

To my cat, Bartleby for learning how to open every door in the house only to use your new found skill to leap up and onto my lap when I'm deep in the writing cave, forcing me to stop and give you love. You're insane but I love you so much.

ABOUT BRITTANY

Brittany Taylor grew up all over the world including places such as California and England. Her love of reading started at a young age. Finally deciding to fulfill her lifelong dream, she took the plunge into the writing world and published her first book when she was twenty-eight. Today she resides in Maine with her husband, two sons, two cats and one dog.

www.brittanytaylorbooks.com